HELLO GIRLS

HELLO GIRLS

BRITTANY CAVALLARO + EMILY HENRY

KATHERINE TEGEN BOOKS
An Imprint of HarperCollins Publishers

Katherine Tegen Books is an imprint of HarperCollins Publishers.

Hello Girls

Copyright © 2019 by Brittany Cavallaro and Emily Henry

ISBN 978-0-06-280342-9

Typography by Ray Shappell

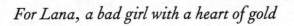

For Lana, a bad girl with a heart of gold

ONE

Winona Olsen watched her father move through the softly lit banquet hall to the stage, as if carried by the current of the room's applause. In his blue pinstripes, his elegant stride reminded her of the great white sharks her mother used to take her to see at the Kingsville Aquarium.

They'd had season passes, and Winona remembered her mother saying dreamily, on more than one occasion, "They even swim when they're sleeping. Can you imagine, Nony? What that would be like, to keep moving even when you're asleep but never get anywhere? You're just stuck in a glass tank."

On the stage at the front of the room, her father stepped up to the podium and shook the presenter's hand.

"You must be so proud," the silver-haired woman to Winona's

right murmured to her through the applause. "What is this, his *third* Changemaker?"

Winona flashed her perfectly symmetrical smile, a duller, narrower version of the thousand-megawatt one beaming from the stage. "Second," she answered.

The woman sat back in her chair, one hand placed over her heart and a look of delighted surprise splashed across her face. Winona knew she'd met the woman before, at some benefit or luncheon or award ceremony—there were only so many philanthropists in northern Michigan and they took turns making speeches and polite small talk at the same few events each year. Truthfully, Winona's father had won far more awards for his philanthropic endeavors than she'd just copped to, but he would have thought it in poor taste for Winona to rattle off the entire list, and *taste* was Stormy Olsen's greatest strength.

His collection of awards and trophies was rivaled by his collection of modern art, his drawers of designer watches, the rows of pristine suits in his closet, and the rainbow of Tory Burch dresses he'd lined Winona's with.

"Well, he just *raves* about *you*, missy," the woman said. "About how you're going to Northwestern next year?"

Winona smiled. "That's right."

The woman settled back into her chair as Winona's father began to speak.

"Wow," he said, voice straining under emotion. Stormy was an emotional guy, and the public appreciated that about him; there weren't many meteorologists who could turn the morning weather report into a human interest piece, but there was just *something* about him that made people want to sit down for a beer or two and swap stories with him. Acts of kindness, big and small, that was what he was about, what he'd instilled in his only daughter, the light of his life, and the town he loved so dearly. *Remember, folks, in the Upper Peninsula, a little bit of sunshine goes a long way!*

The overhead lighting caught on his Rolex and light flashed across the room. Winona realized she'd zoned out—she'd been doing that a lot lately—and jerked her attention back to her father's acceptance speech. She wanted to remember her favorite tidbits to repeat back to him on the car ride home. She knew it would please him.

"... and I really mean this, I do: the people of Kingsville have made it so easy to serve them. They say when you love your job, you'll never work a day in your life, and you know what? In my sixteen years at Channel 5, I'd have to say that's been true for me. Folks, I love my job. But in this last year, partnering with Brain Storm Girls—"He swallowed the knot in his throat as he gathered himself, and the audience tearfully laughed. "Look, I'm no public speaker, I'm a weatherman, so forgive the terrible slew of forthcoming puns."

Appreciative laughter hummed through the room as he picked up the glass trophy. "When I lost my wife, Katherine, years ago, I felt like a tornado had ripped through my life, and I'd been left to pick up the pieces. I didn't think I could ever rebuild the beautiful life we'd had together, but I knew I had to try. I knew I had to do everything I could to empower my daughter, to make sure she knew that the whole world was within her grasp. If the sun wasn't going to shine, hoo-boy, I would build a movie set for her to live in, all sandy beaches and palm trees and blue skies. That's what we do for our kids, isn't it? We hoist the sun up into the sky for them every day until they're old enough to do it for themselves."

That part, Winona thought. *That's the part you should repeat back to him. He'll like that.* She twisted the Cartier bracelet on her wrist, then pressed the metal hard into her skin, a trick she had for imprinting anything important into her memory. *Don't forget. Hoist the sun into the sky until they're old enough to do it.* That was the right line, the perfect one to recite back to him.

"But what I didn't realize," Stormy went on, "was that I was never doing the heavy lifting. The joy of my daughter, the boundless hope and potentiality of children, *that* is what lights up my life. Partnering with Brain Storm Girls has been more than just a job that doesn't feel like work. It has been a second sun hoisted up into the sky for me." He lifted his eyes to the crowd. "And remember, folks," he said. "In the Upper Peninsula . . ."

". . . a little bit of sunshine goes a long way," the room replied, before erupting into applause.

The silver-haired woman to Winona's right pushed her chair back, leading the charge in the standing ovation.

"Absolutely moving!" she shouted down at Winona.

Winona had been so focused on her inner dialogue—*hoist the sun hoist the sun hoist the sun*—that she almost said that aloud in response. Instead she pushed the bracelet into her wrist and smiled wide and lovely. "My father is a rare man."

As Stormy stepped off the stage, he stumbled, temporarily blinded by the stage lights, and missed the first step.

It happened in a second, a tiny blip, but Winona saw it as if in slow motion.

Her stomach rose up like she was on the Tower Drop, and her mind and vision sharpened to present the scene in perfect clarity.

The slick heel of Stormy's Ferragamo wingtip hitting the edge of the step, the part without grip tape, and sliding downward.

His weight thrown back, his body off-balance.

His salt-and-pepper head dropping down-down-down. His toothy white smile—the one that meant he was stressed—stretched across his mouth right up until the last *millisecond* when—

The back of his skull *cracked* against the edge of the stage.

Blood spurting out in a crown around his head. The room beginning to scream. The silver-haired woman shrieking, then collapsing dizzily into the chair. The presenter, for some reason, taking his suit jacket off—because it was hard to get blood out of Italian wool? Because Sturgis "Stormy" Olsen might be cold there, lying at such an odd angle on the stairs?—and scrambling toward the edge of the stage, the five feet ten inches of crumpled pinstripe. The blood, so much blood, glistening in the soft light.

And Winona, sitting there, still as her father's favorite Rodin, as the screams around the room escalated, gruff shouts of "Call 911!" and "I'm a doctor! Let me through!" going up like flares throughout the tumult.

And still, Winona, frozen in her chair.

An orphan in two seconds flat. Totally alone in the world.

Totally alone. A big, empty house waiting for her at the end of a long driveway, and a senile grandfather across town.

Totally alone.

Tears pricked her eyes at the thought. She blinked them away.

She blinked it all away.

Stormy caught the handrail on the stage, and his foot met the second step with ease. He came toward her, like a shark swimming through the applause, and she stood as she knew he expected her to, pushing the bracelet into the tender, burned skin on the underside of her wrist. *Hoist the sun hoist the sun hoist the—*

Of course she had imagined it. Nothing could kill a man like Stormy.

Winona Olsen would never be that lucky.

She accepted the glass trophy her father passed to her, the perfectly practiced kiss he planted on her cheek as he squeezed her shoulders.

It was probably just as well, she told herself. If her dad had died, she would have starved to death.

She didn't have the key to the locks he kept on the pantry.

TWO

Lucille Pryce kicked off one of her hot pink no-slip clogs, then took the other off with her hand and pitched it against the wall. "Why aren't the *lights* on, Marcus," she yelled, slamming the front door behind her. She tried the light switch again. Again. Then she slapped the wall with her open hand. "Marcus!" Her mother's spoon collection rattled in its wooden case on the wall.

The linoleum was sticky against her bare feet as she stalked into the living room. The linoleum was always sticky, no matter how many times Lucille got up before school to mop it so her mother wouldn't do the thing where she walked in the front door, dropped her purse, and blinked, slowly, like she was still in utter disbelief this was her life. There were a lot of reasons why Lucille mopped the floors, and scrubbed out the shower, and worked doubles at the diner, and haggled for the stolen supermarket steaks that Mr.

Jessup sold out of the back of his El Camino so that her mom didn't have to eat something out of a can on her goddamn birthday. But that was the main reason. That blinking, like her mom's whole horrible life somehow got stuck in her eye, all at once.

It had no effect on her older brother. No effect at all.

"I wrote the check last weekend," she said to the figure hunched on the sofa. "I stuck it in an envelope. All it needed was a stamp. A stamp! I gave you the money to walk down to Meijer and get it!"

Marcus coughed. "Meijer's a grocery store, idiot."

"They sell stamps," Lucille said, "at the counter. So what, so you didn't pay it—so you just like left the power bill where?"

He shrugged. She could see him do it even in the dark.

"God*damn*it," she said, and picked up the landline from its cradle on the wall. Then dropped it, because without power, it was, of course, dead. With a growl, she fished her phone out of her purse. It was a secondhand iPhone 4 with a cracked screen and a serious inability to work. When she couldn't pull up the power company address, she texted Winona, and waited. She wouldn't text her mom. Her mom didn't need to worry about this.

Marcus was still hunched over his own phone, like God's own message to the angels was at the end of this level of *Candy Crush*. She didn't ask him for help. She knew it wasn't worth it. Instead she asked, casually, "How much battery do you have left?" The need to charge his phone could spur him into action.

"Twelve percent. But I have one of those external batteries. Don't worry about me." He said it without a trace of irony.

Lucille took a deep breath, dragged her hands through her

knotty hair. It was eight thirty. She'd been the first cut at the diner tonight, but her mom would be there until ten. Then she'd lock up, and since she let Lucille take her car, she'd walk the fourteen blocks home. There was still time to fix this.

If the power company answered their phone after hours. If they could turn the power back on before tomorrow.

The pink-and-green light from his phone turned Marcus's face into a deranged Care Bear's. He had his foot propped up on the ottoman, like he always did, in a blue Velcro cast he'd bought himself off Craigslist six months ago. It was his excuse for everything, that foot. Not having a job. Not going to school. Not eating anything except Oreos and skulking out only at night to buy root beer at the 7-Eleven at midnight, like he was some kind of soda werewolf who was only healed at the stroke of twelve. Before that, it was a burn on his left hand that he'd gotten hitting his new bong. Marcus was twenty, but in terms of his priorities, he acted like a four-year-old who couldn't see beyond the McDonald's ball pit.

When Lucille looked at him, she felt something inside of her chest shriveling up so violently that she was sure, someday, her mother would hear it and know her for the bitch she was.

He just needs to grow up, Lucy, her mom liked to tell her, running her hand over Lucille's thick blond hair while her daughter complained about the PlayStation 4 Deluxe Bullshit Edition that Marcus had just bought while she was working late to pay for her gym uniform.

Yeah? she'd ask. *Then why did I have to grow up first?*

Lucille picked up her work clogs, then went out the front door.

She settled herself on the front step to wait for Winona's response. It was long past dark, but that was always the case up here, a hundred miles north of nowhere. The sun belonged to people who lived in less godforsaken places.

Already the neighbors' porch lights were on. As Lucille pulled out her phone again, Cousin-Tammy-Next-Door stuck her head out her perpetually open window. "You okay there?"

"I'm okay," Lucille called, and put her hand up. "Just waiting on a call."

"Take care, sweetie. Say hi to Bonnie for me."

The fact that Cousin-Tammy-Next-Door didn't say hi to Marcus made Lucille smile. "Say hey to Boomer and Sticks," she said, even though Tammy's calicos were mean little jerks.

Tammy nodded, then snapped her window shut. Lucille's phone buzzed.

Here's the number for Kingsville Electric, Winona wrote, and included it. *Did Marcus screw up?*

Is the Pope Catholic?

When Winona didn't immediately text back, Lucille wrote, *You okay?*

That was when her phone died. She swore, then swore again. Cousin-Tammy-Next-Door's window opened half an inch, and Lucille shut her trap. The last thing their neighbors needed was to hear more about their money troubles, even if they were family. All of Kingsville knew that Lucille's family was trash, the same way they knew that you'd go to hell for killing someone.

Lucille believed in hell. She believed in her mom. She believed in getting out of Kingsville before it sucked the last of the piss and vinegar right out of her.

With nothing else to do, she walked to the end of the drive and opened the mailbox. Coupons for Food Fair, for Meijer, credit card offers in her brother's name that she immediately shredded there on the lawn. A circular from the brand-new Target that was open all night. It reminded her that she'd been meaning to go there with Winona, get candy necklaces from the bulk aisle. More bills, for water and her mom's Visa and cable. Lucille did the math in her head.

She'd been saving up for her and Winona's Chicago Adventure (she secretly thought of it like that sometimes, like it was a Disneyland ride that was also very Adult and Boozy) for months now, but she didn't have anywhere close to what she needed. Not for their escape *and* the family's bills, especially now that the Pryces would have to pay the reconnection fee for the electric. If Lucille still had the stash she'd been hiding away since she was fourteen—

She stopped herself, firmly. She didn't have it. Marcus had taken it from her. He had taken it from her, and that night, at the police station, the world had given her Winona back in exchange.

It was repayment with interest, as far as Lucille was concerned.

As she stood there, toeing the dirt, staring off into the middle distance (the place that correct math answers were usually kept, in Lucille's experience), her eyes focused in on the Crown Vic across the street. A little beaten up, a little rusted out, especially around a dent on the driver door handle.

Lucille didn't know that dent, or that car, which wouldn't be weird outside of Kingsville. But Lucille was 50 percent Pryce, 50 percent Folgarelli, and at least 80 percent related to every soul in this neighborhood. And none of *them* drove a car that looked like it rolled right out of a cop charity auction.

She tilted her head—she tried not to do that, she knew it made her look like a golden retriever—and she squinted, and there he was, a man hunkered down in the driver's seat, texting like he was an actor in an off-brand soap opera. A plainclothes cop. Who ever texted with their elbows up on the wheel? Someone who wanted you to see their phone, that's who. Someone who wanted you to think they were doing anything other than *casing your house.*

Lucille swore for a solid minute before storming back in the front door.

"Marcus," she yelled. "Marcus!"

To her shock, he came hobbling in from the living room. His face was sallow from his processed-sugar diet and his apparent allergy to sunlight.

"There's a cop outside," she said. "He had *binoculars* around his neck, like he's a forest ranger and you're Smokey Bear."

Marcus shrugged, and turned, ostensibly to return to the couch.

"Oh, so I guess this isn't news to you? Of *course* not," Lucille said, and she stormed after him into the kitchen, backing him up against the counter. "Are you dealing again?"

He stared back at her like she was a Super Bowl hologram or a ghost.

"Am I alive? Am I *dreaming* this conversation? Are. You.

Dealing. Again." She looked pointedly down at his foot. "Are you dealing *out of our house* again?"

Marcus had spent the last year running Molly for one of the Upper Peninsula's finest drug lords, who had the delusion of grandeur to refer to himself as the Candy Man. (Lucille was pretty sure that his name had to be, like, Shawn.) But at the end of last year, Marcus had taken a job washing dishes at Denny's, and she'd assumed—naively—that he'd stopped dealing.

Then he had "broken his foot" after dropping a box of dishrags on it.

"I can't exactly get around right now," Marcus said finally. "I might as well work from home."

"Work from—" Lucille's hands seized, and she stuffed them in her pockets. "So you're just making money and hiding it somewhere?"

He scoffed. "Like you can talk."

"I never did anything that jeopardized you and Mom! God, Marcus, they *know* you deal, they're *out there right now*. You have to stop. You know you have to stop."

It was dark in the kitchen, hot without the fans going. In late May, Michigan lit up like a furnace, and it was always worse indoors. Marcus had little ripples of sweat along his temples. He looked like a fish. A sweaty fish. "If you hate me that much," he said, "why don't you just turn me in, then?"

"Because," Lucille told him, "Mom would never let your precious ass sit in a cell for months while they wait for a trial date. So she'd empty out her bank accounts. That's what, two hundred dollars. The Pryce cousins pitch in, the Folgarelli cousins pitch in, nobody wants to have one of us rotting away for the whole town to laugh at, so everyone looks under their couch cushions. That's maybe another five hundred bucks. *Maybe*. Which leaves what, I don't know, another two thousand dollars, and so then we'll have the bail bonds, another mortgage on the house . . ."

Marcus blinked at her.

"You don't think about any of this, do you," she said. "*Do* you. You've never had to. How about the part where I have to work another twenty years to pay it off while you get a law degree and a six-pack in prison? No. You stop dealing. You stop *now*."

But even as she finished speaking, Marcus was edging her backward, his cast thunking hollowly against the floor. "How about this? How about you get out of my face? My little fucking sister giving me orders. Saint Lucille. What if *I* give you an order? Do anything to screw up my setup, and I'll tell the cops that you were in on it with me."

She stared at him, furiously trying to come up with some kind of counterthreat, when he tilted his head a little to the side.

The way she did, when she was trying to work out a problem.

He was her brother. Her blood. They were made of the same basic components—they were just machines with the parts rearranged.

With a hitched breath, Lucille shoved him away. "You *lose*, Lucy," he was saying, but she was already running, sick and shuddering, all the way out the door.

On the front step, Lucille almost tripped over her work clogs and her phone, and she scooped them up with shaking hands. "Tammy!" she hollered. Her cousin stuck her head out the window; she'd probably heard the whole damn thing. "Mind if I come over and say hey to your kitties myself? And maybe I can charge my phone a little too."

THREE

Sometimes Winona felt guilty about not being able to control her thoughts. For even *wondering* what life would be like if Stormy didn't come home from work one day.

Right now, Stormy was driving Winona over the little red bridge that arced across the thawing creek, on their way to their Saturday morning visit with her grandfather, and all she could think was, *What if there's still some ice on the asphalt?*

What if the tires skid, and the brakes don't catch?

What if we flip over the railing?

What if only I survive?

It would only take one wrong move, a tiny mistake.

Stormy made a smooth right turn past the whitewashed fence and glittering lawn into Grandfather Pernet's neighborhood of wide-flung brick mansions and oversized stone cottages. No ice.

"I heard from the nurse this morning," Stormy said in the flat, toneless voice he often used when it was just the two of them, as if he'd used up all his charisma throughout the week and needed to let his vocal cords recover.

Winona's stomach dipped. "Is he all right?"

Stormy glanced up from the road and studied her. Had she sounded too eager? Not concerned enough? Too concerned? Despite their standing Saturday morning coffee dates, her father and grandfather's relationship was less than amicable, and Winona had learned to tread carefully when discussing one with the other.

She'd thought, at first, that the source of the tension must have been her mother's death—that perhaps Grandfather Pernet blamed Stormy for her overdose.

But then, *That Night* had happened and Winona had realized her father hated her grandfather just as much—if not more than—Grandfather Pernet hated Stormy.

"He's having a bad week," Stormy finally answered. "Don't be alarmed if he confuses you for her."

They turned down the long drive, between the two stone lions that guarded it. Her mother had once told her that when she was a child, she'd imagined that at night the stone lions sprang to life, prowled around her parents' lawns and gardens, keeping any evil thing that tried to intrude at bay.

She'd said this like she said most things Winona remembered: wistfully, as if there were a secret, profound meaning Winona couldn't yet decipher. Nearly every memory she had of her mother contained the thought, *I'll understand this when I'm older*, but now, nearly ten years after Katherine Olsen's death, Winona was no closer to understanding who her mother was, or what had happened to her.

Briefly, she imagined the stone lions springing to life, pouncing onto the hood of the car, their massive paws swiping straight through the windshield to claw at Stormy's—

She needed to get a grip on herself. Really, she was being immature, not to mention dramatic. It wasn't like Stormy had even hurt her—except that *one* time, which had probably been an accident—and if she walked around their house feeling like an anvil was on her chest, like any wrong move could bring apocalyptic fire raining down on her house, that was *her* problem, not his.

Stormy was particular but not violent. Except that one time, which had definitely been an accident, now that she thought about it.

Still, that weight pressed in on her from every direction, like it always did when she was near her father, or in his house, waiting for him to come home, or sitting in school, watching the clock tick closer to the end of the day.

The weight only ever let up when she was with Lucille.

Her best friend didn't tiptoe through the world like any misstep could upset the balance of the world, and next year, when they were living together in Chicago—Lucille working in some hip, high-end restaurant and Winona taking gen-ed classes at her father's alma mater—everything was going to be different.

She just had to find a way to convince her father to let her live off campus. So what if he was angry? She'd be eighteen soon enough. She could do whatever she wanted.

"Don't encourage his delusions," Stormy said as they reached the end of the driveway. "But don't upset him either."

Winona nodded. Stormy put the car in park, its sleek black nose pointed toward the second garage where Grandfather kept his 1969 Alfa Romeo convertible. Not that he could drive it anymore. He was mostly blind, and for years his Alzheimer's had been creeping over his mind like smoke, hiding everything he'd known bit by bit.

"Such a shame," Stormy said as he eyed the shut garage, just like he did every week. Winona didn't know if Stormy meant that what was happening to his father-in-law was a shame, or that it was a shame for the car to sit here, unused, unseen, locked away, and undriven.

They got out of the car and followed the flagstone walk to the French doors, which one of the nurses opened before they'd even rung the doorbell.

They were exactly on time. They were always exactly on time.

"Mr. Olsen," the dark-haired nurse, Vera, said. "Ms. Olsen. *Gorgeous flowers!* Come right in." She accepted the vase of pale peach and yellow flowers, along with the twenty-dollar tip Stormy handed her just for opening the door.

"Thank you, Vera," he said, smile beaming at her like a spotlight. The nurse dropped her face and turned, leading the two of them through the maze of flocked wallpaper and picture frames, and Winona performed her own ritual: running her eyes over every photograph of her mother. Katherine Olsen looked like a Van Gogh portrait photographed in black and white: forlorn, secretive, always eyeing something just out of frame.

Just how Winona remembered her.

Just beyond the bright kitchen, in the solarium at the back of the house, Grandfather sat with his back to them, his chair pushed into a square of sunlight.

"Tryggve," Vera said, swapping today's flowers in for the old ones. "You've got visitors!"

"Hi, Dad," Stormy said as they moved into the room.

Grandfather's blue eyes wandered vaguely to his son-in-law, but his face remained blank until his gaze fell on Winona. A line etched between his eyebrows, and she braced herself to hear her mother's name.

Instead, he said weakly, "I knew it . . ."

Stormy clapped a hand on Grandfather's shoulder. "Would you like some coffee, Dad? Vera, could you grab the cookies?"

Grandfather stared Stormy down.

Winona shifted uncomfortably. "Grandfather, would you like coffee?"

Really, she just wanted a chance to slip away, to fold herself into the daybed in her mother's childhood bedroom, run her fingers along the fringe on the silky patchwork comforter and skim the stacks of plays and books of poetry overflowing from her mahogany bookcase.

But their visits were never long, and Stormy insisted they spend every minute with Grandfather Pernet, whose wispy eyebrows had lifted and mouth had formed a perfect O at the sound of Winona's voice. He took her palm between his papery hands.

"Mr. Olsen?" Vera called from the kitchen. "Could you approve these charges?"

Stormy huffed, his dark eyes fluttering between the doors and his daughter, her hand caught in Grandfather Pernet's trembling grip.

"I'll be *right* back," Stormy said. His smile lit up his snow-white teeth as he turned back into the kitchen. "Yes, Vera?"

Winona looked at her grandfather and tried for an encouraging smile. They'd never been close, and ever since that night last year—when he'd called her crying and confused and she'd driven out to pick him up on the side of the road, soaked to the bone, barefoot, and in his pajamas—she'd dreaded these visits.

The way they set her father on edge each week.

The way those watery blue eyes always searched hers.

"Are you having a nice day?" she asked him.

"I *knew* it," he wheezed again, his eyes widening. He reached for her sleeve, his age-spotted hands fumbling for purchase on the crepe chiffon. "I got your letter. I knew you were alive, Katherine. I knew it."

The chatter of the birds went silent beneath the layer of static that rushed through Winona's ears. Even having been warned, she wasn't braced to hear her mother's name, to be mistaken for her.

"No, Grandfather," she said gently. "It's me. Winona."

But Grandfather Pernet was pulling himself out of the chair as he gripped her arm tighter and tighter. "What did he do?" he growled. "What did that bastard *do*?"

She shook her head in terror, tried to unfurl his fingers. "It's Winona," she said again. "Winona."

He slumped back into the chair. "Yes," he rasped. "Winona. He won't have given Winona her letter . . . She won't know . . ."

"What letter?" she whispered.

Stormy stepped back into the solarium, silver coffeepot in hand and a razor-edged smile on his broad mouth, and Winona felt the expression on her face wipe clean instinctively, though she was still holding on to her arm where her grandfather's fingers had dug in.

Stormy walked right between them and began to fill the white china mugs waiting on saucers on the table. "Lovely weather today, isn't it?" he asked.

Winona willed her thudding heart to quiet. She nodded. "It is," she said calmly.

But even as she modulated her voice, her thoughts raced away from her control. Her grandfather had mentioned a letter before.

The night her grandfather had called her, crying and confused.

The night her father had hurt her.

The night she'd met Lucille.

FOUR

Winona was supposed to be writing her French essay, but she was staring blankly at her dark bedroom window instead. Stormy had gone out for dinner with a visiting colleague, so she was home alone, and she'd long since eaten the single-portion dinner their personal chef, Martina, had left in the refrigerator earlier that evening.

Her phone buzzed. A message from Lucille: *It's back*.

The car. The one Lucille had seen watching her house the night before. She was worried it belonged to a barely-undercover cop, and her wasteoid brother was selling drugs to him.

"Marcus," Winona hissed under her breath. If Winona had a time machine, she would snatch Lucille's brother and dump him on the *Titanic*. Maybe save baby Leo DiCaprio while she was at it.

She quickly texted her best friend—her *only* friend—the one-word encouragement they'd been passing back and forth for weeks, whenever their lives in Kingsville proved to be particularly Kingsvilley: *Chicago*.

Lucille texted back: *Chicago*.

Winona sent two old-lady emojis back and waited for a reply, but Lucille didn't send one, and Winona was forced to go back to staring down her homework.

She couldn't get what Grandfather Pernet had said out of her head, and her mind kept wandering back to That Terrible Night, the night she spent a lot of time and energy Not Thinking About. Sometimes she wondered if that was the source of the weight on her chest, but the truth was, the weight had been there as long as she could remember.

That night, Winona had gotten home from school to find a voice mail from her father saying he'd be late. There was a hailstorm rolling in, and Stormy was going to cover it. She'd only been home twenty minutes when her grandfather called her.

Stormy had a rule about Winona talking on the phone with Grandfather without Stormy present. *If he's calling you, there's a good chance he's confused, and if he's confused,* I *need to talk to him.*

So Winona had ignored it, worrying whether Stormy would be angrier if she interrupted him at work or if she didn't tell him about the call.

While she'd been deciding, Grandfather had called her four more times in a row. On the fifth, she panicked and answered. He'd been crying, babbling incoherently on the other end, and by then the hailstorm had picked up, and she'd been fairly sure she could hear it in the background.

The panic had started to set in. She should have answered right away; she should have *called Stormy* right away.

"Where are you, Grandfather?" she'd asked, again and again, until he'd described the nearest street sign. She knew Stormy kept the keys to the Land Rover—which would be hers in a few short months—in his desk drawer.

So she went to get them and drove out to pick up her grandfather, sobbing and soaked on the side of the road. She'd wanted to call Stormy on the way out, but her grandfather had been so scared, so confused. He'd begged her to stay on the phone with him. She couldn't say no.

"If he knows I got lost, he'll move me into a home," Grandfather had insisted hoarsely. "He'll get rid of me, like he got rid of her. That bastard wants my money! He's always wanted my money! Well, I won't be blackmailed out of my own house! I'll spend every dime before I die, if that's what it takes! Don't you tell him, Winona!"

Even now, she remembered the way her stomach had turned at the prospect of trying to keep something from her father.

She had known it was impossible. Deep down, she had known.

But she'd also known he was going to be angry when he found out what she'd done. He might not let her get her license after all. He might not let her have sugar for a month or take her bedroom door off its hinges.

She'd decided to risk it anyway.

But when she'd driven her grandfather home, her father's car had been parked in the driveway.

A neighbor had seen Grandfather wander off, barefoot, and called an Officer Carroway—lucky, because he was a "buddy" of Stormy's. He'd let Stormy know so he could handle the "family matter" privately, and avoid the "town hens clucking."

Stormy had seemed so calm as he explained this to her and Grandfather, and that was how Winona had known he was furious. Other people *lost* their tempers when they were upset; her father *found* his. He was more in control than ever.

"Winona," he'd said. "Go wait in the car. I need to check in with your grandfather."

When their conversation was finished, Stormy met Winona in the Land Rover and they drove home together, leaving his BMW behind. He hadn't said a word, and all that time, the pressure was building. Her stomach was twisting. It was hard to breathe.

They walked inside in silence.

The first words Stormy said, when they reached their airy, tastefully-taupe great room, were, "Stay here."

She stood in the middle of the cream-colored rug and waited while he disappeared into his office. As he walked back out, he lit up a cigarette: the next clue to how angry he was. He rarely smoked.

"Did your grandfather tell you what upset him?" he'd asked.

Winona shook her head.

Stormy took a long inhale and blew the smoke out through his nose, studying her.

"Every year or so, some con artist gets it into his mind to send the poor man a letter saying your mother isn't dead. They're trying to extort a poor old man."

Winona's heart had leaped like a fish from water.

"They want his money." Stormy flicked the ash onto the coaster. "We know your mother's gone, though, don't we?"

It was a strange question to ask, but Winona had been so claustrophobic in her own body right then that she couldn't puzzle over the question's peculiarity. She just needed to anticipate what it was Stormy wanted and do it, so peace could be restored and the weight could lift. She nodded.

"She's gone because she didn't have self-control, Winona," Stormy said calmly. "She made *dangerous* decisions."

Winona agreed.

Stormy held the cigarette away from his mouth and looked at her for a moment. "You're a lot like her, Winona."

Tears sprang into her eyes, and she tried to blink them back. Stormy always thought she was trying to manipulate him when she cried. She shook her head.

Stormy frowned. "You always have been," he said. "But you're *going* to learn to control yourself, darling. You have to. It's my job to keep you safe."

Stormy had reached out and taken his daughter's hand in his.

Then he'd turned her hand over and pressed the cigarette into her skin.

She'd started to cry out, to scream, but his grip on her arm tightened.

"You could have died today, darling," he said while she struggled against him. He lifted the cigarette, and she gasped for breath. Stormy didn't pull away.

"You did something stupid."

He pressed the cigarette to her skin again.

She could still remember the horrible smell, the ash mingling with something like rancid meat, and then the impulse to vomit, like a punch in her gut.

"We have rules for a reason," he said. "Who knows what could have happened today?"

She wanted to fall into a ball on the floor, but she knew he'd think she was being dramatic, so she stood her ground.

"I'm so happy you're safe, darling," he said, tossing the cigarette into the ashtray. "Now go to bed."

And she had, at least until she was sure Stormy was asleep. Then she'd crept out to the police station, seriously thinking she might turn him in.

She'd imagined a kindly receptionist meeting her at the doors, listening to her story and wrapping a warm blanket around her, as if she'd just been pulled from the choppy waters of Lake Michigan. *You're safe!* the receptionist would promise her. *That man will never hurt you again!*

But when she'd reached the police station, the first man she'd seen through the glass was Officer Carroway.

That was when she knew: Stormy Olsen wasn't a man anymore. He'd made himself a god.

She'd met Lucille that night, and her life had changed. But in the end, she still went home, crept right back into her dark house with all the invisible weight that seemed to float around within its walls.

In the morning, their chef made them waffles. There were

flowers waiting on the granite island when Stormy met her at the breakfast table. That morning, he'd given her the Cartier brace-let. He'd gone out to get it before she was even awake, wrapped it clumsily (she suspected even *this* was intentional), and presented it to her with a little card. He was *so proud of her!* He hoped she *knew that he would always be there for her!* She knew immediately the bracelet was meant to cover the burns.

The Louboutins, the *Hamilton* tickets, the new phone, the Land Rover. Each of these had appeared days or weeks after she'd upset him. Sometimes he even cried as he presented them.

But they never talked about their fights—if you could even call them that—and they never discussed what had happened to Grandfather Pernet that night. The in-home nurses had simply appeared the next Saturday, during their coffee visit, and been there ever since.

Nothing but the finest care for Stormy Olsen's father-in-law. Nothing but the nicest jewelry for his daughter.

Winona emerged from the memory and slammed her French book shut.

This was ridiculous. One overreaction, over a year ago, and she was acting like her father was a mob boss. There was a way to settle this, once and for all, but she'd have to be quick.

She hopped off her bed and ran downstairs. She checked, then double-checked the driveway for signs of her father returning, then slipped into his office.

She crept around his mahogany desk and carefully, as though he were listening through a glass just outside the doors, started sliding the drawers open. She'd checked all but the bottom left when she bumped the mouse and his dark computer monitor woke up, the sudden blue light nearly scaring her out of her skin. She clutched her chest and laughed.

She was being so jumpy, and for no good reason.

A photograph on-screen caught her eye, a kitchen nearly identical to theirs.

It was a real-estate listing for a condo.

Sprawling across the top of the listing in bolded font: **EVAN-STON, ILLINOIS.** The Chicago suburb that Northwestern was in. Stormy was condo-shopping. For *her*, for when she went to school? The place was gorgeous: all high ceilings and wall-high windows, white granite countertops and oversized bathrooms.

Lucille would never be able to pay rent on a place like this, and there was no way in hell she'd be willing to live there rent-free. Lucille was too proud for that.

Winona *really* needed to tell Stormy about her plans before he dropped nearly a million dollars on a place she couldn't live in.

She put the monitor back to sleep, then knocked the drawer closed. Something rattled. She opened it again. A crack ran along the width of the drawer, right at the front, as if the bottom of it didn't quite line up.

Her stomach dropped.

It was a false bottom. She lifted the thin piece of wood away, and beneath it found nothing but another file folder.

She tipped it open, and everything in her went cold.

The envelope lay at the top of the stack of pages within, and while the narrow, sloping handwriting across it wasn't familiar, the name and address were her own.

Worst of all was the slice along the top of it, proof the letter—*her* letter—had been opened by her father.

It could still be a fake, she reasoned—but before the thought had even landed, she saw the photograph tucked under it, a bleary action shot of a woman in a crocheted top and yoga pants, jogging down a sidewalk with a rolled-up mat under one arm and the other waving, to someone outside the frame.

Winona's heart jolted; her throat constricted until no air could get in or out.

She was looking at a photograph of a ghost, only ghosts didn't change after they died, didn't buy themselves new clothes or change their hair.

And Winona's mother's hair was longer than she'd ever seen it.

Well beneath her shoulders, with a frizzy wave that Winona couldn't reconcile with the posh, if melancholy, woman of society she remembered. Mrs. Olsen's limbs were fuller, softer than they'd once been, but her face had thinned.

The woman was both her mother and a complete stranger. She would've been more at home in the practiced "bohemian" bedroom in Grandfather's house, with its Persian rugs and towering stacks of Edward Albee and Sylvia Plath, than in Stormy's modern art museum of a home.

And then there was the file underneath it. The name printed right there at the top: *Kate Mercer.* Not her mother's name, but close enough to Katherine Pernet Olsen to call it to mind.

What was this? A dossier?

Her heart was really hammering now, so hard it hurt, and her stomach gurgled loudly as if all the confusion and pain and pressure in her body had turned to hunger.

Her mother was alive. Her mother was alive and her father had a private investigator following her.

Winona eyed the address on the top form. *Kate Mercer*'s address. The *ghost* of Katherine Olsen's address. 1123 Morning Glory Road. Las Vegas, Nevada.

She had either been standing there staring down both for one second, or four hours, when she heard a key rattling in the front door. On an impulse she'd later regret, she snatched the envelope, stuffed the folders back into place, threw the false bottom over them, and closed the drawer.

By the time she heard Stormy's heavy footfall in the foyer, she was at the top of the stairs. She darted into her room and slid the envelope under her pillow.

She couldn't read the letter in this house, not with him right below her feet.

She needed to get out. She needed to talk to Lucille.

She needed to call a Cliffside.

FIVE

ABOUT EIGHT DOLLARS LEFT IN AN UNDERWEAR DRAWER

The day that Lucille met Winona had ended at the Cliffside Motel, but it had begun with Lucille's brother stealing her money.

Ever since Lucille had moved on from candy necklaces and ring pops, Marcus had been raiding her bedroom for jewelry good enough to sell. She'd always taken it as a sign of his particular stupidity. Where on earth would Lucille get the money to buy gold hoops, or one of those Tiffany heart bracelets that the other girls wore, and *why* would she spend that money in the first place?

Every dime Lucille made went into the jar on the kitchen counter. At least as far as her family knew. But ever since she'd started at the Starlight Diner, working for Travis alongside her mom, she'd squirreled away a single dollar from each shift and put it in a sack under her bed. By eighteen, Lucille had been working for four years. She worked five shifts a week, six in the summers. It added up, and she never touched it—for new jeans, or work shoes, or a haircut, she always pulled from the jar on the counter.

Lucille's life was mostly math. Sometimes it shocked strangers to find out she'd aced AP Calc, or that she'd turned twenty bucks on a poker app into a cash-out of a cool five hundred, but she had a lot more reason to bend her brain around numbers than the people who never had to check their bank accounts.

Lucille didn't have a bank account. Not anymore. For the three months that she did, she'd stuffed it with her online poker earnings, until one day she pulled it up to brag to her mom (*your daughter is a five-card stud STUD!*) and watched it vanish. Her mom's lip had wobbled just the smallest amount, and she'd said, *I'm so proud of you, Lucy*, and then she'd looked at the floor and said, *I know it's your money, but I'm so worried about paying to fix the roof and getting new tires for the car and—*

It might've started out as Lucille's money, but it didn't end that way.

But *this* money? Her tip money? That was a different story.

By senior year, she'd already had to change out the singles for hundreds at the bank. Sometimes at night, tossing and turning, she was kept awake by the thought of the money breathing down below her, a thick tangle of life.

She didn't have a plan. No concrete destination, no vision board of what she wanted her life to look like after high school. All she wanted was an option, a possibility. She wanted the opposite of Kingsville, the opposite of the Starlight, the opposite of Marcus, the opposite of her dumbass not-boyfriend Chaxton.

If she hadn't filled in the outline of it yet, who cared. The money could do that later.

So on the days that Marcus raided her room, he took her textbooks to sell on Amazon and the pair of designer jeans she'd found at Value Village to sell to some poor girl on eBay, but he never looked between the mattress and the box spring, where her cloth *Earth Day* sack lived, stuffed with money.

Until, of course, he did.

She'd come home from the library, for once, instead of the diner—she'd been checking out books for her history paper, books that could be returned the next day, before Marcus could find out about them. She kept her textbooks in her locker at school. She kept a watch on her room, her phone on her at all times, an eye on Marcus on the couch.

Today, Marcus wasn't on the couch.

The clock on the stove said 8:02; it wasn't time for his soda run yet. She knew that he was dealing Molly, but she'd never known him to make a house call. Any other place he could be—him running errands for their mom, him out meeting friends—was laughably impossible. Even *his* dealer, she knew, dropped off his supply to their back door. Marcus lived his life through his phone, kept his connections happy, amassed some small sad fortune while his mom and his sister ate food exclusively from Food Fair's finest cans.

Lucille crept into the living room, just in case he was waiting in a dark corner (*he is* not *an actual werewolf, dammit*) when she heard the noise coming from her bedroom. A rustling. The groan of a mattress being eased back onto the bed.

She didn't have to walk in to know what he had done. From the door, she could see it: the *Earth Day* bag flat on the floor, empty. Marcus's ugly-ass Air Jordans next to it, his thick, stupid feet inside them, his brand-new iPhone like a fishing lure on the carpet. Just lying there, like he'd already forgotten about it.

Lucille had always possessed a pretty good memory—she remembered the color of someone's eyes, their dead dog's name—but the next five minutes were blacked out in her head like they'd been censored.

It ended with two black eyes (one hers, one Marcus's), a split lip (hers), and his quiet, steely voice telling her, as he loomed over where he'd knocked her down onto the floor, *Do you know what Mom would say if she knew you'd been hiding money? Because I took pictures. I'll show her. And she'll hate you for it. We're a family, Lucille.*

He had her cash sticking out of his pockets like a cartoon villain.

Marcus left her there, bleeding, on the brown shag carpet. She could hear the front door open, close. A few minutes passed before the hot roar in her ears subsided, and she could ease herself to her feet, stumble over to the mirror. Touching her nose, her lips, her swollen eye, she thought, *I need to clean this up before my mom sees it, this is like an awful* Law & Order *episode—*

Law & Order.

No, she thought, and smiled a bright red smile. *This is gold.*

Calmly, she documented her bruises with a camera. She calmly packed her purse, an overnight bag. She kept on her bloodstained sweatshirt—airbrushed unicorn, rainbows, *Trixie* written across the top, she would kill Marcus dead if this was ruined—and, because her brother had taken the car, she walked—calmly—the three point seven miles to the police station.

In a hailstorm.

That was where she saw her, like a lost deer, or a white marble sculpture, or something. A deer sculpture. A girl in kitten heels and a sheath dress in the rain, no umbrella, standing across from the police station hugging herself. Lucille would have walked on by—a girl with money like that didn't need her help—except for the look on her face. It wasn't self-pity, or fear. It was fury.

She didn't realize she had stopped dead on the sidewalk until the other girl spoke.

"Lucille, right?" Winona didn't turn her head, only her eyes. It pissed Lucille off, until she saw the tears on Winona's face. She didn't want Lucille to see her cry.

Lucille understood pride, if nothing else.

"Yeah," she said. "Winona?" She thought that was her name. The actress from the '90s? Either Winona, or maybe Alicia? It was weird that the weatherman's daughter had a name like that. She would've guessed, like, Victoria or Fluffy or something.

"Yeah. I'm Winona. Winona Olsen." She rubbed her arm absently.

Kingsville was a small town. There was no such thing as being invisible here. They'd maybe talked in the third grade for ten minutes, borrowed a tampon in junior high, but that was it. That was as close as they'd gotten.

"What are you—" Lucille looked down at Winona's arm, at the cigarette burn on her skin, as raw and horrible as a black hole, and swallowed. They both knew what Winona was doing here. "Are you—" But she wasn't okay. "Can I—"

Weakly, Winona started to laugh. "I like your unicorn sweatshirt," she said, and then she started to sob, bent over herself and her dumb silk shoes that were definitely ruined and her sleeveless dress and before Lucille knew it she was digging a hoodie out of her bag, and a towel, and she helped Winona over to the doorway of the church that sat across from the police station like an omen.

She got a better look at Winona's arm in the light. Winona got a better look at her face.

"Who did this to you?" Lucille asked, zipping up her sweatshirt like she was a child. She pulled the hood over her head. It had cat ears. "Was it your boyfriend? I'll kill him."

"You'll kill him?" Winona started laughing again, wildly. "I'll kill yours. Let's go kill them. Our boyfriends. Wouldn't that be fun, if it was that simple?"

Maybe it made her crazy, but Lucille was *there*—a blue sky, a convertible, the two of them with machetes. All she'd ever wanted, really, was someone to ride shotgun, Marcus under her wheels. "I can't think of anything simpler, actually," she said. "Where is he?"

Winona shook her head. "It's not—I don't have—my grandfather—"

"Your grandfather did this to you?"

For a second they just looked at each other. Lucille reached up to touch Winona's arms, to offer any comfort, and then she realized she didn't know where all her burns were. Where her bruises were. She didn't know anything about this girl.

They had matching black eyes.

"No," Winona said. She was whispering. "My grandfather got lost, and I went to go find him. He's my—my mom's dad. My mom disappeared when I was a kid. She was a drug addict, and my dad said that—that if I wasn't careful I'd end up just like her."

It took everything in Lucille not to spit out, *Stormy Olsen? He wouldn't do that.* He'd tipped her mom 300 percent last week at the diner. In celebration, her mom had brought home one of those rotisserie chickens from the grocery store.

She knew Stormy about as well as she knew Winona. But Winona was wearing her hoodie. Winona's body had his burn marks on it.

"That *bastard,*" Lucille said, and it was like a key opening a lock.

"I—I just wanted to help him? He was lost, he wandered out and didn't know where he was and I went to go get him, and he keeps thinking that I'm my mother, he's confused . . . and I swear I'd think that he's just, like, senile, but there's something about him that makes my dad really upset. And I don't get it. My grandfather is going to leave my dad and me all his money, and my mom . . . you know Pernet's?"

"The cookies?" Lucille blurted, before thinking this girl in Tory Burch was definitely *not* referring to the cheapo shortbread cookies that were shaped like blurry Michigans. But to Lucille's surprise, Winona nodded.

"That's my mom's family. That's my mom's money. And my dad *hates* her, and sometimes I think he punishes me for looking like her? For being here?" Winona was hiccupping now, shivering and hiccupping, and Lucille gingerly put an arm around her so she didn't hurt her any further.

"Maybe he's just confused. Maybe he was just angry? He didn't know what he was doing, but he was smoking, and he grabbed my arm, and—"

Lucille nodded. She'd gotten the picture. It struck her then that the two of them were crouched between a church and a police station—two places of confession—and that, for whatever reason, they'd chosen each other instead.

"We should go in," Lucille said. "So you can report."

"So *you* can report. What happened to you? Why are you just letting me talk?" All at once Winona got to her feet. "Where is he? I want to kill him. I want to *fight* something."

"Not in those shoes, you aren't," Lucille said, making a decision. "I was gonna turn my brother in, go stay with my cousin Tammy, but I don't know what I was thinking. A Pryce goes into that police station and all they're going to say is, *Oh, little trash girl, get into a trash girl fight?*"

"I'm not going in either." Winona bit her lip. "I just—I just got in the car and left and this was the only place I could think to go. But the cops know my dad. They're his *friends*. They'll just bring me back to him."

"They might not. Princess like you."

"My dad is king," Winona said with an absurd, shaky grandeur. "I just serve at his leisure."

Lucille had no clue what that meant, but she *liked* this girl. Screw

40

Marcus, and her money. She couldn't get that back. She couldn't help herself—not yet. But Winona?

Maybe.

"You have a car?" Lucille reached up and tweaked one of Winona's cat ears. "I know this place we can get a G&T, maybe make a plan."

"A plan?"

"Of how we make it through to graduation, when we ride a rocket out of here. You ever heard of the Cliffside?"

"That dive? On the edge of town?" Winona laughed. "Okay. The Cliffside."

"That's the one." Lucille paused, wiped some of the blood out of her mouth. "You do like G&Ts, right? That's kind of like a deal breaker for me."

SIX

THE PRESENT, AND CALLING A CLIFFSIDE

Winona opened her messages with Lucille and typed: *Do I need to bring anything for Council tomorrow? Canned soda?*

Within seconds, her phone buzzed. *Yep—canned soda!*

Thank God. That meant Lucille was free to meet.

Last week, Lucille had sent her a text reading, *Don't forget! Chips!* And two weeks before that, Winona had gotten one that said, *Don't forget! Cupcakes,* and two more before that, she'd sent one to Lucille that said, *Do we need carrots at Council tomorrow?*

She hoped that wasn't so many meetings that Stormy would notice. But ever since he'd gotten his Changemaker on Friday, Stormy had been in a good mood.

She might as well take advantage of it. She grabbed her purse off the floor, stuffed the letter into it, pulled her Frye boots on, and hurried downstairs. "Daddy?" she called.

"Yes, sweetie?" her father called back through the open door of his study. He was reading the third Elena Ferrante book.

She fought to keep her mind blank. If she focused on the desk too long, heat would surge into her cheeks. "How was your dinner?"

His mouth stayed in its perfectly even line. "Lovely. And yours?"

"Great," she said. "Martina's really good."

Now was the time for Winona to strike. She smiled apologetically: "Marcy just texted me. I forgot Taylor's sick this week, so I agreed to bring the drinks for Council tomorrow. Do you need anything from the store?"

Her father blinked at her twice, and she did everything she could to keep from trembling and mouthing *please please please please* to herself. It took effort to keep her eyes from darting to her purse, but she was sure if she did, her father would look right through it to the letter hidden inside.

Finally Stormy shifted forward in his chair and pulled his wallet from his back pocket. "A bottle of Pellegrino." He unfolded a fifty-dollar bill and held it up.

She hated when he went for the big ones. It made their system for meeting riskier, because there was always the chance Lucille wouldn't *have* enough money to make change for the bill.

Winona hurried forward and pecked her father on the cheek as she accepted the fifty and the keys to "her" car.

"Don't dally, sweetie," he said.

"Yes, Daddy," she said.

She didn't take off running until she got to the front door. She dialed Lucille as she fumbled over the seat belt—text messages were forever; they had to be discreet. This sort of thing was always better for calls.

"What is it this time?" Lucille answered in her usual clipped, no-bullshit voice.

"A fifty-dollar bill and a bottle of Pellegrino."

Lucille sounded like she was doing a spit take on the other end. "Shit, Non. Fifty?"

"I know. Sorry."

"Not your fault. I'm sure I can scrounge it up, or borrow it from Tammy. See you in fifteen."

Winona pulled out and accelerated to four over the speed limit. For her, this was the equivalent of drag racing through Times Square with a blindfold on, but she had no choice. The Cliffside was on the other end of town, and she needed every spare moment she could get with Lucille.

That was why Lucille—who lived much closer to their usual rendezvous point—always went to the store to pick up whatever Stormy special-requested. It was a real pain, since Stormy always wanted the receipts and receipts listed change.

If Stormy sent Winona out the door with a fifty-dollar bill, then Lucille had to find a way to *pay* with a fifty-dollar bill. Of course, she always got the money back when she traded the Pellegrino, soda, and change to Winona in exchange for Stormy's original bill, but it wasn't like Lucille had fifties and hundreds lying around. Although she'd done her best to keep a few on hand ever since the two of them worked out this system.

They never got much time when they had to meet this way. On nights when Stormy was hosting business dinners or volunteering at charities, they might have a solid two hours together at the Cliffside, but usually he just dragged his Perfect Daughter along with him.

Women in Beverly Hills accessorized with tiny, bedazzled dogs. Stormy had a five-foot-ten human.

It had begun to rain and the tires skidded through it a few times as Winona neared the edge of town, but she didn't slow.

Four months ago, her father had a bad back spasm and had been on muscle relaxers for three days. They had been, unequivocally, the best three days of Winona's life, and she and Lucille had spent all night doing tequila shots at the bar.

She'd been sure her father would wake from his drug-induced slumber and track her down, but when she was with Lucille, she felt . . . invincible. Or more like Lucille was invincible and Winona herself was under Lucille's protection. It was like having two disparate gods warring for control over her life.

And even though the girls didn't get much time together, Winona had started to feel that the nights at the Cliffside were her real life and everything that happened in between was just filler, a job she hated, an acting role that had taken over her life.

The rain had picked up to a vicious downpour by the time she swerved into the empty lot of the Cliffside, its red neon sign stuttering along with its reflection on the rain-slicked asphalt.

She pulled into the spot beside Lucille and Lucille leaned over to swing open the passenger-side door of her mom's nineteen-eighty-whatever Saturn. Winona jumped out and dove through the rain into the seat. "Hellooooo, baby girl," Lucille sang, handing the bag of soda and Pellegrino over first, followed by a wad of bills and coins.

"Here." Winona forked over the fifty. "I'm really sorry about that."

Lucille shrugged it off. "Better than when he sends you with the credit card."

"True," Winona allowed. When that happened, there wasn't usually time for a detour at the Cliffside.

"So what else did you bring me?" Winona asked, false levity in her voice. These first moments when they were together were always precious, reserved for fun no matter how bad things were in both the Olsen and Pryce houses.

"Well." Lucille dragged a duffel bag out of the back seat and reached into it. "TADA!" she cried, pulling a fuzzy pink sweatshirt out of the bag.

"Gorgeous!" Winona shouted, clapping.

"Trés chic, right?"

"Absolutely. Who is it? Givenchy? Chanel?"

"Oh, daaaaaaarling. You know I don't fuck with Chanel. This one-of-a-kind stunner is *Mossimo*."

"Oooh," Winona cooed, pulling the sweatshirt over her J. Crew button-up. "I love their spring collection."

"Isn't it to-die?" Lucille said. "Now, let's get inside and see which rosé Garçon is serving tonight."

"Oaked or unoaked," Winona said.

"Boxed or bagged," Lucille added.

"Only time will tell," Winona said.

The girls darted into the icy rain and through the paint-peeling green door of the motel bar. They always started out this way, no matter how bad things were on either end. Winona didn't consider it small talk.

Small talk was lying. Saying whatever the people her father had arranged around her expected to hear. What she and Lucille did— *shit-shooting*, as Lucille called it—was a lifeline. It was friendship, as a verb. It was an act of love, the way they'd play together, pretend for just a few minutes each day that they were two old widows, with grown children who were always treating Winona and Lucille as if they were going senile, who were always making ridiculous decisions about job changes and moves and which schools would best suit Winona's and Lucille's grandkids, who were, in turn, horrific brats and sweet-cheeked angels.

These aged counterparts of theirs had moved somewhere warm when their husbands died. Sometimes it was Tucson, other nights it was Miami. They'd been on a big Palm Springs kick all winter. Winona wasn't allowed to wear tacky clothes, but Lucille owned nothing else, and she always brought something in a near-impossible shade of pink for Winona to put on before they *visited the poolside bar* or *stepped out for a bite at Château d'Burnetts Vodka* or whatever other names for the Cliffside evolved during their nights there.

As they burst into the bar, the beefy bartender, Glenn, looked up and nodded. He *had* to know they weren't really the twenty-three-year-old Krabapple twins, Kelly and Konstance, that their fake IDs claimed them to be, but Glenn, as a rule, did not Give Shits. The only thing they'd ever heard him talk about was the giant mounted fish over the bar, and Winona had immediately tuned him out. She wasn't much for fish talk.

Lucille took Winona's hand and, virtually skipping, tugged her back toward their usual booth in the corner, just behind the pool table. "Check out the rat at three o'clock," she hissed as she slid onto the sticky metallic-green vinyl.

Winona looked over her shoulder toward the couple leaning tipsily against the bar. A skinny milk-skinned man with a bulging Adam's apple and an hourglass of a woman whose pink spaghetti-strap dress clashed badly with her fire-truck red hair.

"If Stormy saw that guy's *leather*"—Winona made air quotes—"jacket in real life, he would have a conniption."

"Babe, if Stormy so much as *suspected* that jacket existed, he wouldn't be able to get out of his bed in the morning."

Lucille always called Winona's father by his name and somewhere along the way, she'd started to do it too, when they were together. It felt like one more small rebellion, innocent compared to their trips to a skeevy dive like the Cliffside, but sometimes when she said it, she found her shoulders rising protectively, the skin on the back of her neck crawling as if her father were standing right behind her. *Since when is it acceptable to call your father by his first name, Winona?*

To shake the creeping feeling off, she glanced back toward the couple at the bar. "By the way, Luce?" she said. "That's nine o'clock, not three."

"Well, *that's* good," Lucille said. "Three o'clock seems inappropriately early for the kind of business they're conducting."

"Are you sure it's business and not pleasure?" Winona asked.

Lucille shuddered. "Check out his hair plugs and then let me know if you still need that question answered. What do you want, G&T?"

Winona shook her head. "You shouldn't be spending money." And while Winona was technically an heiress, Stormy reviewed her credit card bills with a fine-toothed comb.

"So what," Lucille said lightly, "we came here for the view?"

Winona felt a jab in her gut. It always went like this: the breathless joy of having an ally for a few brief moments, followed by the reality that the two of them were still, largely, alone.

The letter suddenly felt hot against Winona's hip, burning right through her purse.

Winona cleared her throat. "So. How are things at *your* house?"

"At the Pryce Estate?" Lucille's smile faded, and her teeth worried at her lip, the exact expression that meant Trying to Decide What to Divulge. For the past year, Winona had shared all the nitty-gritty about her life with Lucille, but sometimes she suspected Lucille held back from sharing the full picture of what happened at the Pryce house. Like she didn't think Winona could handle it, or something.

Finally, Lucille shook her head. "Bland, boring, aesthetically Byzantine. Two months until you and I bail, so I'm just counting the days. But you called this meeting, Non. That means you start."

Well, how was *this* for being able to handle things: Winona pulled the envelope out of her purse and slapped it onto the table.

Lucille's brows knit together. "What's that?"

"A letter from my dead mother," Winona said. "From eight years after she overdosed."

SEVEN

"There." Lucille dropped two drinks on their sticky table. The last time it had been cleaned was probably sometime in 1982, unless the time last month that Winona spilled a full bottle of nail polish remover on it counted. Lucille didn't think it did.

Winona made a sound of protest, but Lucille pushed the G&T toward her. "Don't tell me these aren't necessary. Your mom is writing you from the grave. Anyway, I think they're doubles. Value for money! I asked Glenn if he would just give us the whole bottle of gin, but he said he needs it to clean the floor later." Lucille, as a rule, didn't babble, but sometimes she found herself rambling on until she could get Winona to smile.

It worked. Unsteadily, Winona grinned. Her hand was pressing the letter facedown to the table like it was going to grow wings and escape.

"Go on," Lucille said, nudging her.

"I'm not ready," Winona said. "Quick. Tell me something. Tell me something ridiculous."

Lucille thought about it. "My phone died earlier because Chaxton kept sending me photos of the flavored condoms that 7-Eleven is selling." Chaxton was Lucille's erstwhile hookup. You could count his brain cells on both hands. "Strawberry. Hazelnut. Blue raspberry."

"Ew," Winona said.

"Ew," Lucille agreed. "The letter, Nony."

"Okay," Winona said. "Okay." After a long, preparatory swig of her G&T, she reached for the letter with two manicured fingers.

It was stuck.

"Our lives," Lucille observed, "are disgusting."

Winona dug at the corner with her index finger, but the letter stayed firmly tacked to the table. "My nails aren't long enough. How are my nails not long enough? They're acrylics. I have *claws*. Are you *shitting* me—"

"Lucy Pryce," a voice above them said. "Oh, and Ivanka Trump. That's super weird. Why are you here with Lucy?"

The two of them steered clear of each other at school. Stormy hadn't expressly forbidden Winona to hang out with Lucille, but that was mostly because he didn't know how close the two of them were. Since they were so close to graduation, the two of them tried not to poke the bear.

Neither of the girls looked up, but Winona bared her teeth for the briefest moment. She kept scratching away at the letter.

For her part, Lucille examined a cuticle. "Jay," she said in the voice she reserved for toddlers who had recently wet themselves. "Why on earth would I explain our campaign strategy to you? I'd hope you would vote Pryce/Olsen this fall, but I don't think they're letting sex perverts in the polling place."

"I understand like, zero percent of the shit you say." He planted his hands between the two of them, and Lucille was forced to look up at him.

Last year, Jay Algren had spent his senior spring texting Lucille at two a.m. on weeknights, asking for nudes. The first time, Lucille sent Jay back a photo of a tasteful selection of buff-colored lipstick. The second time, she told him where he could shove it. The third time, she didn't respond, and then he spent a few days loitering by her locker, talking loudly about all the "poontang" he was getting, like he was an escapee from an MTV reality show in the '90s.

That was last year, though.

This year, he was a cop.

"What are you girls drinking?" he said in a voice that was trying too hard to be casual.

"Floor cleaner," Winona said, then made a tiny triumphant sound. She had pried a corner free.

"She's funny." Jay sounded genuinely surprised. "I thought she didn't talk."

"What do you want, Algren?" Lucille asked. "Ivanka and I need to work on our stump speech."

He stretched two beefy arms over his head. "Just wondering if you noticed anything up with your brother recently."

"Other than the usual mouth-breathing?"

"People in and out of your house who don't belong there. Your brother spending money he doesn't have."

"Those all sound like regular episodes of the Pryce Show," Lucille said. "So no."

Jay Algren eyed her like she was a side of roast beef. "You might want to help me out here. Down at the precinct"—Winona kicked Lucille under the table—"we've been too busy to check on your brother, but we're not going to be busy forever. We could go to Sonic. Talk about it."

"You and Marcus?" Lucille asked innocently.

"No, dumbass," Jay said. "Me and you. Unless you're still with that Chaxton guy."

It wasn't a threat. But it was *absolutely* a threat. And he had no compunctions making it; it was clear that it didn't even ping his moral radar. Why would it? She wasn't a person to him. It was like he was making a trade for a blow-up doll with long blond hair and a sailor's mouth. Or a Pez dispenser full of photos of boobs— maybe, if he opened it right, even *real* boobs too.

Like Lucille was just up for grabs, for *anyone,* even someone as ham-handed as Jay Algren.

"Oh yeah," she said, her voice rising. "I should check with Chaxton. I should check with my *owner* before I make a back-alley Sonic milkshake *deal* with you—"

"God, Lucy, you don't need to get hysterical."

"If you think I care what happens to my brother—"

"No," Jay said. "I think you care what happens to your mom."

For a second, they were all silent.

"Glenn!" Winona shrieked, and the sound was so sudden that both Lucille and Jay jumped. "This man is harassing us!"

The bartender slung his rag over his shoulder and ambled toward them through the crowd. "That right?" Glenn asked.

"You're serving minors," Jay said, looking up a little uneasily at Glenn's towering frame. "I'm not in uniform, but I'm happy to show you my badge."

"The Krabapple twins," Glenn said, arms settling over his chest, "are twenty-three."

"The Krabapple twins?"

"Kelly and Konstance," Glenn said. "Krabapple." ("I'm Konstance," Winona offered. She was slowly peeling the letter back from the table.) "Get out of my bar before I remove you from my bar."

Jay took a step back. "Suit yourself. I'll be back tomorrow, and when I am, I'm gonna *love* taking away your liquor license."

Glenn snorted. "Door's over there, little boy," he said, pointing past the bar with his rag, and Jay made a show of shrugging and walking out. At the last minute, he reached up to the giant shiny fish mounted over the bar, grabbed it by its head, and in a smooth motion, wrenched it off the wall. It came down with a splintering *crack*.

Jay turned, saluted, and left, the gargantuan fish propped over one shoulder.

Winona was still gaping after him, but Lucille was watching Glenn's face. For one horrible second, he looked devastated.

"That was my *muskie*," Glenn whispered. "My trophy muskie."

"A muskie?" Winona asked. "Is that—that's a fish?"

Glenn looked at her witheringly. "It was fifty-eight inches!"

"A . . . long fish?"

For once, Lucille didn't make the obvious joke. She had to respect that Glenn was having an emotion.

It was, after all, the only time they'd ever *seen* Glenn have an emotion.

"Thank you," Lucille said. "Thank you for your sacrifice, Glenn," but he was already walking away.

"Marcus," Winona said, the letter in her hands.

"Marcus," Lucille agreed. "Marcus, and Jay, and it sucks, but I'll be fine. I just need to white-knuckle it through these next two months until we make it to Chicago. Now, can we please finally read your letter?"

EIGHT

It was damp and wrinkled when Winona spread it out between them on the table.

It was also three sentences long.

> *My beautiful Winona,*
> *I'm so sorry to leave you. I didn't have any other choice. One day I promise I'll explain.*
> *With all my love,*
> *Mom*

"Oh," Lucille said.

But Winona was as excited as though she'd been sent a master's thesis on why her mom had abandoned her. "There was a file in the drawer. Stormy had hired a private eye. I wouldn't believe it if I didn't see the photos, but she's *alive*, Luce. And I know that there's more that she didn't feel safe telling me. After all, Stormy intercepted this letter! I'm sure she thought that that could happen."

"Where is she?"

"According to the file, Vegas," Winona said. "There has to be more. I have to go *find* her."

Lucille looked down at the stained, waterlogged letter, and felt her stomach turn. "What you need to do," she said, "is get that back where you found it before Stormy knows that it's missing."

"But—"

Ruthlessly, Lucille grabbed Winona's wrist and turned her arm over. The burn scar was still there.

"I know," Winona said, subdued. "But—my mom. My mom, Luce. She's alive."

"And we'll find her," Lucille promised. "When we get to Chicago this summer, we'll have like, weeks before you start school. You have an address for her? Amazing. So we'll just like, get settled in, and then we'll load up the back of the Land Rover and head west. We'll get your answers. But we'll get them after you're *safe*."

In her darker moments, Lucille thought of herself like Winona's bulldozer. This worked when she roved ahead, mowing down the assholes who got in Winona's way. Like the people at school who mocked her for being uptight, for dressing like a Stepford wife and skipping out on every party. Like Jackson Stufftwaller, who had lost the Student Council election to Winona and then spent the next three weeks saying that she'd had to suck off every guy on the elections committee to beat him. He made the mistake of loudly airing that theory in the hallway outside Lucille's home ec class, and she had literally dropped her Baby Think It Over plastic infant to run out and knee him in the balls. She might have failed the child-rearing assignment for that, but Lucille had always thought she should've gotten extra credit. She was going to be a kickass mom.

It had been like that since the beginning with them, Lucille and Winona. Lucille couldn't shake the idea that Winona had a spine made out of something hard and beautiful, like a pillar of diamonds, and that the world was doing everything it could to flay away her skin until it was exposed to the open air, glistening and awful. But if Lucille could just put herself between Winona and the world, if she could just *protect* her—

This, though. Them getting to Chicago. It could be Lucille finally clearing a path all the way out. Or it could be her reversing her Caterpillar right over Winona instead. Her diamond spine. It was a confused metaphor, but that made Lucille like it.

No. She shook her head. Everything would be fine when they got out of Kingsville.

"I keep imagining her in a bungalow," Winona was saying, her eyes faraway. "Somewhere in the desert. Maybe she makes her own essential oils. She grows big flowers on a trellis outside her door. She doesn't have anyone to bother her. She isn't using. She's just . . . herself. But a new version of herself."

Lucille was a little choked up, despite herself. It was a shame, she thought, that they weren't moving to Vegas in the first place—Winona could live in her mom's spare bedroom (or on the futon in the Instagram-curated living room, cuddling a hibiscus throw pillow while she slept like the angel she was), while Lucille, in a green plastic visor, would be down at the blackjack tables on the Strip. Around six a.m., flushed with success, she'd wander in to find that Katherine Olsen's perfect new boyfriend would have dished up eggs and bacon. While Winona got ready for her Shakespeare class at whatever Ivy League school was in Vegas (there had to be one, right?), Lucille would be counting her bag of winnings at the kitchen table, divvying them into three piles—one for her, one for her mom, and one for Nony.

In her imagination, the sack on the table would say *Earth Day*.

"We'll find her," Lucille said through misty eyes. Her phone was buzzing on the table between them, but she ignored it. "I'm so happy she's alive. I'm sorry I jumped all over you. I just—I just worry."

"I know," Winona said. "Honestly, it's probably a pipe dream anyway. She left me. You know? Phones exist, in the world. She could've called. And it's not like we're going to have infinite funds this summer. You can't just like, drive cross-country for free."

Lucille cackled. "We could stop at every casino between here and Vegas and you could loose me on the tables."

"You are so gross." Winona grinned.

"I've only ever counted cards in the app before," she said. "But I think I could try in like, a strip mall casino in Iowa City."

"Iowa City," Winona intoned, like it was a holy site.

"We could dye our hair blue for the occasion."

"We could wear shower caps and decorate our walkers."

"Oh, darling," Lucille said. "My Harry *always* decorated my walker for me!"

Winona cackled. "We could go all out. Steal my mom's Rolex. It's mine, anyway."

"In that case, how about we steal Marcus's stash before he pays his boss? What's he going to do? Call the cops?"

"God," Winona sighed. "We'd need a lot of money. At least a couple grand. And a car."

"A convertible," Lucille said. "Scarves in our hair. Reflective aviators."

"A red convertible," Winona said, and her voice grew unexpectedly bitter. "Like my grandfather's car. Maybe he'll leave it to me, and after Stormy finally dies at the age of 108, I can joyride it once around the neighborhood before I croak right there over the wheel."

Before Lucille could say anything, her phone buzzed again. Winona turned it over. "Oh, *ew*. And maybe we can save some money to bribe Chaxton to back off because *he just texted you his pecs*."

She practically hurled the phone across the table.

"Those aren't pecs," Lucille said. "Are those pecs? It's so close up, it looks like—like Wonder Bread? Like the buns they sell in the grocery store."

"Like an art exhibit."

"'All this could be yours, baby,'" Lucille read out loud. "Oh my God, he's such a weird man infant."

"Look, I know I just agreed to run away to Vegas with you, Luce, but I would never stand in the way of true love. If you want to stay here, I'll understand. Do you think your babies will be all shiny like his pecs?"

"I think he oiled them for the photo." Lucille drained her G&T. "Somewhere Harry is just *roooooolling* in his grave."

"What Jay said—about your mom. Will she be okay?" Winona asked softly. "When you leave this summer?"

It was like Winona to think of Lucille when she was going through so much, but Lucille still felt her back stiffen.

She loved her mom with a devotion that scared her, sometimes, for its ferocity. Her mom, scrambling to hold on to their house. Sperm Donor Leonard (she refused to call him her father) skipped town to go drill oil in South Dakota when Lucille was still sleeping in a crib. He promised to send back the money. He didn't send back any money. Or letters. Or any word, anything at all, and one night, when Stormy was out of commission and she and Winona had spent all night at the Cliffside getting shithoused on tequila shots, Lucille had gone home and dizzily done the thing she'd swore she'd never do: she looked up Leonard Pryce on Facebook. In his profile photo, he had a GO ARMY hat—her dad, who'd never served in the armed forces—and a baby in his lap dressed in pink.

Lucille passed out, but not before sending him a message, one she didn't remember until she saw it on her phone in the morning. *How long until you leave your new family to drill for oil in hell?*

Sperm Donor Leonard didn't love her mother. Marcus didn't

love her mother. So Lucille loved her *for* them, took care of her the way they *didn't*, and if Lucille stopped to think about it for too long, she would start to wonder if all that fierce love covered up a thick ugly knot of resentment at the center of her. Because her mother took care of Marcus, and Lucille took care of her mother, and Marcus routinely dug through Lucille's jewelry box to see if there was anything gold that he could hock at the pawn shop.

Lucille couldn't have wants. She couldn't have needs. What she had was a hole that she shoveled her love into, a hole she couldn't see the bottom of until she met Winona.

"You need to get home," Lucille said. "You need to put that letter back."

"I know," Winona said, already taking off their old-lady disguise. As she was pulling the fuzzy pink sweater up and over her head, her phone started buzzing in her pocket. Two calls in quick succession. Stormy, double-tapping.

A warning. And, like an answering echo, Chaxton texted Lucille a picture of—*oh, yep, that's definitely porn*.

"How much do you think he's good for?" Winona asked, nodding at her phone.

"What do you mean?"

Winona's lips bent up into a smile. "Broken security camera. Oiled-up man baby who's desperately in love with you. How much do you think we need to get to Vegas? Two grand apiece? Four grand total?"

"How much is in a 7-Eleven register?"

Lucille paused. "You want to knock over a 7-Eleven."

They looked at each other for a long, long minute. Winona's eyes were big and brown, guileless as a doll's, but there were dark things there, swimming closer to the surface than usual. *Dare you,* Lucille found herself thinking, *dare you, dare you, dare you—*

But Winona broke first, into peals of breathless laughter, and then Lucille started cackling, their arms linked on their way out to the parking lot. Because what were they going to do? Put on ski masks and grab rubber guns and storm Chaxton's convenience store castle? That kind of thing only happened in movies.

"We're not that far gone yet," Winona said, getting into her car.

"Nah," Lucille said, and rapped on the roof twice, a send-off. "Unless you want to meet me by the slushie machine later!"

NINE

Winona kissed her father on his cheek.

She handed over a Pellegrino, a receipt, a handful of change, and a set of keys to the car her father had bought for her. Then she said goodnight and went upstairs to wait.

She listened for his heavy footsteps on the stairs, carrying him up to his nightly shower. She listened while she combed her long, auburn hair, and while she washed her face with her Clarisonic.

She listened as she patted serums made from grapevines into her fair skin and she listened the whole five minutes she waited before moisturizing.

Winona took her Cartier bracelet off and set it on the side table like she did every night. If ever she forgot, she was sure to wake up feeling like it was tightening around her, a vise threatening to cut her hand off. Sometimes she even felt that in the day, but she knew better than to leave it off.

Her scar had never fully healed and if Stormy saw the marred skin the bracelet hid, he'd think she was trying to manipulate him, punish him. She couldn't risk that, so she took the bracelet off each night and put it on as soon as she opened her eyes every morning.

She climbed into bed and turned off the lights and she kept waiting, watching the crack of light along her cracked-open door (house rules) for signs that Stormy was going to bed.

Every minute that passed, her dread deepened. She knew she should find an excuse to go downstairs, but she was too afraid what she would find.

Maybe he has a private investigator following me too.

Maybe he knows about the Cliffside, about gin and tonics, about Lucille and the apartment in Chicago.

She told herself that if Stormy were angry, he would not be sitting silently down in his office. She repeated it until her heart slowed and her eyes grew heavy, until she found a way to drift out of her panicky body and float over it.

Shit. She startled awake with the realization: she'd fallen asleep.

She opened her eyes.

NO!

Her room was bright. Sunlight slanting through her drapes. Birds chirping. She glanced at the clock: 8:03 a.m.

She'd fallen asleep. She'd missed her window.

But maybe—*maybe* there was still time. There had to be. She leaped out of her bed and snatched the letter from under the pillow where she'd slept with it all night. She tiptoe-ran down the hall, down the stairs, through the kitchen, to the office doors. Through their glass inlays she saw the empty leather chair, the empty mahogany desk.

He wasn't in there!

She reached to open it.

"Winona, darling," a low voice drawled behind her.

She jumped, clutched her chest, just barely kept the lid on a scream that was rising up through her like a jack-in-the-box.

She turned around, and slowly padded around the corner into the vault-ceilinged great room.

Her father was sitting on the white sofa, his back to her as he looked out the windows toward their yard, sipping his morning coffee. He didn't turn to her, but the sharp, precise cut of his hair along his neck seemed to stare at her suspiciously.

"Get the scissors from the knife block, please," Stormy said.

She had the envelope crumpled in her hand. Heart thudding, she slowly tucked it into the waistband of her pajama pants.

"Sure, Daddy," she said just above a whisper.

She turned back to the kitchen, went to the naturally grained knife block. The butcher knife, she noticed, was missing.

It's in the dishwasher, she told herself. *Of course it's in the dishwasher.*

She slid the kitchen scissors free and walked back to Stormy.

She held them out to him, and her arm felt heavy, like the Cartier bracelet was a solid steel anchor.

Stormy stood as he took the scissors, seeming to tower over her despite his mere two inches on her.

"Sit down," he said.

She didn't ask why. That would only make things worse.

She lowered herself to the sofa.

Slowly, he walked around her, his black dress shoes *ssff*ing on the Persian rug, then *click*ing on the wood. Almost tenderly, he pulled her glossy auburn hair back and draped it over the back of the couch, running his fingers through the curls. "You're so like your mother, Winona," he said thoughtfully.

Now her heart stopped. For a second, she was sure she was dead, witnessing her own last moment of consciousness before her brain got the cue that her body had given up.

"Always so self-destructive," Stormy said, his voice low and restrained.

She was alive after all. Every muscle in her body drew uncomfortably tight.

"I've tried and tried, but I can't seem to make you understand," he said coolly. "*Rules* are there for your protection. If I *tell you* not to go into my office, and then you *go*, what can you expect to happen, Winona?"

Winona suppressed a shiver. Shivering would make this worse. He would feel like she was manipulating him, trying to keep him from disciplining her.

She needed to accept her punishment. She needed him to know she accepted her punishment.

She couldn't stop shaking as he lifted the long curl out to the side of her face, wrapped it around his palm in her peripheral.

"I know what you did, what you think you *found*. What I struggle to understand is why you're hell-bent on hurting yourself," he said. "You want what you want in the moment and care *nothing* for the consequences—how it will affect you or anyone else."

The scissors sung open, *shwing*. Their joint tested the end of her hair.

She tried to apologize. No sound came out.

The scissors skidded up along her hair as if Stormy were curling ribbon on a package. They went straight to the root, to the soft skin behind her ear.

"I'm your father," he said. "I know best."

She tried to nod. The edge of the scissors was pressing into her skin now. It didn't hurt. It didn't hurt, she tried to remind herself.

Any second, it might.

"If I *tell* you to eat your broccoli," Stormy bit out, "it's because your body needs nutrients." The scissors pressed a little harder. "If I tell you to go to bed, it's because you need your rest. If I tell you your mother is dead, Winona, it's because it's for the best. Do you understand?"

"Y-yes," she whispered.

"Speak up, darling."

"I understand," she got out.

The scissors released their pressure. They slid back down the strand of hair, but stopped a few inches from the end. *Snip.*

Three inches of curl fell onto her shoulder.

"She was a disaster," he sighed. "She couldn't control herself. But you'll learn, darling. You're half me, and you'll learn to be good. I'll do whatever it takes to teach you. I won't give up on you, darling. Next year, in Evanston, it will be a fresh start for you, and you'll see."

This time, she managed to nod. "Yes," she gasped. "You're right."

"Poor darling," he said. "You were mixed up."

"I was mixed up."

"Of course you were confused, after the way your mother abandoned us. No one could blame you for that, darling, but you've got to learn to respect the rules. The time for this silly rebellion is over. Next year, we'll be happy. We'll have a new, beautiful home in Evanston. You're going to love our condo, darling. It's nothing like this, of course, but it's closer to the city, and a more metropolitan upbringing would suit you."

All the blood in her body went cold. This time, she knew her heart hadn't really stopped.

Our condo.

Our condo.

Our. Condo.

"I'm going to help you learn self-control," Stormy said, "and you're going to make me proud."

Then, piece by piece, he cut her hair off.

The scissors only slipped once, an accident. A prick against her neck.

"When the blood's dried, we'll take you to the salon," he said. "Get that cleaned up as well as we can. You've made a mess of yourself, Winona."

TEN

No one kept a schedule like Stormy Olsen.

He didn't let the stolen letter or the impromptu haircut or the trip to the salon affect their evening.

That night, like every night, the locks came off the pantry door an hour before Martina arrived, and went back on an hour after she'd finished the dishes and left. He called this gap of time, if ever forced to reference it, "breathing room."

It was the portion of each night when he sat sipping his favorite Scotch while Winona played the piano, just like she was doing now, her glossy auburn bob curled expertly around her chin.

What had happened that morning was in the past.

What mattered was, they were back on schedule. Back to perfection.

Stormy was swirling his Macallan in its snifter. Winona's long fingers were flying across the ivory keys.

It's like you live in a fucking Jane Austen novel, Lucille had once said.

But there was nothing Austenian about this time of night in general, and especially not tonight.

The real purpose of the "breathing room" was to be sure Martina didn't circle back to the house for a forgotten purse or phone or house key—like had happened with their *last* housekeeper—only to see the locks that kept Winona from going back to the kitchen to binge.

Stormy had had Martina sign an NDA, of course, but still he *worried about the embarrassment you might feel, darling, for your condition.*

As far as Winona knew, she didn't *have* a condition. She remembered eating too much cake just once, on her thirteenth birthday, so much that she made herself sick and vomited the whole night's worth of food back up.

It hadn't even stopped her from wanting more the next day, but he'd thrown it out by morning. Three days later, the padlocks appeared. *You must learn to control your vices, darling.*

"Beautiful," Stormy said flatly, pulling Winona back to the present as she finished the song.

"Thank you." She turned the page of her sheet music, set her hands back on the keys, and resumed playing.

Whether she'd actually *had* a problem or not, she'd developed a complicated relationship to food in the years since the locks first arrived, but ever since she'd found that letter, it was like her appetite had woken up, starved and angry as a post-hibernation bear.

She'd never been hungry like this.

All night, in between much darker thoughts, she'd found herself consumed by cravings for chocolate cake and whipped cream, syrupy cherry juice and Magic Shell on black raspberry gelato, fatty cuts of pork and duck-fat fries and fettuccini swimming in alfredo. Even while she was chewing her grilled salmon and steamed broccoli across from her father at dinner, she'd been hungry. Even as she was pushing the empty plate away and dropping her linen napkin on the table for Martina to take home with the wash, she hadn't felt sated.

Her fingers nearly fumbled on the piano keys again, but this time she caught herself, face burning, and sunk back into Mozart. She was grateful for something to focus on.

She'd never fully conquered the irrational fear that her father could read her mind.

She chanced a sidelong glance at him. He sat on the gold-embroidered brocade sofa, one leg crossed over the other, the crystal snifter lolling against his knee. His face was impassive. Outside this house, he was charismatic, animated, but in the privacy of their home, he was a different animal. Sometimes Lucille called him the Reptile King.

Winona jerked her gaze back down before he could latch onto her eyes.

He doesn't know about the apartment with Lucille. He doesn't know about the plan. He can't, she promised herself, but her chest began to ache. It didn't matter anyway.

All those plans were obliterated, their ashy remains raining down around her.

But she couldn't think about what next year in Chicago was going to look like. If she thought about it, she would cry, and if she cried, things would get worse.

She threw herself into the song and when it ended, she felt a little better, calmer, lighter.

And then Stormy stood, glass emptied, and slowly crossed the room to stand beside her at the end of the bench, and everything in her that had finally unraveled tightened again, braced protectively. Her breath caught in her throat, which had swollen as he closed slowly, purposefully in on her.

His free hand lifted to the back of her neck and squeezed lightly. His thumb was just over the scab where the scissors had poked her, and every muscle in her body was tight, ready to snap.

If he gave just a little bit more pressure, she wouldn't be able to breathe. If his hand moved just a little to the right, he'd be holding her by the throat. She could feel him holding back and her face was itchy with heat and the memory of the scissors tracing a strand of hair up toward her scalp sent a fiery rush through her stomach.

He knows about the Cliffside, about our system, he knows about every time I've lied to him, he fucking knows—

But he simply bent and brushed a kiss on the side of her head as he did every night. His hand released. His face drew back. He straightened and looked down his sharp nose at her. "Why don't you finish your homework and get to bed, darling?"

She blinked back the tears pricking her eyes. She gripped the edge of the piano bench to stop her trembling and nodded obediently. "Yes, Daddy."

The sound of the words made her sick. He waited for her to stand and head for the stairs before he turned back toward the kitchen.

Halfway up the stairs, she thought about the photograph she'd found.

Pictured her mother's long, wavy hair, her yoga pants and her full-cheeked smile and the lean muscle of her arm as she waved to someone, a friend Winona had never met. And then she imagined her mother's house in Vegas, a small adobe ranch with a rock garden around its front porch and wind chimes dancing in the breeze, maybe a bright red bistro table and a pitcher of fresh-squeezed lemonade whose condensation raced in sugary rivulets down the glass.

Winona felt a yearning for this imaginary place so powerful she had to stop for a second and grip the banister to keep from crying.

Just like every night, she told herself. *You don't need to be afraid, because this is a night like any other.*

But suddenly a deadly calm came over her, and she knew that it was a lie.

In thirty minutes she'd hear the shower come on down the hall. In thirty-three, she'd be on the move.

She stepped into her bedroom and eased the door halfway

closed—just enough not to raise Stormy's alarms while she was sifting through the dresses, handbags, and shoes that would bring in the most money.

She glanced over her shoulder before pressing up onto tiptoe to ease her luggage down as quietly as possible.

WHAT ARE YOU THINKING? her own voice was screaming inside her head, but she couldn't stop. It was like the hunger in her had wrested control of her body from her mind, like her gut was in control now.

Quickly, she stuffed a handful of bras and underwear from her drawers into the bag, then draped an orange Kate Spade dress on top of it. A few more dresses and a Chanel bag.

Clothing drive, clothing drive, clothing drive, she repeated as she worked. *If he catches me, it's for a clothing drive.*

He would be disappointed to see all those beautiful pieces he and his personal shopper had *just* picked out for Winona going already, but he'd be pleased it would reflect well on The Family. He'd be disappointed how little all that spent money had amounted to but unwilling to consider the thought for too long, lest it remind him that still, after all these years, he wasn't completely accustomed to the wealth he'd married into.

Wealth that Winona's mother had been willing to relinquish in exchange for her freedom.

The image of the adobe ranch rushed through Winona again like a drug. A giddy thrill. She was going to see that house.

You think Lucille's just going to go along with this?! that same voice demanded. *Us just up and leaving tonight?*

Yes. Yes, she would. She had to. Winona would make her understand.

She froze at the sound of shoes on the steps. Her cheeks were burning.

But his steps were already moving off in the other direction, and then the water turned on down the hall.

She was out of time, *no more breathing room*.

She closed the suitcase, tucked it back into the corner of her closet, and moved in a heady daze into the dark hallway. The master bedroom's door was ajar. Winona held her breath as she turned to sidle inside, wincing as her hip caught the knob and the door whined farther open.

The bedside lamp was on, but did little to dent the darkness of the cavernous room, as did the light eking out around the French doors that led to the en suite bathroom. She crept to the side table, closed her eyes, said a prayer, and eased the drawer out.

Her father's parody of a keychain, laden with the keys to every locked compartment in her life, lay on top of a King James Bible. They weren't religious; Winona's best guess was that Stormy had put the Bible there because that was simply where Bibles belonged.

Her fingers bumped the keys, and she bit the inside of her cheek as they jangled.

She counted to three, then slipped the keychain into her palm and slid the drawer closed.

Then she went to his closet.

This room, more than any other, was a perfect embodiment of its owner.

It was easily four times the size of Winona's closet, nearly as large as the master bedroom itself, and every square inch curated and organized to perfection in its walnut shelves. There were drawers with plush lining for Stormy's watches, for his cuff links, his ties and tie clips and belts. There were shelves for his leather shoes and briefcases, shelves for his monogrammed luggage of every size, and then there were the dozens of suits lining the back wall.

Winona moved as quickly as she could in the dark and it still felt too slow, too clumsy, too loud as she bumped the walnut console in the center of the space. She followed it to the back wall, turned on her phone's flashlight, and rustled through the heavy trousers hanging there, searching for the locked valet box where he kept his most valuable possessions hidden.

No. No. No.

Had he gotten rid of it?

Moved all its contents to the locked basement? Or his locked hobby garage? Her heart began to pound more forcefully.

Her hand hit the smooth black leather of the valet box, and her stomach lifted hopefully.

She shined the light onto the keyhole.

She had six keys to try. The first key didn't make it a millimeter in. She flipped it over, just to be sure, then moved on to key number two. No luck.

The water shut off in the next room.

The keys slipped out of her hand and jingled as they dropped to the carpet. Winona froze, rigid. *He can't have heard. He can't have.*

He couldn't have, because she couldn't live like this anymore. She couldn't accept a world where he had heard.

In that world, she thought he might kill her.

KILL, she thought. It hadn't occurred to her before. He could *kill* her.

She picked the ring back up. Her fingers were shaking so badly that she flubbed the key twice before she got it partway in. She thought she might've found the right one, but she couldn't get it to turn, and when she tried to pull it back out, it jammed.

She heard the glass shower doors warble as they opened on the far side of the closet wall.

She jerked the key free, but by then she'd lost track of which she'd tried. Her heart was racing so fast she felt like it could explode.

She chose a key at random.

She almost couldn't believe her eyes when it clinked right into place and turned.

There it was. Her mother's watch, her engagement ring, her wedding band. And something else Winona hadn't expected.

The salty, iron-tinted taste of blood flashed through her mouth at the sight of it.

Sleek, black metal that matched the leather so wholly it made the handgun look like some repulsive fetus hanging out in its womb. Like it had sprouted there, right in the heart of her father's deepest secrets.

A gun. He has a gun. He had a gun in this house all this time.

When he burned her. When he held a pair of scissors against her throat. When he gripped her arm and the back of her neck just a little too hard. He'd had a gun right down the hall. The dark room swung in front of her. She grabbed hold of the box to steady herself.

The gun was staring at her.

If it were hers, he couldn't hurt her. If it were hers, she could take whatever she wanted and walk out of the house, even if he caught on to what she was doing. She'd be safe.

Right?

She heard the bathroom door opening and fear shot through her body so fast she felt like she'd bitten down on some kind of terror fast-release tablet.

She grabbed the rings and watch, closed the box, and yanked the key out.

Now what?

She hadn't put the keys back in his drawer!

Fuck, fuck, fuck!

She heard the soft click of the door, then the light switch. She threw herself forward to the far side of the console that occupied the center of the room.

The carpet had muffled the noise of her movement as her father was entering the room, but now, as she listened to the soft pad of his steps on the rug, she was aware that he was no more than four feet away from her, separated by nothing but a glorified dresser.

If he leaned forward far enough, he'd see her.

She listened to the quiet roll of a drawer opening and let her breath out, dragged half of another in. The soft sifting of fabric. The quiet rustle of silk. Her muscles ached from the unnatural crouch. Her lungs burned.

His steps were moving toward the door, but he hesitated there, and the light didn't go out. She flicked a glance back at the valet box.

Her stomach balled up as she realized a couple of the suits she'd brushed aside were still tucked up at the corner of the box.

She'd made a mistake. That had to be what he was looking at.

The light flicked off. The closet door closed.

Was he messing with her?

She stood on shaky legs and moved toward the slatted doors of the closet. The bedside light was still on. Her father was sitting up in bed, looking at his phone.

Winona waited there for him to glance at the drawer, to *sense* her betrayal.

She waited until he set his phone down. She waited until he turned the light off, and still she waited as he lay down. Waited until he went to sleep, and then waited some more.

When she was sure he was really out, huskily snoring in a way his vanity never would have allowed him to fake, she slowly, quietly slipped out.

There was no point in putting the keys back now.

When she made it back to her room, she was exhausted and exhilarated and more than anything, hungry. But something was still holding her back. One last shackle.

She slipped the Cartier bracelet off and set it on her dresser.

She was hungry for the world, and she was going to have it.

Starting with a 1969 Alfa Romeo.

ELEVEN

ZERO DOLLARS

There had to be money in Marcus's stash.

Lucille hadn't been able to stop thinking about it when she'd gotten home—how easy it would be, in one fell swoop, to get Jay Algren, Mall Cop, away from their house, away from her and her mom. She just had to remove the problem. Physically.

No drugs? No cash? Marcus wouldn't be able pay his supplier, and he'd have to deal with the consequences himself.

And maybe Lucille could take back what he owed her in the process.

It was laughable, how quickly Lucille found it taped up underneath the sofa. It was the literal first place she looked. After she'd gotten home, she'd lingered by her bedroom door for what felt like an hour until Marcus had finally gone into his bedroom. The second she heard his door click shut, she was *there* in the living room, hands under the couch, and she'd made it back into her bed with the ziplock bag hidden underneath her shirt before he'd even started the car.

Under the covers, she examined it by phone light. Molly. Coke. Pills she recognized. Pills she didn't. She snapped a photo, then ran a reverse image search.

Roofies.

Oh my God, Lucille thought, fist pressed to her mouth. *Is he selling them? Is he giving them to girls?* But there wasn't really a difference between the two, was there?

She shook the bag again to shift its contents. There wasn't a single cent inside it. Either Marcus had a secret bank account—he was old enough to not need a parent's approval to get one, he could've been putting it away for years—or he immediately spent every dime he made. Or he had a different hiding place for his cash.

But the Pryce house was small, and Lucille couldn't think of anywhere else she didn't see all the time (the linen closet? The pantry?), except Marcus's room, which he kept locked. Her mom let him get away with it. *He's an adult, Lucy. He needs his private space.* Never mind Lucille's bedroom—no lock, crooked hinges, her things easy come, easy go.

Lucille turned her phone light back onto the baggie. Rattled it. Grinned.

Even if she couldn't do anything with Marcus's stash (she *definitely* wasn't going to sell drugs), she could take it. Take away his livelihood. Stop him from hurting other people. Other girls.

It was good enough for now.

As she turned off her flashlight, her phone began to ring in her hand. When she saw the name on-screen, her stomach dropped. "Winona? What happened?"

She was so sure what her friend was going to say, so terrified to hear her crying about whatever Stormy had done to her, that she couldn't register what Winona *actually* said until she repeated it. "I'm at the *door*, Luce—come let me in!"

Lucille kept her phone to her ear as she ran down the hall, heart now lodged in her throat. She swung open the door, expecting blue and purple skin, blood flecks, snotty streaks, tears, horror, pain—everything she imagined on a daily basis since she'd come to care about Winona.

Instead Winona was standing in the doorway with her cheeks flushed, her once-long hair lobbed off at the chin but just as conservative-chic.

But there was something about the New and Not Quite Improved but Laterally Transformed Winona that unsettled Lucille.

It was the fresh scab across her neck, a place no one without a very territorial cat could expect an injury.

"We have to go. We have to go *now*, Luce. I have the car—the Romeo—we need to get out of here before Stormy finds out I'm gone."

Lucille knew better than to ask questions when her best friend was shorn and bleeding on her front step. "Let me pack a bag," she whispered. "Two minutes. Promise."

Thank God her mom slept like the dead.

She left Non inside the front door and ran to her bedroom.

Marcus's baggie went into her duffel, first thing, and then she tossed in the next few things she thought of: toothbrush, charger, two pairs of off-brand Keds. Everything on her dresser. A bunch of cutoff shorts and tanks, a tangle of glamorously ugly Cliffside apparel, her Members Only jacket.

She dragged her bag down the hall. "Where are we going? Chicago?" she asked.

"Vegas," Winona said, leaning against the wall for support, and Lucille saw then that she was shivering. Blood was seeping out of her cut, dripping down the line of her neck.

Gently, Lucille led her friend into the kitchen. "Straight there? No Chicago? Non, I don't know if that's a good plan—"

"Stormy bought us a condo in Chicago," she said as Lucille dabbed at her neck with a napkin. Lucille blinked at her, confused, and Winona clarified. "Not *us*. Him-and-me us. Twenty-four-hour Stormy surveillance."

"With a side of physical abuse."

"He'll be my jailer."

Lucille grabbed another napkin. The cut wouldn't stop bleeding. "And Northwestern?"

"I have three months to figure it out. But I—I don't have another night I can spend in that house." Winona swallowed. "I know we don't have any money. But we don't have any time to fix that."

"How much do we need?" Lucille echoed. "Four grand? Here, hold this. Put pressure on it."

"Four grand," Winona said.

Lucille looked at her for a long minute—the splatter of blood, the figure-skater bob, the steel in her eyes—and then she turned to look desperately around the kitchen, as though a bouquet of cash might have been delivered while her back was turned.

They were quiet for a long minute. Lucille thought she heard a cough from Marcus's room, and tensed. *We need to go*, she was about to tell Winona, but her phone pinged in her pocket with a text. She knew it was probably Chaxton, but her nerves made her pull it out anyway.

Where are you, it read. *I miss you baby. Last night until the cams get fixed at work. We could do an-y-thing u like.*

He was persistent. And inconsistent (*You? u? Which was it?*) and gross and *oh my God, there might be a way for us to fix this problem.*

"I'm ready," Lucille said. "But there's somewhere we need to stop first."

"Fine," Winona said, walking to the door. "Good—anywhere."

Lucille hoped she really meant that.

TWELVE

ZERO DOLLARS

This was a bad idea.

In the course of Winona Olsen's life, she'd had plenty of those, but she'd never followed through with any of them. She hadn't skipped class to go stalk the filming of her favorite Food Network show when they came to town, or given herself a secret stick-and-poke tattoo the night Lucille did her own inked sparrows, or cheated on her physics tests (once she'd accidentally looked over at Lucas Graywater's paper and when she saw what he'd written, she knew for certain that he was right, and *still* left the question blank out of guilt).

Winona Olsen had never even had bangs!

Stormy didn't think they would suit her face.

Taking the Romeo was her first true rebellion and even that had been as simple (and legal?) as taking the spare key to Grandfather

Pernet's front door out from under a mat, and the keys to the garage and car from the drawer in the writing desk just inside the foyer.

But now Lucille was looking at her with a raw-edged excitement, hissing under her breath like the world's best snake-charmer, "This will work, Non," and Winona wanted to follow through.

She *had* to follow through.

She couldn't go back.

Going back would mean death, if not literal, something worse: a death of the soul. She thought about the old black-and-white *Twilight Zone* episodes she and Lucille sometimes ad-libbed over when Glenn had them playing on mute at the Cliffside. A group of strangers awakening at the bottom of a deep pure-white vault, with no chance of escape, only to discover after twenty-some minutes of planning and persevering that they were nothing but toys at the bottom of a child's box.

If she went back, that would be her life.

They'd already called Chaxton. He was in, which was probably the biggest indicator of how deeply, thoroughly, wholly bad this idea was.

"We park the car two blocks back," Lucille went on. "It's nothing but old warehouses back there. People who won't talk to cops. We're in and out. He gives us a head start, then hits the panic button, and when the cops show up, we're long gone and the description he gives is a two-hundred-pound man with a snake tattoo."

She wanted to do this, but they had to be smart. "What about our shoes?"

"Babe, if you want to rob a gas station in your Louboutins, that's your prerogative, and I support you."

"So the cops show up, and Chaxton describes André the Giant, and then they find these two sets of tracks back through the old industrial district. Size eight Louboutins and size seven and a half Keds. What then?"

"Excuse me," Lucille said, bumping Winona's foot with hers. "But the designers at Target would never forgive me if I didn't point out that these are *not* Keds."

"Luce," Winona chastised. "Be serious. We have to consider every possible thing that could go wrong."

Lucille arched her eyebrow. "Which means that you're considering it, period."

Winona felt—in a distant, scientific way—startled to realize that she was *more* than considering it. Her grandfather's stolen (really, more like "borrowed") car was already parked out front, after all. "Shoes," she said again.

The smile faded from Lucille's slightly crooked mouth. She thought for a moment. "Oh my God," she blurted. "It's perfect. It's so fucking perfect."

Sometimes they were so used to being in each other's heads that Lucille forgot Winona wasn't literally telepathic. "What, Luce?"

Lucille opened the hall closet and picked up a pair of Air Jordans. "Babe, put your Louboutins in the trunk."

THIRTEEN

They brought ski masks, but that was more for fun than anything else.

Fun?

What the hell was Winona thinking? You didn't rob gas sta-
tions for *fun*.

And yet, there she was, in the dead of the night, dressed like a
cartoon bank robber and driving a red convertible with a trunk
full of loot. Neither of them had spoken since they pulled away
from Lucille's place, probably because the stupidity of the idea was
starting to set in.

Winona was 99 percent sure they weren't going to go through
with it.

They would get there, she kept telling herself, and park
between the old ketchup factory and the old shoe factory, and

they'd stare each other down until they both exploded into laughter.

You thought I was serious! Lucille would scream.

You thought I would actually go along with something that crazy?

Winona drove slowly, giving either of them ample opportunity to give the ruse up.

Why weren't they giving the ruse up?

She was parking.

They were getting out of the car, shakily locking it behind them. Their eyes met over the top of the car. Lucille gave a half smile. Winona returned it. *Thank God*, she thought.

Then Lucille pulled her ski mask down over her face and led the way.

Winona pulled hers down and followed. She felt numb, or maybe like she'd left her body. Like she was very drunk and watching a movie, slurring out, *Yeah, right, that would* never *happen in real life*.

She would never be tripping through a craggy, asphalt wasteland at two-thirty in the morning wearing Lucille's brother's shoes.

They walked the way they'd driven: slowly.

Not slow enough. They were emerging from the gnarly range of trees behind 7-Eleven into its cluster of Dumpsters.

"Lot's empty," Lucille whispered.

Winona looked her in the eyes; maybe it was the ski mask, but she saw no sign of laughter in her friend's face. "Are you ready?" Lucille whispered.

Winona's stomach and her heart were on two very different

trips. The former wanted to vomit, but the latter was thrumming, *You're ready to get out. You're ready to be free. You're ready for life.*

The fact of the bird-shit-stained gas station in front of them barely factored into it. "I'm ready."

Lucille squeezed Winona's shoulder, then reached into her sweatshirt pocket for the water gun she'd brought. "There's no going back."

"Promise?" Winona said.

She pulled out her own plastic gun and ran through the dark lot into the ghastly glow of the convenience store.

FOURTEEN

ZERO DOLLARS

When Lucille rehearsed this whole scene on the car ride here, ran it through in her head, the lights in the 7-Eleven were pink neon, and she slipped through the front door like liquid, Winona at her heels, and there was a song playing, too loud, like in a commercial, something dance-y, electronic. Maybe Winona made Chaxton put all the Haribo Gold-Bears in a bag while Lucille took on the cash register. Maybe that was when the music got louder. In her imagination, the stickup was Day-Glo, or hyperreal, because even though Lucille was the one driving this thing (even if she didn't have her hands on the literal wheel), it felt like a dream to her.

I didn't say goodbye to my mom, she thought wildly as the bell on the door of the 7-Eleven chimed, as the two of them stumbled inside. *Has she called? I should call her. Winona and I could leave tomorrow—I could just pick up some milk and Cheez-Its and Non could take me home—*

"This is a stickup," Winona sang out, like she was in the chorus of *Hello, Dolly!* again.

Lucille couldn't see. Her mask was twisted a little to the left, and as she fumbled to right it, she saw (thank God) that the store was empty. Empty, and poorly lit, the freezer doors all dark except the one closest to them: frozen pizzas.

I could just get a pepperoni and take it home—

Why was she thinking this way? *Your mother doesn't care about you,* she told herself firmly, *and in the end she'll be happy you got out. You can make your own rules. She could come visit! She'd love Vegas! She'll forgive you. You're fine.*

Fine.

"I'm over here, Luce," Chaxton was saying. "It helps if you point the gun in the right direction. And if it isn't, like, bright purple with dinosaurs on it."

She swung her head around until she could see him through the eyeholes of her mask. Chaxton Smith: his parents had balanced out the workaday last name by naming their son after a sneeze. *Chaxie,* his mom called him, on the one night he persuaded her to come to his house for dinner (takeout Chinese, the Detroit Lions on the television). He still lived with his parents; he'd "tricked out" their basement with a pair of pinball tables he'd bought broken and secondhand, which he was perpetually in the middle of fixing like they were a pair of Camaros.

Most things about Chaxton made Lucille want to get out her own toolbox, but she wasn't in the business of fixing people. Or at least she knew a lost cause when she saw one. There was no conceivable mold she could pour Chaxton into that would improve the raw materials. If you gave him a corporate job and threw out all his cargo shorts, Chaxton would still be Chaxton, and the only good thing about him would still be this: he was built like a fitness model and had tan, freckled skin that was always warm to the touch, and if he wasn't talking, Lucille could pass a happy few hours in the back of his truck. He sort of wanted to marry her, which was sad if she stopped to think about it, but Lucille refused to let herself pity him. *She'd* always sort of wanted a Dalmatian, but you didn't see her crying about that, did you?

"This is a stickup," she said to Chaxton, and he mouthed back, *You're so hot.* "Empty the drawer."

"Yes, of course, I'll put the money in the bag."

"Oh," Winona said. "Right. Put the money in the bag." She tossed it at his head, and he caught it one-handed. It all had to look real from at least the outside windows: Lucille had seen enough cop shows to know that other businesses had cameras, and they might be able to catch a (blurry) shot of them from a distance.

"After this, what are you guys doing?" Chaxton asked as he pulled stacks of bills from the register. There wasn't ever that much in a business like this—two hundred dollars tops; the rest went to the bank each morning—but "not that much" was still more than what they currently had. Which was "nothing."

It was taking too long. Lucille's eyes kept straying to the big front window of the 7-Eleven, to the headlights of cars driving by. The two of them in all black, in plain sight, like a pair of girls in bad Halloween costumes.

"Why?" Winona asked Chaxton. "We're not, like, sticking around."

"I need to pick up my sixty-seven dollars," he said. One-third: that was his take. "I can't have it in my pockets when the police get here."

"We'll Venmo you," Lucille said, too fast, and she realized that what she was looking for out the front window wasn't the police, or a pair of unlucky strangers, but her mom. Or Stormy Olsen. For someone to swoop in and drag them home by their hair. She was losing control. "The cigarettes, too, Chaxton."

"You don't smoke—"

"The cloves. Why do you even *sell* cloves, I thought this was a 7-Eleven. And the Haribo Gold-Bears—Winona, grab them. The Rolos, too. Is there Cracker Jack? Dammit, Chaxton, hurry up—"

He handed Lucille the *Earth Day* bag, full again, and Winona quietly stuck the candy on top of the cash, and softly, on the 7-Eleven radio, was Meatloaf's "Paradise by the Dashboard Light," and their parents weren't coming to get them. No one was ever coming to get them again.

Was Lucille afraid? Was she happy?

Both, she decided.

Winona reached out and squeezed her shoulder. A tendril of her auburn hair had escaped her mask to lie against her neck.

And then, through the front window, headlights. Some poor fool was headed here to buy Slim Jims.

"Out the back. Run!" Chaxton said, and in that one moment and one moment only, he was incredibly, incredibly hot.

FIFTEEN

TWO HUNDRED DOLLARS (MINUS CHAXTON'S SIXTY-SEVEN)

Somehow, Winona knew as soon as they got into the car that they'd gotten away with it. That they would continue to get away with it. It had been too easy, and not in that way like, *It was too easy . . . what are we missing?!*

They had two hundred dollars, minus Chaxton's cut, which frankly, Winona wasn't convinced they'd end up paying. Probably he'd made a big deal about it just so he could seem selfless when he told Lucille to keep the money.

God. Poor Chaxton.

Then again: Chaxton.

As they approached the highway, Winona punched the gas a little harder, reveling in the throaty purr of the car. She was officially speeding as she whipped the wheel around the curve. Lucille erupted into laughter as Winona unnecessarily stomped the brake, sending the back tires skidding outward, the car half spinning into the far right lane like they were in the seventh installment of an increasingly improbable Vin Diesel franchise.

Maybe they were.

They'd done something impossible and it had turned out to be quite easy. Winona had the startling realization that perhaps nothing was impossible. That perhaps she would never again be as surprised by life as when they fled the 7-Eleven with a haul of candy and rumpled dollar bills and chests full of something like helium.

"Oh my God," Lucille kept saying through breathless laughter as Winona recklessly spun them through the lot, finally stopping the car when they were sprawled across three spots. "Oh my *God,* Non!"

A giddy, wordless shriek tore out of Winona.

It was possible Winona Olsen had never screamed before.

Lucille kicked her feet against the dashboard as she writhed with laughter. She screamed too, a short, spastic spurt, which made Winona dissolve into giggles.

"Oh God, Non," Lucille said again, when she finally got control of herself. "What now? I mean, did we just peak? Is life a slow decline from here on out?"

Lucille had meant it as a joke, but Winona was surprised by the angry thud in her stomach in response. "*No,*" she said sharply. "This is just the beginning, Lucille."

"You know what we need?" Lucille said. "A soundtrack!"

She fished an aux cable out of her purse and plugged in her phone, then turned on a Carly Rae Jepsen album at full blast. They didn't stop speeding or singing for the next six hours.

SIXTEEN

A 5 A.M. TRUCK STOP AND TWO HUNDRED DOLLARS (MINUS CHAXTON'S SIXTY-SEVEN)

Which made it five a.m. by the time they pulled into the truck stop on the Indiana side of Chicago.

"You make it sound so picturesque," Lucille said through a yawn. "I'm pretty sure everyone else just calls it Gary."

Winona pulled the Romeo into a parking spot in front of the 24-hour Pizza Hut. "Tell me this isn't the most picturesque thing you've ever seen."

The truck stop was *big*, at least the size of the mall in Traverse City. The Pryces used to go school shopping there when Lucille was a kid, back when her mom still had her receptionist job and money wasn't as tight as it was now. It always gave her a fuzzy feeling, that mall—the giant parking lot, the Gap Factory outlet store, the Orange Julius stand in the food court, her mom's hand cupping the back of her head.

And there was a goddamn Orange Julius *here*, in this truck stop. There were at least a hundred different pumps for gas. There was a movie theater and a chiropractor and a Taco Bell and a barber shop and a dentist and something called a *DOGOMAT*, all caps, with no further explanation, and those were only the things that were within Lucille's current line of sight.

The two of them got out of the car and stared out across the neon lights of the miniature truck-stop city.

"Am I hallucinating?" Lucille asked. "Are we even on Earth or, like, on Tatooine? Is this . . . suburban Tatooine?"

"No," Winona said in a hushed voice. "It's a truck stop."

It was *hot* on the asphalt, in a way that was surprising for daybreak in the Midwest. There had been a blizzard in the Upper Peninsula just three weeks ago; the week after was rain, the snow on the sidewalks melting and refreezing overnight. And then, this Monday, Lucille had woken up to 83-degree weather, the change in temperature so drastic that the wood of the Pryce house doorframe warped and tore out of the wall. (Marcus had been supposed to fix it. Lucille did instead.)

Now she was in cutoffs in a truck stop in Indiana and it was so warm it felt like they were in the middle of some Star Wars desert. And at least that far away from home.

Lucille noticed she was thinking a lot about home. *Stop that*, she told herself. *Stop that*.

"I'm definitely hallucinating," she decided. "I guess we haven't slept, and I'm sure there's probably some urban legend that says if you listen to Robba Ransom's *Kill Kill Murder Death* eight times in a row, you go immediately into an acid trip, do not pass go—"

"Don't you dare malign our queen that way," Winona said. Robba Ransom was, quite literally, a drag queen; her dance album was full of songs called "Candydeath" and "Slay (Literally Slay)," and they had ridden her energy all the way down from Grand Rapids.

"I just listened to that album eight times in a row," Lucille said. "I'm pretty sure I *am* Robba Ransom. Did you like, research this place?"

Winona averted her eyes. "I might have looked up a list of the best truck stops in the United States. This one is number four."

They stared into the glowing windows of the convenience store, transfixed.

"Encyclopedia Olsen. Number four," Lucille said. "It's like a wonder of the world. Right here, in the Indiana side of Chicago."

"This is probably as close as we can get to Chicago without spending, like, four billion dollars," Winona said. "Maybe we should stay here? Or near here? We can crash out for a few hours and then get back on the road in the morning. I think it's only going to be like, three more days to Vegas?"

"We need snacks," Lucille said.

"We only have two hundred dollars," Winona said, and doubt was clouding her voice. "Can we really afford snacks? God— can we even afford gas? This thing takes *premium*." She eyed the Romeo like it was a dog that had shat on the rug.

The high-shine recklessness was starting to wear off Winona a little, which would probably be fine, in most cases—she didn't want to encourage Winona to go full-on femme fatale shoplifter or anything—but Lucille had the sneaking suspicion that right underneath Winona's manic energy was terror. She was afraid of Stormy Olsen, Lucille knew, but she was even more afraid of running away from him. Who could blame her?

If he got his hands on Winona, Stormy would snap her neck like a twig, and then he'd turn her funeral into a charity gala.

No. Winona was *not* getting cold feet, not now.

Lucille grabbed her by the hand and propelled her to the front door. "We are getting snacks," Lucille said. "Oreos. And more Haribo bears, I ate them all. And beef jerky because protein is *very* important and maybe a couple of those trucker hats that say WE'RE NUMBER 4? I have no idea what that means—"

"Number four truck stop in the country," Winona supplied.

"—but I want the hot pink one, neon goes best with my hair. Blondes wear neon *very* well—"

Winona scoffed.

"And so do Winonas," Lucille said. She took a heavy step forward. The automatic doors whooshed open.

The place was empty enough that they could hear the buzz of the fluorescent lights. At the counter, a grizzled old man was rolling and unrolling a long stream of scratch-off tickets.

"So you have our list," Lucille said, squaring her shoulders. She pointed to the gleaming rack of candy across the store. "I want some souvenirs."

"Luce," Winona hissed, "we don't have any money—"

"Hello," Lucille called to the clerk, ambling up with her thumbs in her belt loops like she was a movie cowboy. Was it attractive when girls walked like that, or only men? Sometimes, when

Lucille had spent too much time with Winona, she forgot how to be a person that the rest of the world could understand.

"Hello, girls," the clerk said. "You two are out real late." He had a beard like Santa Claus and a gut to match. Over his T-shirt, he wore a fishing vest hung with hooks and lures.

"Really early," Lucille said. She leaned her elbows on the counter. "We got up early to help with the harvest—"

His eyebrows went up. *Oh shit, it's May, people plant things in May—*

"—of my aunt Pam's organs," she finished. "Went brain-dead in a car accident last week. I had to be up all night holding my mom's hand. Juliet over there was my moral support."

Behind her, she could hear Winona rustling through a box of candy. The clerk's eyes sharpened over Lucille's shoulder, and she took a step to the left to block his view.

"I've been meaning to buy a lottery ticket," she said, sending her voice up half an octave. "Since I just turned eighteen."

His eyes snapped back to her.

Here, fishy, Lucille thought, because this old man was definitely fishy, and not in the femme-y drag queen way. (A Robba Ransom song began pulsing in her head: *fishy fishy serving fish fishy fishy look delish!*)

"Just *three days ago,*" Lucille said, darting her tongue out to touch her lips. "And there are *so many* kinds of lottery tickets, and I just don't know which one I want!" She could see Winona, out of the most peripheral of her peripheral vision, inching her way over to the trucker hat rack.

"There are a lot to choose from," the clerk said. He couldn't look away from her. "It can be really hard to decide, if you don't know. Do you want me to explain?"

With a happy sigh, Lucille bent over the plastic-topped counter. "Yes," she said. "That's all I've ever really wanted—someone to explain all the different scratch-offs to me, in *detail*."

Five minutes later, Winona had snuck to the women's restroom—*That isn't part of the plan*, Lucille thought, until she realized there had been no plan—and Lucille was learning all about the Triple Double Lucky Tender card.

"Tender?" Lucille asked, letting her lips settle into a pout. "Like a chicken tender?"

"Tender means money here, I think." There was sweat beading above the clerk's lip. It was almost as though him realizing the magnitude of Lucille's ignorance was the grand erotic moment of his life.

Around the corner, Lucille could hear the restroom door creak open.

She beamed at the clerk. "Ooh, let's do one together!" She fished out a five from her pocket and dangled it between them. "Break a five?"

He took it slowly from her, pulling it out from between her fingers, and Lucille giggled and said "*rrrrrrrr*," like she was a big, stupid, pornographic cat, and when he turned around to open the register, Lucille windmilled her arm, a signal.

Winona dashed out from the restroom hallway, with her shirt stuffed full of cookies and candy and what looked like a neon-green pair of Crocs, and she ran for the automatic doors like she was about to give birth right then and there to her contraband convenience store baby.

The doors opened.

The doors closed.

"My friend's real tired," Lucille sighed when the clerk finally turned back around, a clutch of singles in his hand. "I think she's just going to go nap in the car. But I just really. Really. Want to know if you can teach me how to get this Triple Double Lucky Tender jackpot."

When she finally ambled out to the Romeo, Winona had the top up, and she was stuffing her face with pork rinds.

"Protein?" Lucille asked, sliding into the passenger seat.

"Protein." Winona's whole face was shining with sweat and exhaustion and glee. "You realize you just cheated on Chaxton with that Santa man."

"Poor Chaxton," Lucille said. "Always the bridesmaid, never the bride."

"They're gonna call us the Gas Station Robbers."

"Please," Lucille said. "How prosaic. They're going to call us the Pigtail Snatchers."

"Ewwwww *amazing*. No—the Ponytail Pilferers."

"No, I want that one to be our band name. What about the Baby Burglars!"

"I'm not stealing *babies*," Winona said. "Please! Have some dignity. Speaking of dignity, I got you Crocs."

Lucille grabbed them off the floor and divested them quickly of their tags. "You have the best worst taste."

"I *know.*" Winona stuffed the rest of the pork rinds into her mouth. "We should get out of here before he realizes that we made off with at least fifty bucks' worth of useless crap."

"There's a motel back by the highway exit," Lucille said, and grinned. "Good thing we don't have a recognizable car or anything."

"Good thing."

They drove and ate in silence until Winona pulled into the Super 17 parking lot. "Did you hear what he said to us?" she asked. *"Hello, girls!"*

"Hello, girls!"

They sang it back and forth to each other like a song.

"Hello, girls!" "Hello, girls!"

Until it was nonsense.

With a snort, Winona slammed the car into park. "I hate it when they do that. Hello, *girls*! Like we're *children*. Like we're the littlest of little girls in our prettiest princess costumes, and simultaneously hot and sexy ladies. We just robbed a clerk who couldn't stop staring at your Child Boobs."

"Okay, *that's* the name of my band," Lucille said, and yawned big enough to split her face open.

SEVENTEEN

ONE HUNDRED SIXTY DOLLARS AND A SEEDY MOTEL ROOM WITH BLACKOUT CURTAINS

Winona opened her eyes on the alarm clock. At first, she thought it was four a.m.

That she was lying in her fluffy canopied bed in her tastefully spacious home.

That in one hour, she would hear her father stir down the hall and soon after, she would smell the nutty scent of brewing coffee.

Then she remembered where and when she was—that she'd fallen *into* this sticky motel bed with Lucille two hours *after* four a.m.—and she leaped out of bed and hurtled across the room to the blackout curtains. Lucille groaned as Winona threw them back on the sunlit parking lot.

Winona spun back to her. "Luce! Luce." Lucille grabbed a pillow and held it over her face. Winona hurried back to perch on the edge of the bed and shook her friend's shoulders. "It's four p.m.!

We were supposed to check out like . . . four hours ago!"

Lucille grumbled something unintelligible through the pillow.

"Lucille!" Winona said, and jerked the pillow away. Lucille had her eyes scrunched up, determined to keep the room dark, and Winona yelled, "I can't hear you with a pillow over your face!"

"I *said*," Lucille bit out, "that places like this don't expect a speedy checkout any more than they expect you to partake of their alleged continental breakfast!"

"Well, what about *Stormy*?" Winona hissed. She hadn't said his name since the night before, and even now, she whispered it as if it were a powerful incantation.

It had the same effect on Lucille, whose eyes flew open. She sat up in bed.

"He'll have realized I'm missing hours ago!" Winona said. And from there, it was only a matter of time until someone discovered the Romeo was missing too. "We need to get back on the road!"

Lucille essentially tumbled out of the bed and sprinted for the bathroom. "*Shit*."

"Where are you going?" Winona screamed after her.

"To pee!" Lucille screamed back through the partially closed door. "Don't scream at me!"

"Don't scream at *me*!" Winona screamed, and Lucille let out a bloodcurdling shriek. Winona catapulted herself off the bed and ran toward the bedroom. "What? What?!"

Lucille's scream had already dropped into a low, miserable groan, so apparently, she *wasn't* being murdered. She looked up at Winona from where she sat on the toilet, oversized T-shirt hanging off her bony shoulder and zebra print underwear bunched around her ankles, and she stomped her bare feet on the linoleum as she groaned some more. "I just started my fucking period!"

"Lucille!" Winona gasped, clutching her chest. "You can't just scream like that—I thought you were dying!"

"In four hours, I'm going to feel like I am, and I won't have my heating pad!"

"Look on the bright side: there's no Chaxton Jr. spawning in you."

All at once, every hint of misery wiped off Lucille's face. "Touché. Grab me my DivaCup, would you?"

"Exqueeze me," Winona said.

Lucille waved her hand. "Front pocket of my duffel bag."

"You want me to grab your vagina bowl?"

"Dude. It's clean. Don't be weird."

"I *know* it's clean," Winona said. "That's the point! You want me to handle it and then you're going to use it."

Lucille stared at her blankly. "It's not like you're in the middle of eating Doritos. Now, vámanos, before the Murderous Meteorologist shows up!"

Winona huffed, grabbed a tissue out of the box on the sink, and ran back into the bedroom for the DivaCup, careful not to touch it directly.

They were on the road four minutes later, Beyoncé's latest album just *barely* drowning out Lucille's period groans. "It feels like someone's running my insides through a noodle press," she shouted over the music.

"How Italian," Winona said. "You must get your reproductive system from the Folgarelli side of the family."

Lucille wagged her head back and forth against the headrest and moaned some more. "The first few hours are always the worst for me."

"The first cut is the deepest," Winona said.

Lucille gasped. "How dare you quote Sheryl Crow in the middle of a Bey song and leave me so tempted to cut it short!"

Winona shrugged as they pulled into a gas station. "I can't control when inspiration strikes."

Forty-three dollars later, they pulled onto the highway in silence. Winona's mind tried to wander back to Kingsville.

She didn't let it.

She turned the song up and sang along for a while, and soon, the worst was over for Lucille.

Soon, the worst would be over for both of them. Although, they didn't necessarily know what came next . . .

"Not Northwestern," Winona said without really meaning to.

Lucille's blue eyes cut to her. "What?"

Winona looked away from the road, the scrubby, trash-littered weeds on either side of it, and met Lucille's gaze. "I don't want to go to Northwestern."

Lucille's brows pinched. "Nony, don't let Stormy take that from you. If you want to go to Northwestern, you can't—"

"I don't," she said, dragging her eyes back to the road.

In one instant, the pressure lifted from her chest. Maybe not all of it, but so much that, after all these years, she felt like she might float through the fabric top of the convertible in its absence. "I never wanted to go," she admitted. "I wanted to keep him happy. I wanted to keep the peace so things would be easier, but I've never cared about school. I *thought* I did, because it was always such a relief to be there, as long as I was doing well. But I don't know if I even *like* school really. If it were up to me, I might not even go to college."

When Winona glanced over, Lucille's eyebrow was arched and she was fighting a smile. "Well, I've got good news for you, Nony. It *is* up to you."

Winona laughed. Lucille did too, until another cramp wrenched the sound into a groan. She clutched her stomach and closed her eyes as she tipped her head back against the headrest. "So no Northwestern."

"No Northwestern," Winona said with a nod. After years of doubting herself, it was strange to be so sure of something. She couldn't stop herself from adding, "At least not right now."

"Then what *do* you want?"

Winona thought it over for a minute. She didn't know. That was the point. She needed time, time she hadn't had, to figure out what she liked, what she wanted. There was *one thing*, though, an image that burned bright in her imagination. "Wind chimes."

"Wind chimes." Lucille giggled again. "Just wind chimes?"

"I don't know." Winona shrugged. "I just picture my mom's house having them, and I want some too. And I want our apartment to have posters pinned to the walls and stacks of mail that don't get sorted into a system as soon as they arrive. I want *clutter*, and I don't want to hold my breath whenever I spill something. I just want . . . I don't know. It's hard to explain . . ." She trailed off for a moment, looking for the words. "Stormy's been thinking about buying a plane—did I tell you that?"

Lucille's jaw dropped in Winona's peripheral.

"Yeah. He wants a private jet, with his name on the side. And last year he donated that huge chunk of my mom's money to get the library its new Sturgis 'Stormy' Olsen wing. He's always looking for places he can leave his mark." Her hand instinctively went to her wrist, like she could rub the scar away while she drove.

"Can you imagine caring about that?" Winona said. "I've *never* wanted my name carved in stone. That would never in a million years occur to me as something valuable. I may not know the details of what I want, but I think I know what it adds up to. I just want to have a small place in the world that *truly* belongs to me. To not feel, for just one fucking second, like I'm wandering through someone else's world with someone else's permission to be there. So yeah, I want wind chimes and the occasional trip to KFC and a tiny little apartment that's just for us, whether it's in Chicago or Las Vegas or anywhere else. And then maybe, in a few weeks or months, I'll have a better idea of what my corner of the world might look like."

Lucille smiled faintly at her, but the expression didn't reach her eyes. Usually, Lucille was so solid, but Winona detected something soft, gooey, wavering in her friend right then.

"What is it?" she asked, bumping Lucille's elbow.

"Do you think he lied?" she said. "Stormy, I mean. Do you

think he lied about *all* of it, not just the overdose? The pills, the drinking, everything he's told you about your mom?"

Winona turned her eyes back on the road. She couldn't pretend the thought hadn't crossed her mind, as light and airy as a little helium balloon bobbing around in her skull.

"No," she answered finally. "Not about all of it."

There was one night in particular that Winona remembered when she'd stayed home with a babysitter while her parents went to some black-tie charity function. Back then, Winona slept well, and she'd fallen asleep long before they got back. In the middle of the night, she'd awoken to a commotion down the hall. Her parents must've just gotten home.

She'd wanted to see her mother in her sparkling black gown one more time—she never wore a gown twice—so she'd crept, bleary-eyed, down the hall.

The master bedroom had been shut tight, but Winona had heard her parents' voices behind it. First, the low, gravelly hum of her father saying, *Look what you've done, Katherine. Look,* and then, what sounded like her mother crying.

Or maybe coughing! she remembered thinking. The noise had been halfway between the two. Was her mother sick? Was she sad?

Winona couldn't have been more than six years old, too young to know it was unwise to open your parents' bedroom door, but old enough to feel dread at what lay on the other side.

Are you proud of yourself? Stormy had been asking as Winona finally turned the knob. *Fucking pathetic.*

She hadn't often seen her father surprised, but as he looked over his shoulder, half-silhouetted by the dim glow of the bedside lamp, he'd been stunned. Winona remembered the way his mouth had opened and closed in an oddly fishlike expression as he searched for words.

And then she remembered how her eyes had swept over the sliver of room she could see through the door, taking in first the sparkling spray of glass shards on the wine-stained white rug and then the woman kneeling there, right in the middle of it all, still dressed in her beaded black gown, though one strap had fallen and her makeup was smudged and teary.

She'd looked right in Winona's eyes and whimpered through tears, *I'm sorry. I didn't mean to.* Her eyes had filled with tears as they went back to the shattered wineglass on the floor. *I didn't mean to.*

Then Stormy had swept forward and caught the door, buffering Winona back. *Go back to sleep, darling. Mommy's not feeling very well.*

She didn't think he'd lied about her mother's problems, but now she also couldn't help but wonder if there was more to the story. She'd know soon enough.

Winona smiled at Lucille. "It's okay, though. Things are different now. I can feel it. We're going to have everything we've ever wanted, Luce."

Only now Lucille looked as lost in thought as Winona had just been, her face angled out the side window.

Winona shifted uncomfortably in her seat. "Did I upset you?"

Lucille shook her head. "I'm just . . . I guess it sucks to realize

I've never had a chance to want anything other than money. Money to fix the roof. Money to pay the internet bill and get my mom a mammogram. There's never enough, and I'm always trying to make the dates line up right so I don't owe it all at once. Marcus gets to guiltlessly pine after sneakers made by children and I can't remember a time when I was able to want anything more than *enough*."

"So," Winona said. "I want freedom, and you want the chance to want."

"And here we were, totally unaware that we were living in a country song."

The girls laughed, but Winona wondered if it felt as hollow to Lucille as it did to her. "You know, I think we can have it all," she said finally. "I mean, as long as we keep aiming low."

"Aiming low is my middle name, baby."

"I'm serious," Winona said. "We're going to find our little corner of the world, Luce. It's going to belong to us."

"And where might this corner of the world be?" Lucille asked. "Maybe Chicago. Maybe somewhere else." *Vegas*, she thought but didn't say. Winona shrugged again. She didn't really know the answer. Once she was looking into her mother's eyes, maybe she would, but right now, she could only think one hundred miles ahead.

"No one's going to take it from us," she said. She held her hand out and Lucille gripped it tight.

"No one," she agreed.

The music went up, the top went down, and their hair went

everywhere as the hot air beat against their skin. They drove like that for hours, only interrupting their desperately clutching hands to tear through the rest of their truck-stop junk-food bounty. It wasn't enough to fill the ever-deepening chasm of Winona's stomach.

"I think I have a tapeworm," she announced around nine that night, when her stomach gurgled angrily in the silence between songs.

"Nah, it's just all those empty calories," Lucille explained. "Your body knows they're useless."

Winona looked down at her stomach. "Martina's carefully balanced meals seriously failed to prepare me for this!"

Lucille sighed. "I was raised on garbage food, so what's my stomach's excuse?"

"I guess we'd better stop for a real meal," Winona said.

"We need to be careful with our money. It's harder to steal gas than snacks."

Winona frowned. Not that she didn't love a sleeve of Oreos, but now that Lucille had mentioned the empty calories, she was craving something heartier. "I want mashed potatoes."

"Oh, and steak, while we're at it," Lucille said.

"And rolls dripping with butter," Winona said. "I would totally knock over an O'Charley's right now."

"I would rob the fuck out of an O'Charley's," Lucille agreed through a ripple of laughter.

"Call Chaxton. Make him get a job at an O'Charley's."

Lucille started laughing so hard tears streamed down her cheeks. "Oh, Chaxton. Poor baby Chaxton."

Winona was giggling now too. "Poor Chaxton? Poor *us*! We're the ones who haven't seen an O'Charley's in two and a half—oh, wait! Look! A casino. Casinos *totally* have steak."

She gestured toward the billboard on their right.

KING MIDAS CASINO: Find Out If You've Got the Golden Touch.

"ARE YOU KIDDING ME?" Lucille shouted at the sign. "KING. MIDAS. CASINO." She held up her middle fingers as they sped past. "Read a book, fuckers!"

"Come to our casino!" Winona panned. "Where you will never again touch food or your loved ones without turning them to solid gold, and it's considered *winning*! Please consider visiting our sister locations, Pandora's Big Box Store and Curiosity Cat Supply."

"If winning at that casino results in some Midas-like power, I wonder what happens to the losers." Lucille heaved a sigh and gave her hair a melancholy flick. "Unfortunately, I'll never find out. Ever since I got addicted to this app, I'm just *too* good at poker. I can't lose! It's been a *really hard* time for me, and I hope you'll respect my privacy."

"Oh my God." The idea popped into Winona's head fully formed and beautiful, like a hybrid flower created in a lab for precisely this occasion, rather than grown from the dirt by luck and circumstance.

Okay, so maybe she'd leave the deluded metaphors to Lucille— the point was, Winona had an idea!

Her gaze snapped between the highway and her best friend, slumped back in the seat with her shoes kicked up on the dashboard.

If she didn't make a decision fast, she'd miss the exit. She clicked the turn signal on and moved into the right lane.

Lucille's eyebrows knit together, and she eyed the odometer. "Are we out of gas again? What are you doing?"

"I'm getting my best friend a steak," Winona said. "Well, actually, *she's* getting us a steak. But I'm driving."

Lucille's eyes widened as the exit lane curved around a marshy plot of grass, and the hideous red-and-black facade of King Midas Casino rose into view, a cement block of a building with a tower of motel rooms sprouting up one side. Probably they meant for it to look luxurious. In the brown-and-gray expanse of Nowhere, Illinois, it looked more like a blood-colored guard tower in a prison yard. "Time to put that math brain of yours to good use," Winona said.

Lucille looked at once thrilled and terrified. "Can we just do this?" she said. "Can we just walk into a casino and play poker?"

"What are you even saying right now?" Winona asked. "I literally don't understand your confusion about this. It's a building, with a door, and these Krabapple IDs are burning a hole in my pocket. But if you have a problem with *just walking in* and would rather be airlifted in, we can always call Chaxton."

"I've only played on my phone," Lucille said, chewing her lip. "What if I mess up?"

"You're too good," Winona said with a grin. "We can't lose."

Lucille gave her a Cheshire grin. "We really can't."

EIGHTEEN

ONE HUNDRED TEN DOLLARS AND A WHOLE LOT OF WET N WILD

They had some serious preparation to do before they dared walk into the King Midas Casino.

"Do you think they sell those see-through visors at the gift shop?" Lucille asked, yanking her airbrushed unicorn sweatshirt over her head. "The granny ones?"

"What's the point of them, anyway?" Winona was adjusting her frilly socks over a pair of orthopedic loafers. (Lucille had found them at the "shoes by the pound" section of the Kingsville St. Vincent de Paul.)

"I don't know, but they make your face *green*," Lucille said, leaning into the trunk. Her cosmetics bag must've been unzipped when she'd tossed it in there, because her makeup had spread out and rolled to the far back corners of the trunk. As she found each missing piece, she smudged it on her face—a tube of Revlon Cherries in the Snow, her blue glitter liner, her knock-off Orgasm blush. It would probably be better if she had a mirror, but Lucille wasn't exactly going for Artistry. She was going for Old Lady Realness.

Behind her, she heard a car pull up. "That your car?" the man called out.

"Ain't she a *beauty*," Winona said in a pretty good imitation of Lucille. (Lucille, head still in the bowels of the Romeo, gave her a thumbs-up.)

"Not as pretty as you." Lucille heard the car door swing open. "Mind if I take a look?"

"Um," Winona said. "Yes? No. Yes, I mind."

With a groan, Lucille straightened and slammed the trunk shut. "Who the hell are you? Oh. Of course." A skinny man in convertible cargo shorts, climbing out of his pickup. "Can I help you?" she asked, hands on her hips.

The man took one look at her, and scuttled back into the cab of his truck like some deep-sea indigestible lobster. "Holy shit," he said, "never the fuck mind," and he peeled out of the parking lot without turning on his lights.

Winona was bent over wheezing, one hand clamped over her flowered hat. "Lucille," she said between gasps. "You look like you escaped from a clown torture basement."

She grinned and touched her cheek. Her finger came away sticky with blue glitter—she'd meant to put blush there, but oh well. "Only if I'm the torture clown," she said, "and not the torture-ee."

Lucille had always liked uglying herself up; it was a hobby, had been for a long time. She'd hit puberty at twelve and immediately grown what her mother called a very "obvious chest," and that, in combination with her riot of blond hair, meant that she first got catcalled while she still had streamers in her bike handles. It wore her down after a while. It wasn't just the catcalling, of course—it was assholes like Jay Algren looking her up and down like she was a racehorse; it was the long, lingering stare of men older than her father when she dropped their dinners down at the Starlight Diner. Sometimes, for Lucille, those looks grew indistinguishable from the "nice boys" gazing earnestly into her eyes when they asked her out to homecoming, and she found herself brimming with an effervescent sort of rage that made her tell nice boys like Michael Gellar to stuff his corsage up his ass.

Lucille liked her body, her hips and her neck and her belly button, she liked her *Baywatch* hair and her blue eyes, but she hated the narrative that floated around it. That *this* body, the body she was born into, meant that she was perpetually Open for Business. Not just sexy business, but power business—dudes looking to put her in her place, to make her shut up so they could appreciate her better as the toy she should know herself to be.

So sometimes Lucille didn't wash her hair. Sometimes she put it up into space buns and wore sweatshirts four sizes too big and said everything on her mind at the top of her lungs, watched the men around her wince. Sometimes she smeared on her red lipstick like she was the Joker and waited tables that way until her boss, Travis, made her wash her face in the back.

Sometimes she and Winona dressed like old ladies and pretended that the world had no use for their bodies anymore, that Winona and Lucille finally belonged to Winona and Lucille.

With all these scams (*look at us*), all these tiny robberies (*see us*), with every speed limit blown, every shriek out the top of their convertible, every time they held each other's hands, propped each other up, called Stormy Olsen by his proper name (*can't you see us?*), they made the world refocus its gaze.

See us. See us. SEE US.

And if they couldn't see Lucille and Winona for who they were, they would pay for it.

In cash.

When Winona and Lucille walked through the automatic doors of the King Midas Casino (and Crappy Motel), the rush of air-conditioning physically blew their hair back. Winona grabbed the brim of her flowered hat.

"Which of these bitches wants to *dance*," Lucille said.

NINETEEN

ONE HUNDRED TEN DOLLARS / ZERO DOLLARS / ALL THE DOLLARS

Lucille slapped her WE'RE NUMBER 4 trucker hat on her head ("to hold my wig on!" she told the old men by the entrance) and ambled inside, Winona at her heels.

She needed a second to think. Most of the time, she was pretty okay with Winona seeing her fall on her ass, but the stakes were higher now. Literally.

Should she start at the poker tables, and deal with the variable of other people—some who might be World Series of Western Illinois Poker champions, some who might be stupider than Chaxton Smith? Or should she begin at the blackjack tables so she only had to deal with the dealer and the cards, try her hand at counting for real? Should she plop down at the penny slots to make a plan while Winona pulled the lever? Should she walk right back out the door?

Her train of thought broke off into a bunch of little toy trains and then raced off in different directions. She furrowed her brow and stared out across the sprawling complex, at the plastic chandeliers and the waitresses in red-and-black corsets, hauling around their drink trays with the efficiency of the deeply bored.

She didn't realize that Winona had wandered off until she reappeared with a paper bucket of chips, THE MIDAS TOUCH!!! emblazoned on its side.

"Gum?" Winona asked, holding out a stick.

Lucille popped it in her mouth, chewed, and blew a bubble. "So you started with twenty bucks?" she asked, peering into the bucket. This was definitely more than twenty dollars' worth of chips. "Whoa. Fifty?"

"One hundred ten," Winona said casually.

Lucille swallowed her gum.

"I know it's maybe risky," Winona said, "but it doesn't *feel* like a risk. I watched you make all that money on that app—"

"It's a totally different thing! This is a totally different situation!" Lucille could feel the gum lodging itself somewhere in her liver. Was the esophagus connected to the liver? At that second, she couldn't say for sure, and *she* was the person that Winona had just bet all their money on.

"Oh my God," Lucille moaned. "We're going to have to hitchhike to Vegas! We're going to have to get a ride with some trucker who will play the Eagles for eighteen hours straight—"

"Oh *God*," Winona said.

"And then we'll have to *murder him*," Lucille finished, grabbing the bucket of chips. "No. I need to cash these back out."

Winona snatched it back. "No one is murdering anyone," she said firmly. "Except you. In blackjack. You're going to murder all the blackjack . . . people."

"Nony," Lucille said. "Do you even know what blackjack is?"

"Yes?" Winona said hopefully. "Look! There's a table there!"

"Listen. I think you need a primer," Lucille said.

She explained it to Winona as quickly as she could, the system she used. Blackjack was a pretty straightforward game: the goal was to get cards that added up to twenty-one without going over. Number cards were worth their "pip," or their number: two was worth a two, et cetera. Face cards, like the king and queen, were worth ten. And the ace was worth either one or eleven, according to the player's choice.

"You go through a couple rounds," Lucille told Winona. "You have a few chances to bet."

"And *you* win by counting cards. So does that mean there are fifty-two cards in a deck and you're keeping track of how many?"

Lucille was shaking her head. "No. It's—look, it's not worth explaining, because I'm not going to be able to do it, anyway. I'll do one round, and then we'll split a steak, and then we can, like, go rob some unlocked cars in the parking lot."

They chose their blackjack table because the dealer had smiled encouragingly at them when they walked by. *Probably smelling an easy mark*, Lucille thought. She settled down next to the four other players—an older couple holding hands, and two solo dudes, both greasy-looking, both smoking. One of them eyed Winona. One of them eyed Lucille, but was interrupted in his inspection by a phlegmy coughing fit.

Lucille settled down at the table and gave the dealer a queasy smile. She put down a twenty-dollar chip.

"Hi," she said. "Um . . . high ho, let's go?"

"That's my girl." Winona patted her reassuringly on the back.

The dealer's smile had disappeared. She looked at Lucille impassively, taking in her sweatshirt, her blue-glitter-blush, her wild, frizzy hair. "Hit?"

"Hit," Lucille confirmed, and as the cards were dealt, she started adding them up.

This was how Lucille counted cards: the high-low system. She kept track of the high cards (the ten through ace), which were worth +1; kept track of the low cards (the two through six), which were worth −1; kept track of the "neutral" cards (the seven through nine), which were worth nothing.

As the players were given their initial pairs, Lucille averaged them out in her head. The greaseball next to her had a +2; the greaseball on the other side had a −1. The couple on the far end each had a zero. Lucille had a zero too, and the dealer had two cards that averaged to a +2.

The total was +3, then. They were playing with six decks total; Lucille saw them in the dealer's shoe. She divided the three by the five and a half decks that were left, and made a decision.

"Stand," Lucille said.

She did this math in about four seconds.

Another hand. Another. Winona wandered away and came back with a giant puff of cotton candy; she fed big purple bites to Lucille as she worked. Lucille's small stack of chips decreased, increased, decreased—

And then it increased, increased, increased.

After the dealer's eyes narrowed one too many times, Lucille shoved her chips in her bucket and stretched in a way she hoped was natural. It wasn't as though counting cards was *illegal*, exactly, but as Lucille had recently learned, things weren't illegal until you get caught.

"Next table?" Winona asked.

"Next table." Lucille fished out a ten-dollar chip. "I'll go break this for you. While I'm working, do you wanna go play the Evita slot machine? I haven't heard it sing, so I don't think anyone's won for a while."

"Oooh," Winona said. "Yes! How much are we at?"

"You want an apartment in Vegas?" Lucille said. "After we meet your mom? Right now I think I can get us one of those shitty places that's within a five-mile radius of a pool."

"A *pool*. I could have a flamingo float."

"Not yet, you can't," Lucille said. "But maybe in like, half an hour?"

A sallow-faced group of grandmothers shuffled by. One was a good foot taller than the others; in her right hand, she carried an inexplicable megaphone.

"Okay," Winona said. "Half an hour."

Half an hour later, Lucille told her that they were getting a condo. Not on the Strip, she cautioned, but within driving distance. Pretty soon after that, the two of them decided on a house. Something tasteful, small. Mediterranean-style, maybe, or shingled and Pepto-Bismol pink, with a chimney. And a window seat. And a gazebo. Then they added a garden, with leafy bunnies cut out of the hedge. Then a guest cottage that they could Airbnb, but only to people who brought their dogs. (Winona still hadn't gotten over the DOGOMAT she hadn't been able to explore.) Then a penthouse.

"With a butler named Rhett!" Winona had squealed, as Lucille clapped her hand over her mouth in sheer joy.

They were catching their breath on one of the cushioned benches by the wall. Beyond them, a weeknight bachelorette party was playing a pair of Dolly Parton slot machines. "Baby needs a coat of many colors!" the girl in the veil was screaming.

"We've only made five hundred dollars," Lucille said, coming down a bit. "It's still not enough for a first and last and a security deposit payment, but—"

"But it's literally *five times* what we had when we came in." Winona's eyes were shining. "And we didn't make it. You did."

"Hallmark moment, Nony." Lucille was equally allergic to praise and schmaltz.

But Winona shook her head. "I found you something, while you were playing." She pulled out her phone, a real-estate app already up, and shoved it at Lucille. "Look."

As far as Lucille could tell, Winona was just showing her a picture of an empty room, and not even a particularly nice one. The windows were small, and the shag carpet was brown.

"Swipe left," Winona said, watching her face.

A picture of an empty kitchen.

"Keep going."

A bathroom with scuffed and cracking linoleum.

"That is," Winona said triumphantly, "our new place. I've pored over the rental listings in Vegas, and this is the one."

Lucille glanced up at her. "Wait, what? In Vegas? It's kind of a shithole, Non."

"But we can actually *afford* it. And there's a little porch, where we can sunbathe and drink smoothies—and hang chimes! I mean, if you really want, we could install the hedge bunnies ourselves."

Lucille chewed her lip.

"Listen. Seriously listen to me. That could be our home base. We could make a *life* from there. It's two miles from my mom, so we'll have family there. Real family. That cares. And then we can make plans! We were talking about me going to college—what about *you*, going to college?" She grabbed Lucille's hand. "Like, I know you just want to wait tables, and I'm sure you could make good money doing that—but what if you waited tables while you took some classes?"

"School is expensive," Lucille said gently. "And we don't have anyone else to lean on. I'm not going to blow my money on college, especially when we'll have rent to pay."

"Maybe not right away. Maybe next year. Maybe when we're, like, comfortable." She shook her head again, like there was a fly in her ear. "I don't know, Luce. I've never seen anyone do anything like the math you did while holding a conversation and eating fucking cotton candy"—she held up a finger—"and I know you have a zillion comebacks to that. So sleep on it. Okay? Worst-case scenario, no college at all, and you just card shark all night long. In your green visor and your glitter Keds, the queen of the entire world."

Lucille looked back down at the apartment. Swiped left.

A picture of a boiler room. A picture of a busted closet door.

"I want it," Lucille said. "Why do I want it? How much?"

"First, last, and a security deposit. Thirty-six hundred bucks." Winona grinned crookedly. "Minus whatever we spend tonight. Winner winner steak dinner."

Sitting there, in the freezing King Midas Casino, a tiny bubble of *want* appeared inside of Lucille Pryce's chest, and for once, she let it grow.

"I'm starving," Lucille said.

"I *know*," Winona said.

TWENTY

AN *EARTH DAY* SACK FULL OF COLD HARD CASH AND THE ENTIRE CONTENTS OF THE PATSY'S WALK-IN FREEZER

The plan had been steaks, and there was, in fact, a steakhouse at the casino—an Outback, to be precise—but after wandering the whole place, they settled for the bar called Patsy's in the back instead. As hungry as they were, they were *also* five hundred dollars richer, and Lucille was determined to use some of her winnings to stay the night somewhere that didn't have bedbugs.

This had horrified Winona, as it hadn't occurred to her that their *last* motel might've been crawling with them. "Did you check the mattress?!" she'd demanded.

"Hell, no!" Lucille had said. "I wasn't about to disturb *anything* in that room and risk finding a hidden crime scene."

So now they were passing under the neon glow of the PATSY'S sign to see what kind of bar food they could scrounge up. Everything, both in the bar, and in the casino beyond its dirty windows, looked just a bit different to Winona from how it had when they'd first wandered in.

The row of gray-faced men who sat at the slot machines looking like they'd been put under some kind of enchantment, their glazed eyes fixed on the colorful cherries and coin stacks spinning past with each pull of the crank.

The waitresses in their stretched-out fishnets and cheapo red-satin bustiers. The sticky vinyl booths in the back of Patsy's and the sea of denim and flannel and bad cologne at the bar. The red cast of the whole place, glinting against the beer bottles and chipped tumblers, the cigarette-burned felt of the pool tables. As Winona watched it all move around her, she felt like the world itself was a slot machine and she and Lucille had rigged it so that when it stopped, it'd read JACKPOT, straight across, every time.

The world was a flower that had reached its season: it was brightening, opening its petals to her, and now she understood she could take any part of it that wasn't bolted down and stuff it in the Romeo's trunk.

She followed Lucille through the crowd right up to the bar. "Patsy, darling!" Lucille yelled in the general direction of the bartender, a woman with long black hair, a lip ring, and a tattoo on her lightly muscled arm that read PARTY OR DIE.

Her gaze turned toward Lucille and Winona without betraying any amusement at their Granny Chic getups. She was ostensibly *not* partying, which could only mean that this was the face of death.

"Two of your best steaks," Lucille said.

The bartender *fwapped* a laminated menu onto the counter, then went back to cleaning a glass. As soon as Winona's eyes hit the menu, her salivary glands went into overdrive.

Cheese fries. Bacon-topped burgers. Stuffed potatoes. Calamari—*where on earth is this place getting calamari?* It didn't matter. She would eat it if they'd caught it in the storm drain in the casino parking lot.

"One of everything?" Lucille said.

Winona's mouth was so full of drool that if she spoke it would pour down her chin like a waterfall. She nodded, dazed.

Lucille put the order in, and added two G&Ts with a wink she probably expected would get them a discount. Garçon was still not amused. She was still not partying.

Winona liked to think the girl was Glenn's cousin. Or maybe they'd just gone through the same Bartending Preparatory Academy to train their faces to relax into a deadpan. Within a few minutes, their sweating gin and tonics appeared on crumpled napkins in front of them, along with a laminated number 13 to flag down the servers when their food came out.

Do they know? Winona found herself thinking, as she followed her friend back through the sweaty press of the crowd. *Can they tell what we just did?*

Counting cards was frowned upon, right? Or was it illegal?

She could still feel the energy from back at the table sparking off her, as if she were a downed electrical wire in a lightning storm. She had to be broadcasting it: *I AM A WANTON CRIMINAL AND I HAVE NO PLANS TO STOP.*

She looked around Patsy's, searching for proof, but was still startled when she found a pair of blue eyes watching her from the corner. Even more surprised when she noticed they were attached to a young man—somewhere between eighteen and twenty-three—with the face of an angel. Except for his mouth, which was thoroughly devil.

He smirked at her, and Winona gave herself whiplash spinning back around in the booth. Her cheeks were burning. She was now positive that the change in her was, in fact, a physical, visible thing. At least to the boy with the slicked-back blond hair and pouty mouth.

That boy had taken one look at her and known what they had done, she was sure of it.

She wondered briefly if she should feel guilty about the gas station robbery, or the stolen off-brand Crocs, or the cards her best friend had just counted. The first cold slug of gin burst through her skull, obliterating the thought. She was happy. At least that was the closest word for what she felt. At this rate, they'd have carved out their little corner of the world in no time. Lucille could finally relax, figure out what she wanted—maybe even put her ridiculous brain to use—and Winona could decorate it with tacky posters and thrift store fringe lamps, clutter it up to her heart's content.

Northwestern was out of the picture, for now, and wind chimes were well within their grasp.

Lucille felt it too. She couldn't stop grinning. They were having one of their telepathic conversations. It went something like:

Do you believe it?

I know!

I can't believe it!

Me neither!

We made all that money!

I know!

I know! *It's so weird. I can't get over it.*

"What should we do?" she asked. She couldn't sit still, and she didn't think Lucille was loving being stationary either.

"Pool?" Lucille suggested.

Winona was freakishly good at it—it was one of Stormy's party tricks, pulling his daughter out to wow his dinner guests in the billiards room in their basement—and Lucille wasn't bad either. "All three tables are taken," Winona pointed out. "God, that guy in the lizard-skin button-up really should *not* be betting money on his abilities. Look, watch how he holds the cue."

Luce glanced over her shoulder for a beat and when she looked back, her eyes had that Lake-Michigan-Under-Sunset glint in them. "Oh my God," she hissed. "You beautiful genius."

"Thank you?" Winona said.

"I'm going to ask you to do something extremely counterintuitive and possibly quite difficult, Non."

Winona's heart sped at the challenge. "What's that?"

"I need you to be bad at pool," she said.

A slow smile tugged at Winona's mouth. The rest of their conversation happened in their heads. The girls made their way back to the crowd of grizzled men at the center table, heels sticking to the beer-slicked floor.

When Lucille stopped at the corner of the table and flipped her hair, Winona could have sworn a spotlight fell onto her friend's honey-blond head, drawing every eye—or at least, every eye they needed.

There was one set of blue eyes in the corner that Winona could tell were only watching her. She turned her back to him and focused on the men who really mattered at that moment.

"Hello there, girls," the Lizard-Skin man said.

"You *boys* have room for a couple more?" Lucille said.

TWENTY-ONE

FIVE HUNDRED EIGHTY DOLLARS AND A NEW KIND OF HUNGER

Lucille wasn't good at pretending to be bad at things, and pool was no exception.

Back at Kingsville High, people thought that Lucille Pryce was coasting along on fumes. The common consensus: she was dumb (because she was too tired to raise her hand in English), she was lazy (because sometimes her homework was late if she'd waited tables for six hours after school), and that she was "easy" (a word she hated; as Winona put it instead, Lucille was simply a connoisseur of manflesh).

Basically, Lucille had to spend a lot of time proving people wrong, and that wrong-proving did not usually involve twirling her hair around a finger and slurping her gin and tonic through a straw.

But here they were.

They lost the first three games in spectacular fashion, eating fries dripping with cheese and chewing overcooked burgers between every turn. Winona—going by Juliet now, which Lucille found hilarious—scratched right out of the gate, putting the cue ball into the right pocket with a shaky cue and a nervous laugh. "My brother told us to wait here for him," she said. "I'm so sorry! I know I'm doing this wrong. Thank you guys for playing with me!"

"We're just sorry to take your money, honey," the lizard-skin-shirt man said. He and his friend had put down fifty bucks, and "Juliet" and "Enid" had matched it from Lucille's spoils. The bills were growing damp under Lizard-Skin's sweating beer.

"It's okay," Winona said. "He gave it to us to have fun with, and we're having a lot of fun!"

Lucille loved watching Winona unshackled, the veneer of worry scrubbed clean off her. And what was underneath was glorious: a sort of reckless, gin-soaked exuberance that led her to confidently pocket stripes when she and Lucille were playing solids, before draining off her drink like she was Beyoncé in a Pepsi ad.

Lizard-Skin and Silent Friend were staring at her like she was the holy grail. They weren't the only ones. Roadside casino regulars were, apparently, old and endlessly skeevy, or young and beaten-down—except for the boy in the corner. Blond-pompadoured, pillow-lipped, heavy-lidded, he was hot in that *I just woke up next to you in our house of sin* kind of way, especially in his tight pants and brown leather jacket. He wasn't even trying to hide how much he was looking at Winona—he had one hand on a beer and the other under his chin and he was studying her like he was at a museum or something.

And Winona saw it too. (*The beautiful painting was gazing back at him*, Lucille thought triumphantly. It was a good image.) Lucille would be the first to tell you she didn't know every nook and cranny of Winona's life, but she could tell you for sure that she'd never been kissed. *Who do you think Stormy would kill first, me or my swain?* Winona had asked, when Lucille had tried to set up a double date one Friday. *It would be a slow killing. He'd disembowel him with a butter knife.* No, Winona got one Stormy-sanctioned prom date a year (*every American girl needs to go to prom, Winona*) and that was it.

This beautiful, probably stoned dude in the corner? Stormy would be sharpening his butter knives, especially at the way that Winona made eyes back at him over her drink, over her shoulder, over her cue stick.

Lucille—connoisseur of manflesh—was tickled pink. She'd always gotten more attention, because of the confidence and because, well, she encouraged it, but Winona was the real beauty, and the girl had just helped her mastermind a pair of (minor) robberies. She deserved this.

Three lost games later, and Winona was flushed pink with success. There were three hundred dollars sweating under that glass now.

"One more game?" Lucille asked Lizard-Skin and Silent Friend in her sweetest voice. "Her brother's coming to get us soon."

Seven hundred at stake—all their cash from the 7-Eleven and

the blackjack tables, and two hundred from these Idiot Twins that they could add to their pot. This was called going double-or-nothing. Lucille didn't like those odds, but the adrenaline screaming through her *loved* them.

Her phone buzzed in her pocket. Chaxton, probably, wanting them to send his sixty-seven bucks. But no, his text said, *Cops at my house. What do you want me to say. Also r you OK?*, because of course he had to leave a paper trail for the police to follow straight back to them.

Lucille hoped that the cops were just following up on the 7-Eleven robbery, and not trying to track the two of them down. Either way, Chaxton was a dumbass. (The sky was also blue.)

Who is this stop texting me she fired back.

Lucille?? It's me Chaxton!

This is Marlena Von Engelhoven I am blocking this number. She couldn't deal with this, not when the stakes were so high. Even as Lucille was watching, Winona was calmly putting one ball after another away, calling each and every pocket like she was on the World Series of Bad Casino Bar Pool. Silent Friend looked like he was going to snap his cue stick in rage.

"Juliet," Lizard-Skin was saying slowly, "have you been trying to pull the wool over our eyes?"

Winona giggled nervously. "I think I'm just getting the hang of it!" They seemed assuaged by either the giggle, or the hair flip she followed it with, a Lucille signature that Winona had apparently picked up as quickly as she'd pretended to master pool.

Lucille's phone buzzed again, but this time with a call.

Her brother. Not Winona's imaginary one: *hers*.

Shit, she thought, *shit*, and then she took a deep breath and picked up. "Marcus."

"Lucy," he said. "Where's my stash?"

"What? I can't hear you. Can you say it louder? Like, go walk over in front of Mom and enunciate."

Lizard-Skin and Silent Friend were staring at her now. Even Sleepy Blond Hottie had torn his eyes away from Winona to look. Lucille held up a finger; she'd take the call outside, and let Winona finish the game on her own.

Lucille wandered out the side door, the one meant for townies coming into Patsy's to drink. The parking lot was still packed with Ford Fiestas and Honda Fits, and she ducked and dodged through the crowd of girls smoking by the entrance, through the mess of dented Volvos and Subarus in the parking lot. Lucille watched them, fascinated, as Marcus stumbled through the longest speech she'd ever heard him make.

"Lucy, Mom is worried, but I'm covering for you, and I'm doing that because I, uh, love you. I love you a lot. And you have my stash. I know we haven't really, um, gotten along in the past few years—"

Split lip, Lucille thought. *Black eyes. My hundreds of goddamn dollars.*

"—so I thought maybe I could make it up to you because I guess, uh, you feel like you need money—"

"You can start by paying me back the four hundred seventy-two dollars you owe me, fuckwad," Lucille spat, and one of the girls outside the bar shouted, "Yes, honey, make him pay you!" She gave her a thumbs-up and moved farther into the parking lot, toward the street. The noise inside the casino bar was getting louder.

"I, uh, can't do that, because I bought neons for my car, and I don't have the car yet, so I haven't even seen how the neons look on it. But we're a family. It was *family* money, Lucy. Look. Lucy"—he kept saying her name like they were on a game show"—I want to help you. You can *keep* the stash. And you can help with the business. It's better money than working at that stupid diner, I don't even know why you and Mom do it instead of dealing."

"Because it's *legal*, Marcus. And because I'm not in the business of getting girls raped."

"They're just sleeping pills," he snorted. Where was he even taking this call? For sure her mother was home already. Had he actually gotten off the couch and gone into the backyard? "Look. Lucy. I'm going to send you a customer. Okay? You can keep seventy-five percent of what you sell to him. And then I want my stash back. Where are you right now?"

"Why would I tell you?"

"You're off the highway right outside of the Quad Cities, at a casino called King Midas Casino," Marcus said with ruthless accuracy.

"What," Lucille hissed, "the *fuck*, Marcus."

"You're using my old phone, dumbass. The Candy Man gave it to me. It's not like, a nice piece of tech"—Lucille gritted her teeth—"but he made sure it had a tracker in it. The Candy Man wants to protect his investments."

"And you have access to that tracker," Lucille growled. "You're tracking me."

"How the hell else do you think I got into your room when you were gone? I know where you are. All the time. Off with your lesbian girlfriend at the Cliffside. You think I'm so stupid," he marveled. "I'm a fucking *genius*. And now I'm going to turn you over to the Candy Man and get a really nice reward."

"Marcus, what are you involved with? Do you have any idea?" She couldn't breathe.

"I have a boss," he said patiently, "and that boss has a boss, and that's the Candy Man. And he runs the Midwest. And right now I have a customer on his way to see you. Sell him what he wants, turn your car around, and bring me the rest."

"I'm not doing that—"

"That stash is worth *five thousand dollars*," Marcus said. "He'd kill you for that much money. He'd kill *me*. I'm doing you a favor. One shot to make this right."

"Some favor," Lucille said, but she was distracted, because the noise in the bar was hitting new decibels. The girls by the entrance were rushing back in, cigarettes still in hand.

"I can do you the opposite of a favor instead," Marcus said, then swore, then said, "I gotta go," and the line cut out.

Lucille picked a path back to the motel, listening to the last remnants of snow slide off the roof. She didn't plan on dealing any drugs to anyone, much less one of Marcus's "clients," but she had to do something with that stash in case the police did, in fact, catch up to them. She'd flush it, she decided, before she and Winona cut out in the morning.

So Marcus was looking for them. Was Stormy looking for them yet? Probably.

With a perfectly polished pearl-handled gun.

Lucille looked over her shoulder to the street, but it was empty. Not a police car in sight. No sign of Stormy's black BMW sedan.

Stupid. She was being stupid. They were in *Illinois*, for crying out loud! Everything was fine.

Everything was fine.

She stepped back into the bar at the King Midas Casino (and Crappy Motel), and right into the middle of a bar brawl.

TWENTY-TWO

NINE HUNDRED SIXTY DOLLARS, UNLESS THESE GUYS KILL US

She probably shouldn't have shown off, but something had come over her as she lined up her final shot. Truthfully, something had been coming over her. First there was the breaking and entering in her own home, then the stolen Rolex, the stolen car, the robbed gas station, the *other* robbed gas station, the poker tables, the increasingly bold eye-flirting with the thoroughly unapproved-by-Stormy blond boy in the corner.

It was like every impossible thing she'd done tonight had simultaneously inflated her and left her hollow, hungry for more.

And now, here she was at the end of the game and the winning move was too easy, practically illuminated with pulsing blue arrows like a pool phone game for beginners. She'd barely have to tap the cue ball to ease the eight off the nearest bank and into the pocket.

Instead she called the pocket nearest to her and the two men, the one whose face was as shiny as his dark green shirt and the one who hadn't said a word yet, exchanged a look like, *Thank God this girl is the idiot we pegged her for.*

As Winona leaned over the pool table and slid the cue between her fingers, she gave up trying to hide her smile. *Pop!*

The eight ball hit the nearest bank, careened across the table to glance off the far side, and ambled toward her like a puppy toward a bag of treats.

She straightened victoriously before the ball even sunk. She looked right at the shinier of the two men, trying for a giggle at the sound of heavy resin dropping into the net of imitation leather.

"Does that mean I win?"

The two men stared back at her, and she leaned over to snatch up her loot, counting the soggy bills in—what she would soon realize—was a much too showy fashion.

She became aware of the hulking shadow first and looked up, expecting to find the reptilian man with the shiny-pink face who kept calling her "sugar." Instead she found his beefy friend.

"You little bitch," the man drawled.

"What," Winona said stupidly. She looked around, expecting to find the rowdy room suddenly empty. *Bitch* was a word she'd only ever been called in the privacy of her own home. The effect of hearing it here was twofold: she felt both embarrassed and gripped by terror. Her shoulders rose; her skin went hot and tight on her face as she braced for the worst.

The bulky man took another step in, his snaky friend close behind. "You think we're some kind of idiots?"

"I—" Winona stammered. The man's red-tinted hand flashed out toward her, and she flinched away from him, biting down on a scream as she tripped backward, hard, into the booth behind her.

The woman whose lap she'd tumbled onto yelped and thrust her away. She hit the floor and the not-so-silent man bore down on her—not to hit her, she realized, but to make a grab for the four hundred bucks clutched in her hand.

Somehow, this was worse.

She'd been burned and stabbed with scissors, and she'd survived all that. But she'd never reveled in her freedom only to have it ripped away from her. The man bent over her and reached down for the money, and the rest happened so fast she could barely follow.

A hand snatched at Silent Friend's shoulder and yanked him backward. He spun and a pool cue sung through the air, hitting him across the stomach with a meaty *thump*.

The girls in the booth behind Winona screamed, and she scrambled onto her feet and out of the way as another *smack* sent him reeling back right where Winona had been crouched seconds before.

In the meantime, Lizard-Skin had hurled himself at his friend's attacker: a blur of fair skin, blond hair, and brown leather.

The pouty-lipped boy. He was smaller than either of Winona's pool opponents, but he was fast and scrappy, and when he got caught around the stomach by Lizard-Skin's green-clad arms, he threw an elbow up so hard blood spurted from the man's very shiny cheek.

People came running. High-pitched screams went up like fireworks. Glasses skidded off tables as the three men careened through the bar. Winona knew she should run, but years in Stormy Olsen's house had melted all her natural flight-or-fight into an instinct more akin to Playing Possum.

She stood rooted to the spot, heart racing, until the blond boy had been flipped onto his back right onto one of the billiard tables, and then she found *herself* screaming, *herself* running into the fray. "Leave him alone!" She grabbed for the nearest beefy elbow and was immediately thrown backward, the side of her head clipped in the process. Her vision swam. The room spun. She was adrift in a sea of garish color and horrible noise, and then one low, resounding sound cut through it:

"OUT. NOW."

Winona blinked back the assault of stars sparkling across her vision in time to see the tattooed bartender hauling the two men off the split-lipped boy sprawled on the pool table. The men blinked stupidly, their blank expressions taking their sweet time to pass from guilt into anger when they understood what was happening.

"These little bitches started it!" Silent Friend spat in Winona's direction, and she caught Lucille's shocked face in her peripheral vision. "If you're gonna kick someone out, it should be them!"

The girl bartender stared into Winona's face, and Winona felt herself shrinking under her observation, stripped of all her stupid, unearned bravado. The girl's gaze flicked back to the men. "Those girls," she said flatly, "they stay." She jerked her chin toward the bar-back, and he sailed forward as the bartender turned her focus to the tangle of lean limbs and blond hair stirring on the table.

He sat up slowly, lazily, with a crooked smile, despite the trail of red from his full bottom lip to the midpoint of his pale throat. A lock of hair had fallen across his forehead, and his white T-shirt had twisted up to reveal a slice of pale stomach. He looked like he was rising from the world's most sensual nap, not recovering from being decked by the human equivalent of a rusty sledgehammer.

"Are you okay?" Winona ran toward him, forgetting he was a total stranger until she reached out for his hand and felt the rough calluses of his fingers, and the quirk of his crooked mouth sent her pulse leaping.

"Fine, fine," he said in a gentle voice that surprised her, only because she'd just watched him break a pool cue on someone's ribs. His eyebrows pitched up in the center. "What about you? Those guys were pretty nasty."

Winona nodded frantically. "Fine. Thanks to you."

The boy had slid off the edge of the pool table, but he hadn't let go of Winona's hand, and as soon as she realized this, she was both humiliated to still be clutching his warm palm and dreading the moment she'd be forced to let go. Winona was tall, nearly six feet, but somehow, now that he was standing, his easy, lounge-y posture made him seem to hang over her.

"What are you drinking?" the bartender asked the boy. "It's on me."

"Bourbon," he said with a polite nod, like he had fully expected this. Like he was a person well accustomed to both climbing off pool tables and being offered free drinks. The bartender betrayed no particular interest in him, just offered him a nod, turned to

Winona and Lucille, offered *them* a nod, and sauntered back toward the bar, mumbling, "A bourbon and two double gins, coming up."

Lucille and Winona exchanged a look. Remembering herself, Winona dropped the boy's hand.

What the? Lucille silently asked.

No idea, Winona silently answered.

She turned back to her rescuer. He was swiping the blood off his mouth with a shy grin, as if it were a particularly incriminating shade of lipstick he hadn't wanted her to see.

When they'd been separated by two pool tables and a crowd of casino-bar rats, it had been easy to flounce around, playing the confident vixen, catching his eyes whenever she laughed, casting him intense looks over her drink, but now they were face-to-face, and she was forced back into being herself.

Winona blushed.

It was possible Winona Olsen had never truly blushed. At least, it had never felt quite like this.

He looked right at her and his smile deepened. "Are you really all right?" he asked again. "That got pretty ugly. Do you want to sit down?"

She and Lucille exchanged another look.

What the? Lucille asked.

I know, Winona answered. She looked back to the boy. "You're really bleeding," she stammered, unable to think of anything else to say. "Wait . . . here." She turned and dumped a discarded drink's ice into a napkin and thrust it toward him. "For your lip."

Her face went fully red either when his long fingers brushed hers again, or when she stumbled over the word *lip*. She caught Lucille openly grinning at her.

Oh God. This was all so humiliating. Worse than being called a bitch in public. She almost wished she'd handed over the four hundred bucks.

Almost.

But then she thought about his rough touch. About all those glances they'd volleyed back and forth.

Winona had never had a boyfriend. She'd never even had a kiss. She'd known her life was too complicated and secretive even for friendship, but it was like her body had just realized that was no longer her life.

She *could*, theoretically, kiss this handsome stranger, leather jacket and bloody mouth and all.

Lucille cleared her throat meaningfully, and Winona a little bit wanted to die when Lucille said, "Thanks for taking care of my girl. Her name's Juliet, by the way, and I'm Enid. That matters less."

Winona didn't know how to shoot daggers. She would have to study Lucille the next time she did it so she'd be ready.

The boy shifted the ice-napkin against his lip to his other hand and thrust his right one out to her. "Silas."

"Winona Olsen," Winona accidentally said, and shook it. "A pleasure."

Dear Lord, why had she let her father turn her into such a weird, tiny businessman? Why couldn't she be a badass like Lucille?

Silas held her gaze too long, grinning, then pulled clear and shook Lucille's hand. "And it was a pleasure taking care of your girl . . . Enid. Those assholes were trying to take her money."

Lucille gave Winona a raised eyebrow as she perched on the edge of the booth behind them, her natural command drawing Silas and Winona along with her.

"I'm sorry you were dragged into it," Winona managed. She started sifting through the bills crumpled in her hand. "Here. Let us repay you."

He shook his head, and his grin widened as his hand dipped into his back pocket. He retrieved a slim black wallet and held it up between two fingers. "You don't owe me anything. I already took my cut."

Lucille's eyes went wide as she took it and flopped it open. "You took his wallet? When? How did I miss that?"

"Trick of the trade."

Lucille's mouth dropped open as she tugged a stack of bills from the wallet. "Shit. Who carries around wads of money like this?" Present company excluded, of course.

Silas gave a one-armed shrug and leaned back in the booth, his sparkling blue eyes (like Lucille's, on steroids) wandering between them. "That's the joy of a place like this," he said. "Lots of people who don't want their purchases tracked by Visa. Thus, lots of cash. I don't mind sharing."

"You're a con artist?" Winona blurted.

"Non," Lucille said gently, like, *it's rude to point out that your savior is also a criminal! Duh!*

Silas's brow furrowed and his gaze dropped to the table, an

embarrassed expression that made Winona want to run her fingers through his hair.

Not that that would fix anything. She just thought it would feel silky between her fingers and it might make him smile.

"I only con assholes," Silas said defensively. "Besides . . . I was watching you girls all night." The spark jumped back into his eyes. "It's not like *you're* totally innocent either. Bet you're just as bad as me."

No, Winona was definitely not, but she was willing to be.

Lucille straightened her shoulders and lifted her chin. Their drinks had appeared, as if by magic, and Lucille took a dignified sip of hers. "We're not con artists by trade," she said. "We're businesspeople. We go where the business is. Speaking of which." She jerked her chin in Winona's direction. "That was Marcus on the phone. He wanted to send us a 'customer.'"

"Wait, what?" Winona said. "Here? In Illinois?"

"He's apparently part of an operation." Lucille shrugged. "He was tracking me through an app on my phone—I just had to delete it. Idiot. He shouldn't have told me."

"And he wants to send us—a customer?"

Lucille nodded and crossed her arms, kicking back against the booth. "Do you believe that shitbrain? Wants us to offload his stuff and then give *him* a cut. The only cut he's getting from me is a swift one in the general region of his testicles."

Winona shuddered.

"So by entrepreneurs," Silas interjected, "you of course mean young, beautiful drug dealers in three-inch heels with no sign of a can of mace, let alone something that could actually protect you from landing *right back* in the situation I just rescued you from."

Lucille flashed him a vicious smile Winona wished she could bottle and spray onto herself when she needed courage. "Look, I really do appreciate you taking care of Nony, but this isn't necessarily your business. Besides. You might have rescued . . . Juliet, but the bartender rescued *you*, and that's because of her *fellow female feeling*, if you will. So basically, you're welcome."

"*Enid*," Winona chastised gently.

"No, you're right," Silas agreed, standing with his rocks glass full of bourbon. "I didn't mean to intrude. But look, girls, if you need anything, I'm in Room 211. Try not to get yourselves killed. I'd hate to have gotten punched in the face for no good reason."

Silas turned and started to amble away. Winona's stomach sunk disappointedly with every step.

"You're forgetting your wallet," Lucille called after him, clearly delighted by how this whole conversation had gone down.

"I didn't forget it." He looked over his shoulder and caught Winona's eye. "I left it for you."

When he turned back, she fumbled it open and a receipt from the bar tipped out, a phone number scribbled on it.

Didn't that mean Silas had stolen the wallet and slipped the phone number into it before the fight ever started? Something about this made Winona's whole body buzz.

"Wait!" Lucille shouted suddenly at Silas's back. "You have a room."

Silas stopped again, waited a full three seconds, then turned around. "I'm not from around here," he said. "I'm passing through."

"People actually stay here?" Winona said, more to herself than to either of them.

He flashed her an amused smile. "Not people like you. It's a sordid kind of place. I'm only here by necessity."

Lucille lurched to her feet and her eyes flicked to Winona. For once, Winona wasn't following the movements of her friend's brain.

"Let's make a trade," Lucille said quickly. "You let us use your room for an hour, and we'll give you two hundred bucks."

"Lucille," Winona interrupted. "What's going on?" Why on earth would they *ever* want to set foot in this hideous casino's rooms-by-the-hour, and especially *for* just one hour?

She accidentally glanced at Silas and her cheeks colored. Okay, so there were reasons, but she doubted that was what Lucille had in mind.

"I don't need money." Silas held his arms lazily out to his sides. "This place is full of it."

Lucille shifted uneasily between her feet. "Drugs, then."

Silas cracked a smile. "Even less use for those."

Lucille huffed. "There's got to be something we can trade you. We only need the room for an hour."

Silas crossed his arms and narrowed his eyes, and when his gaze wandered to Winona, Lucille sidestepped in front of him. He smiled. "You got a car?"

"We're not giving you our car."

"Not asking you to," he said. "Mine broke down, and I'm trying to get to Denver."

Lucille chewed her lip. "Fine. Denver. You let us use your room and we'll get you there. Do we have a deal?"

"Luce," Winona pressed again. "What's all this about?"

"Marcus," Lucille answered, like that should explain everything.

"Marcus?" Winona said, but right then, Silas was watching her with a faint smile, and she couldn't picture Marcus Pryce for a thousand dollars and a restraining order against her father.

"Okay," Silas said without looking back to Lucille. "It's a deal."

TWENTY-THREE

FOUR HUNDRED DOLLARS, AND ONE BLOND DRIFTER

After Silas ambled back to his room (did he ever walk like he hadn't just clambered off a horse? Men were the *worst*), Lucille spread her metaphorical plans across the table and pulled Winona in for a conference.

"Look," she said, showing Winona her phone. The text from Marcus read: *He'll be wearing green sneakers. He wants the blue pills.*

"Viagra?" Winona asked mock-innocently, and Lucille snorted despite herself. Her stomach was starting to sour from the vast amounts of processed beef she had consumed.

"I looked up the ones I didn't recognize," she said, pulling the stash bag out of her jacket. "The blue ones are rohypnol. Rohypnol like *roofies*. Like, the girl blacks out and the dude can—"

"You don't need to finish," Winona said. "I know."

"I feel sick."

"We both knew Marcus was a scumbag," she said, taking her hands.

"Yeah," Lucille said miserably. "He's a scumbag."

With a half smile, Winona dug into the *Earth Day* bag below the table. "I got that Cracker Jack you wanted," she said, pulling it out. "There are nuts in it, if you want to pretend it's healthy."

Lucille ripped the box open with her teeth. "I don't know if healthy is on the menu," she said. "Look. This guy that Marcus is sending—there has to be something more to it. Marcus isn't going to have him like, put a hit on me, is he?"

"A hit? Oh my God, Luce, like—what have we gotten into?"

For a long moment, Lucille eyed her over her handful of Cracker Jack. "We survived a bar fight, got you a grifter boyfriend, and now we're about to roofie one of my brother's friends," she said. "Before we skip out of the Quad Cities in Trygg Pernet's fifty-thousand-dollar car."

Lucille didn't really know why she did this, gave these our-lives-are-shit round-ups to Winona in the brief moments where she went all Disney princess. It wasn't that she wanted to *shock* her exactly, or ruin her night, but when she watched a Winona-shaped balloon drifting up toward the ceiling, she felt the need to give it a little tug to come down.

Usually it worked.

"I know," Winona breathed, hands under her chin. "Isn't it amazing?"

Lucille stopped chewing.

"So what's the plan?" Winona was saying, already getting up

from the booth. The vinyl squeaked against her legs.

Lucille looked at her dress and thought, *We need to get this girl into a pair of jeans.*

"We knock out the date rapist, leave him in Silas's room, and then—"

"You forgot where we take his money. That's the best part."

"I love that part," Winona said dreamily.

"And then I'm sort of stuck," Lucille said, shaking the rest of the Cracker Jack into her hand. The toy toppled out with it. Winona picked it up—it was a red plastic ring—and held it between her thumb and forefinger, like a specimen, before sliding it onto Lucille's hand.

Lucille looked down at it. "Because, like—I know we've been avoiding talking about it, but how long is it going to be before Stormy comes looking for you? I don't come home sometimes, my mom might text but I can just say I'm staying at your place, but you—"

Saying this had the effect that her summary didn't: it deflated Winona completely. Slowly, she lowered herself back down into the booth. "We're so close," she whispered. "So, so close."

"I know, Nony." Lucille touched her best friend's cheek. "We're going to get rid of this guy, we're going to dump him in the motel room, and then we're going to haul Silas's beautiful ass all the way to Denver."

Winona visibly brightened at Silas's name. She did that sometimes, like when she and Lucille saw a wolfhound puppy on a sweater in Target, or when she flew into Lucille's arms after too many weeks kept apart by Stormy Olsen. Never for a boy, though, had Winona's brown eyes gone all soft chocolate, and Lucille was pretty tickled by it. For sure, she liked it better than the look it had replaced: abject fear of her father.

One day, years from now, Lucille Pryce was going to storm back into Kingsville and fillet that man right in the middle of his forecast on Channel 5.

Winona went up to get a glass of water from their bartender—their unexpected, wonderful hero girl bartender, who had now gone back to pretending they were transparent ghosts—and Lucille scanned the bar. The fight had thinned the crowd a little. There were some regulars lingering by the bar, a few beaten-down-looking couples in the booths.

She was taking all this in—because it was either that or think about her mother, taking off her makeup with Pond's cold cream before lying down on the lumpy mattress that Lucille had always vaguely thought she'd replace for her someday—when Marcus's customer walked into the bar.

Ginger hair, a ratty beard, built like a brick shithouse, and at the bottom of that whole mess, a meticulously clean pair of green sneakers that Lucille couldn't place but knew were expensive. His T-shirt said, *MAKE ME A SANDWICH.*

"Are you *shitting* me," Winona said behind her, but Lucille barely registered it. Her job had just gotten a lot easier. If there was anyone she despised even a smidge more than Stormy Olsen, it was a slogan-wearing misogynist.

Lucille went to wipe her palms off on a napkin, then stopped. Instead, she strode up to Ginger Sneakers and gestured at his shirt.

"Do you need a pill first? For indigestion?"

He visibly startled, his tiny eyes flashing away from her, like he expected to find the Secret Service closing in on him. "What?"

She even hated his voice. "Your shirt," she said. "I thought you were here for pills, not sandwiches."

This garnered the exact same reaction: the twitch, the flick of the eyes. She sighed. Were people who bought drugs usually this bad at it? Did he expect her to be wearing a sandwich board announcing herself as the Dealer?

"I'm Marcus's sister," she said, and stuck out her hand, which he took in his sticky one. "Can I buy you a drink?"

In short order, she had him fixed up with a beer at the bar. "I have to get home," Ginger Sneakers said as Lucille sipped at the dregs of her gin and tonic.

"You have a family?" With her clean hand, she'd been fingering the pill she'd taken from the car and stuffed into her pocket, but at that thought she hesitated. What if he wasn't as bad as he seemed? What if he got ketchup on his clothes at a cookout and borrowed the horribly un-clever shirt from a coworker he despised?

Ginger Sneakers's mouth twisted. "No. I have to make it to my CrossFit class in the morning."

"Cool, cool," Lucille said, and when he looked down to check his phone, Lucille reached out as though she were grabbing her drink and, instead, delicately dropped the roofie at the top of his beer.

From the other side of the bar, the bartender caught her eyes for a brief second, then looked away.

Was this a bridge too far? This was definitely not a victimless crime. Even if her victim would have had victims. Lucille bit her lip as she watched the pill fizzle out and fade.

"Why do you have all that clown makeup on?" he asked.

She lifted her eyebrows. "Because I want to?"

"Makes me wanna puke," the guy said.

"I'm sorry for your boner," Lucille said brightly. "Look, Marcus didn't give me details. What did you want? Three? Five?" she asked.

"Fifteen," he said without looking up. "Make sure they're all there, or I'm taking it out on your brother. It's bullshit I had to come all the way out here. I drove here from *Des Moines*."

Yep, he was going down. "Okay," she said. "Let me grab it."

"Hurry." He picked up his beer, then drained a third of it.

Winona was watching all this go down back in their booth, eyes wide, eating gummy bears. Lucille gave her a stage wink as she pretended to go through her things, then went through them again. Then she swore, loud enough for Ginger Sneakers to hear.

"It's back in the room," she told him. "Can you come with? You can bring your beer."

He rolled his eyes and lifted his glass. "I can finish it here," he said, and downed it. "If you want, I can teach you how to drink one down. Not everyone nurses one like a girl."

Lucille sort of wanted to throw up, sort of wanted to throw around confetti. "Yeah," she said. "That would be good. Maybe after this?" Already he was following her out of the bar and into the elevator bay that rose to the motel rooms, like he was a Pekingese, like the pills were dog treats.

"So, CrossFit," she said, looking back over her shoulder. *Here, doggy. Good doggy.* The elevators made a soft chiming sound and the silver doors slid open. Lucille and Ginger Sneakers stepped in and as the doors closed again, she forged ahead. "Don't those exercises have girls' names? Don't you guys like, come in in the morning and say, *Yeah, I'm just gonna crush Ashley today, I'm gonna crush her hard*." The doors chimed and opened again on the second floor. Lucille stepped out. "And then like the other guys in the room grunt, *Ashley, kill it*, and if anyone walking by heard it, they'd be asking where you all buried the body—"

There was a slow, creaking *thump*, like a bag of wet cement toppling over. Lucille stopped. Turned around.

Ginger Sneakers was blinking, sleepily, from the floor of the elevator. Then his eyes shut.

At the very end of the hall, where the emergency stairs spat out, Winona was silhouetted, eating green gummy bears. "I'm out of the red ones," she said.

"I'll get you some more." Lucille eyed Ginger Sneakers. "Think you can get the left ankle? I'll get the right. We can drag him."

Winona popped another gummy bear into her mouth and hurried over the red-and-black chessboard carpet to the elevator. "Sure," she said, reaching down and pulling out his wallet. In a gesture that looked almost practiced (Lucille's eyebrows went up), she pulled out five hundred-dollar bills, a twenty, a ten, three singles—

"Shit," Lucille said.

Then Winona shook out the wallet and collected the quarters

off the carpet. "We'll total it in the car," she said. "Ew. I need to wash my hands."

"Perfect. And we'll get Silas, and then," Lucille said, grabbing the hairy ankle above his sneaker (Air Jordans! *Why did everyone wear Jordans?*), "on the way out, I'll tell the bartender that the guy who wanted to roofie us is passed out in room 211."

TWENTY-FOUR

NINE HUNDRED THIRTY-THREE DOLLARS AND TWELVE CENTS AND SOME REAL TALK

Lucille had crashed out in the passenger seat between the slant of the window and Winona's shoulder, but Winona hadn't slept a wink. The only other time she'd stayed up all night was when she'd found her grandfather soaked on the side of the road, and that had left her feeling like dough rolled out to oppressive thinness by the time the sun came up.

This was different. She and Silas had talked all night—at least, all four hours he was driving them west while Lucille snoozed restlessly against Winona's shoulder, waking every half hour or so to stir, only to realize there was really nowhere else for her to move before she eventually drifted off again in the same crumpled position. The Romeo was technically a two-seater, and so none of them—her or Lucille or Silas—were comfortable, but Winona was happy.

Silas was on his way to Denver, for a job at his cousin Armie Quinhole's chop shop.

"That can't be true," Winona had said immediately, through a laugh she noted sounded more like Lucille's than her own.

Silas's brow had flicked up in amusement. It did that a lot. "And why is that exactly, Ms. Winona Olsen?"

"Because that name is impossible!" she'd shrieked delightedly.

Silas gave a grin and a casual shrug. "Do you know many Winonas?" he asked. "Or Lucilles and Silases for that matter? Some might say *we* were impossible."

The way he'd said *we*, suggested there was a *we*, would have sent Stormy into a full-blown conniption.

It thrilled Winona.

"*Have* you met another Winona?" she couldn't resist asking.

He grinned at her through the faint blue light of the car's console. "Of course not."

She didn't know what that meant. She didn't know why it made her stomach feel like it was turning inside out. Was this feeling the explanation for Lucille's weird attachment to Chaxton? To all the boys before him? Was this a feeling other people had all the time, or was it particular to her, to her and Silas? Honestly, it reminded her of the giddiness of those early days with Lucille, when everything was hilarious and wonderful and interesting, and each moment was a desperate quest to unearth *more*, to *know* more, to *absorb* more of one another.

"Tell me about yourself," Silas asked after a long silence, no sound but the purr of the car on the pockmarked highway.

"Are you seeing anyone?" She kept waiting for the mountains to spring up around her, but so far it had been mostly drab and flat, though the sky, by contrast, was a phenomenal dome of constellations.

She laughed nervously, suddenly aware that Lucille was asleep, that it was up to her to keep this conversation going. Thrilled. Terrified.

At school Winona kept to herself. There was very little she could share about her life that didn't pull on a thread that led back to what she sometimes thought of as the Stormy Knot. The knot that encompassed her mother's addiction, those forlorn days spent gazing at sharks in too-small tanks, that night her mom had broken the glass on the floor and looked up at Winona with sorrow and apology for what she already saw coming, those years after when her already-domineering father shifted into something both more and less than himself, as if he'd been replaced by a robot capable of deciphering his preferences but not of reasoning out whether they ought to be enforced as rules.

She didn't tell the girls at school anything she thought might point back to the Knot, and so she didn't tell them anything at all, unless they leaned over to ask when a paper was due or whether she had a spare pencil. And as for boys, she somehow managed to speak to them even less.

Her father wouldn't allow her to date ("until she was seventeen," although that birthday had come and gone without mention of the predetermined rule), except when it came to senior prom, and then he'd essentially handpicked her date from a suitable pool of colleagues' children and planned and paid for every minute of their night—ostensibly to guarantee his daughter the Cinderella experience, though actually to guarantee that she was never alone with her date for more than a few minutes.

Winona had spent the night crying in the girls' bathroom.

Not about her date, but about the fact that she was increasingly convinced she would never kiss a boy (or a girl for that matter; if she was gay, would she even know? She wasn't sure she was straight either). She'd never even truly talked to a boy in any real way. Worst of all, she'd had to deal with that reckoning on prom night while Lucille, her only friend and ally, was stuck working at the diner.

That was the last story she would ever actively choose to share with a handsome older boy with perma-parted pillow lips who'd just asked to be given the grand tour of Winona Olsen, and so she was horrified when she realized she'd been replaying all of this in startling detail out loud.

It was practically an out-of-body experience, and when she jolted back into herself, she looked over at Silas, expecting to find him trying to cringe her out of existence.

Instead he was silent, thoughtful for a moment, with his eyes heavy on the road. After a beat he cleared his throat. "Your dad sounds like he could give my old man a run for his money."

His father?

Silas gave her a soft, understanding look that unwound something she'd been holding tight to her chest. "I'm guessing choosing your prom date wasn't the *only* bat-shit thing he did?"

Winona instinctively covered her wrist where the Cartier brace-let used to sit. Silas's eyes dipped to her hands in her lap. His mouth jammed shut, and his brow dipped, and then his eyes were back on the road.

"I'm from Denver originally," he said, stoking the dead embers of the conversation back to life. He gave her a cautiously meaning-ful glance. "I had people I needed to get away from too." He shook his head. "Happens to the best of us."

Again they were silent for a long moment. Silas's voice was quiet when he next spoke: "It's not just you. You're not alone, Winona. You're safe now."

And just like that, the knot came undone. The Stormy Knot. Winona's secret history. That tangle in her chest that she now realized she'd spent the last ten years guarding from the world, keeping it wound tight.

She told him everything, everything she could think to say, and he told her about himself too. There was no joking, no deflecting, just the quiet murmur of their voices over the hum of the engine, just the electric current that passed between them whenever they reached to bump the heat up at just the same moment.

By the time they pulled into the motel outside Iowa City—a parallel universe iteration of the Cliffside that basically just reversed the layout, replaced all the red vinyl visible through the bar door with blue, and swapped out the green room doors for sickly orange—she knew the strange scar at the inside of his left eye was from a firecracker his mother had thrown at his face.

He had two brothers and a sister, and he was the youngest. His oldest brother had died in an accident on an Air Force base in Virginia when Silas was only nine, and that was when his family had changed, just like Winona's. His other brother was in prison for "accidentally burning down a church he was living in," and no one had heard from his sister since she got married to a man she met at a bus station in Indiana.

Sometimes Silas worried she was dead, that her husband was as mean and stupid as their father had been.

He told her good things too. Like how he'd hated swimming until he drove across the country to California and saw the ocean for the first time, and how, if he could do anything, he would write books.

Jack Kerouac shit, he said, and Winona pretended to not absolutely despise Jack Kerouac, and she thought maybe she really didn't, that maybe she'd just misunderstood it before, and now she replaced all the protagonists with baby-faced blond boys with a split lip that creased deeply when smiling.

The time flew by, and then they were waking Lucille. She was rubbing her eyes as she stumbled, leaned up against Winona, into their room. Silas had offered to pay for it; it was a good deal, he'd said—he'd been through this way before.

Winona felt all wrapped up in his care, in his attention to detail. The girls collapsed into their bed while Silas went to shower, and as tired as she should have been, Winona lay awake, flat on her back, listening to the water pounding against the tub, the occasional splash and splatter of moisture slicked of skin, and she thrummed with raw energy.

This was her life. All along, she'd been cosplaying as Stormy Olsen's daughter, and now here she was, holed up in a gorgeously cheap hotel room, her best friend's face pressed into her shoulder, snoring softly, and a beautiful boy who understood her, who had whispered in the car that he thought she was brave, now showering on the far side of a very thin wall.

She searched herself for guilt and found none.

The water turned off and the flimsy door opened and Silas stepped out into the fluorescent-lit sink alcove outside the bathroom proper. He'd twisted his white towel around his hips and his pale abdomen rose out of it, nearly the same color but imbued with a greenish pallor. He stood in front of the mirror and ran a wide-toothed comb through his blond tangles, pushing it back off his face, and he was so beautiful, so self-assured that Winona forgot she wasn't daydreaming, that he could see her too, as she openly stared at his long, vaguely crooked spine. He had a purplish bruise between his shoulder blades in the approximate size and shape of a pool ball, and when she gasped at it, he turned around, briefly silhouetted, and gave her a smile she could barely make out except in the right corner where the light struck it.

"You aren't sleeping?" he whispered.

She propped herself up on her elbows and Lucille rolled away, burying her face into a pillow.

"Me neither," Silas whispered back. Winona didn't point out that he'd just been in the shower, and that was an unlikely place to doze off. She liked that he was relating to her, even if it was sort of a lie. "Are you hungry?" he asked.

She nodded. She was starving.

"Get dressed," he hissed, tipping his head toward her duffel bag full of shift dresses and A-line skirts. "I know a place. You're going to love it, Winona Olsen. It's so you."

TWENTY-FIVE

ONE THOUSAND DOLLARS AND TWELVE CENTS, A BOX OF DONUTS, AND AN ARGUMENT

Lucille woke up from the kind of sweaty, sour-mouthed sleep that she'd tried, over the years, to avoid at all costs. It wasn't a hangover, at least not the way they looked in the movies—it was a kind of slowness, a forced reckoning. The Cliffside. It was always the Cliffside's fault. She reached out to the bedside table for the glass of water she'd left there and frowned when she couldn't find it. A rookie mistake. She had to quiet the buzzing in her head before AP Calc, or Mr. Erwin would give her the stink-eye.

Gently, Lucille pushed herself up on her elbows, her head humming with static. Or was it the white noise machine next to the bed? It sounded like a dentist's drill in the background. She blinked at the painting over the television: a child's teddy bear, the ribbon around its neck unwinding. In the corner, a puppy waited to disembowel it.

Where the fuck was she?

All at once, Lucille was devastatingly awake. The sheets were scratchy against her legs and the bathroom door was open to its murky, damp insides, and they had maybe killed someone last night and definitely picked up a drifter and carried him across state lines in their stolen convertible and *Winona was not there.*

Winona, the only responsibility she hadn't given—wouldn't give up.

Lucille wasn't someone who panicked. Today was no exception. She pulled on sweatpants, a tank top. Twisted her hair into a topknot, washed her face, filled her water bottle and took it over to the window. These were important things to do: she was priming her mind like the pump for a well, or like a gymnast stretching out her legs.

It hadn't escaped Lucille that Silas was gone too, and that his bed hadn't been slept in at all. *That baby-faced piece of shit gangster,* Lucille thought, twisting the top of her water bottle with shaking fingers. The night before, she had slept pretzeled up next to Winona in their ridiculous two-seater convertible, jerking awake every few minutes before falling back down into sleep. She'd caught only a few words: *jail, prom, arson, Stormy.* Winona always using her father's first name like some kind of talisman, like naming the demon stripped it of its power.

Silas who had run off with Winona like she was a machine he could strip and sell for parts.

With a single furious hand, Lucille pushed the slatted blinds across the window and let the light come streaming in. This

motel, wherever they were—the only way it was really different from the Cliffside was that the doors for each room faced the
parking lot.

Their space was empty, the ROOM SEVEN PARKING ONLY
sign flaking away on the asphalt.

Lucille squinted. *Was* it flaking?

Or was there something in pieces, scattered across the words?

She shoved her feet into her slide-ons and slammed outside, the
front door thudding back against the still-open dead bolt. It was
shockingly hot outside, and Lucille squinted against the sun and
the empty parking lot and the hollowing-out roar in her ears that
came on her like a wave.

The thing in the parking space was Winona's phone, in pieces.

She couldn't call the police. She couldn't get her mother. She
couldn't call Winona—of *course* she couldn't call Winona, that was
the main issue, not being able to run out and find her best friend
and wrap her in a sweater and then turn back to face the rest of the
world with her teeth and her knives and there was *nothing*, there
was *no one else*—

She didn't remember going back inside, didn't register how
she emptied her duffel bag on the stained floral comforter,
searching through it until she seized on the bowie knife in its
orange plastic sheath.

Lucille and her mother had scrubbed their house clean of
every last thing belonging to Sperm Donor Leonard—except
for this knife. When Lucille, age twelve, had found it in the back
of the undersink cabinet, she'd stuffed it farther under a heap of

old dried-up sponges so that it would avoid her mother's purge. It seemed like a good thing to have.

She held it up now. The plastic made it look less real, and so she slid the blade out of its sheath to let it glint in the light.

If this two-bit grifter thought he was going to snatch away Winona, he better not be all that attached to his fingers and toes.

That was how Winona and Silas found her as they bustled into the room, Winona with her arms full of PARTY CITY bags, a devil-horn headband in her hair, Silas with a case of donuts and a finger through Winona's belt loop like it was a leash, like he owned her.

Winona didn't own jeans. She was wearing her best friend's thrift store 501s.

Lucille had worked herself into such a fury that the only way out was through. She held up the knife between them like she was lofting a candle, and said in her very calmest voice, "Where. The Fuck. Were you."

That was the moment where they finally seemed to *see* her, the girl in the tank top holding a knife like it was a gas canister. Silas startled, but Winona reared fully back into him, like a horse preparing to bolt, and Lucille remembered (too late) that her father had probably greeted her at home like this more than once.

Lucille's fury went out all at once, a candle blown out. She shoved the knife back into its sheath. "Silas. Right? That's your name."

"Yes ma'am," Silas said, and his arm was fully around Winona now, like *Lucille*, of all people, would hurt her.

"Her phone is in pieces in the parking lot." These weren't questions.

Winona said in a whisper, "We went out for breakfast. Stormy had put that app on my phone—you know, Where Is Your Child Tonight?—and when he activates it, it calls the police and hacks my GPS, even if it's off, and when I remembered, I told Silas and he thought the best thing to do would be to destroy it completely."

Silas juggled the box of donuts under his arm. "Easiest thing seemed to be running it over with that car. I'm sorry to have worried you, but it *was* all my fault. Not Winona's."

"That makes sense," Lucille said. "Now get your hands off her."

Silas narrowed his eyes, but released Winona all the same, and took a step clean out of the room onto the sidewalk.

"Non," Lucille said, finally tossing the knife onto the bed, "can you get the donuts from him and shut the door?"

Winona shifted her weight. The devil horns jiggled in her hair. "Um. Why?"

"Because I'm starving," Lucille said, "and because Silas needs to go get us some coffee and then wait, outside, in the hot sun alone, until I've had at least three almond cremes."

To her credit—thank God—Winona didn't look over her shoulder to get Silas's approval. She just reached backward, took the box, and kicked the door shut behind her.

TWENTY-SIX

ONE THOUSAND DOLLARS AND TWELVE CENTS AND ENDLESS GLITTER

There were angel wings in the bag for Lucille. "There was a costume store right next to the place where we got breakfast," Winona was saying as she polished off a chocolate long john, "and we'd just scored at the restaurant, and I've been like . . . I don't know how to describe it, Luce. Like, giddy. Like when we used to pretend we had those old husbands—"

Used to? The last time they'd done it had been last night. Lucille looked down at her latte. Silas had gotten her an extra-large hazelnut with whipped cream, which made her forgive him the tiniest bit. She could see him through the window in the parking lot, talking to someone on his phone, his blond hair flat and chemical in the sun.

"—it's like everything is sugar, you know? Or like, hot"—she took a swig of her coffee—"and beautiful and I just want to live here, in this new world. It's like being at the Cliffside on a Tuesday night, with you, but *all* the time. He's been there. He knows me. I feel like I'm just . . . safe."

Lucille was, uncharacteristically, out of words. The bowie knife was still beside them on the bed, and she wondered, vaguely, if she put it away, if she would be her old self again. "You said you scored at the restaurant. How did you do that?" she asked finally, and her voice was even raspier than normal.

"Oh," Winona said, flushed, "the waitress was horrible, she kept ignoring us because she thought, I don't know, that we couldn't pay? I guess I don't look the way I usually do—"

You don't, Lucille thought, raking her eyes down Winona. The jeans, the T-shirt, the topknot. Even the horns. *You look like me.*

"—and I was kind of upset and Silas was like, *No, I got this*, and we paid and tipped, but when we got out to the street, he had her tips. Like, *all* of them. A roll of cash! It was amazing, like magic, and since he'd already paid for this room, I told him he could use it as payment, but he wanted to buy me a costume so 'my inside could match my outside,' and . . ." Winona trailed off. "What? What's wrong?"

Lucille looked down at her diner waitress hands. "Nothing," she said, putting the half-eaten donut back into the box. "Nothing's wrong. Tell Silas to get back in here, so we can get on the road. I need to take a shower."

She wasn't the least bit amused by Silas anymore. The sooner they could drop that jackass wherever he was going, the better.

In the bathroom, washing her hands, she caught Winona's

stunned eyes in the mirror. She looked like such a little girl, sur-rounded by fake feathers and pastries and pillows, a child set up for playtime by parents who adored her. Except she was six feet tall, cross-legged in a motel bed, and, as Lucille finally saw as she shut the door between them, in tears.

The shower was hot; the towels were rough; Lucille put on the same clothes as before and spread her hair across her shoulders to dry. She thought she'd heard Silas come back in, but when she opened the door, he wasn't there.

Winona was. She'd cleaned the room meticulously—their bags were all packed by the door, and the devil horns were nowhere in sight. It was as though she'd been tidying her bedroom frantically before Stormy came home, putting all the parts of herself away, out of sight. Now she was sitting on the edge of the bed, clutching something in her lap.

"Winona?" Lucille asked.

She looked up, and her face was pale, haunted.

Lucille took a few uneasy steps into the room, any anger about Silas and Winona's little stunt with the waitress evaporating in this new atmosphere. Something had changed while Lucille was in the shower. "What is it?"

Winona seemed surprised to see Lucille standing there in front of her. She opened her mouth, but no sound came out, and Lucille crossed the room to pull her own phone from Winona's hands.

Winona had pulled up the Channel 5 website, and a video of Stormy's morning weather report was paused on-screen, the crack in the glass running straight through his forehead. At the sight of him, fear curled around Lucille's neck like a viper, its coils tightening slowly, inevitably.

Her skin crawled as she hit PLAY and Stormy's crackling campfire of a voice came to life.

"Heeeeeello, folks! I hope you're all enjoying this beautiful May day, or as I like to call it, fifth-winter. After yesterday's surprising highs, today you can expect a mix of sunshine and possibly flurries, with a side of your neighbors curled up in the corner, crying." He winked, and went on. Something about a storm, and a promise that at least this one "isn't worthy of a first name! That's when you know we're in trouble, folks, when we're so desperate to barter for a little sun that we start calling the storms by our stubborn uncle's name! Of course, I'm not complaining. My name's Sturgis, and I've been called by a weather pattern's name my whole life!"

And pause for the laughs at home.

Lucille happened to know for a fact this was a lie. Winona's grandfather had told Winona, in one of his half-lucid rants, that "Sturgis" had adopted his nickname after marrying into the Pernet family, because he thought it made him seem like he belonged to a "higher class." Like Bunny, or Bitsy, or Tuppy.

Grandfather Pernet thinks that's what made Stormy choose *to be a meteorologist*, Winona had told her, and they'd laughed at him together.

Now Lucille wanted to throw tomatoes at his face. She wanted to make the crack running through his face on-screen a reality.

He was still talking, waving an arm around the map behind

him, but his words had turned to static in Lucille's ears and the contents of her stomach curdled violently.

She hated his George Clooney voice, and that shit-eating grin, which had once seemed so charming, but now struck her as custom-made for some kind of demented Disney World animatronic brought to life for the express purpose of instilling nightmares in all the little girls riding past.

He was convincing as the charming weatherman, the doting father, but once you noticed one little detail that was awry, maybe the flat-black deadness of his pupils or the twitch in the corner of his mouth, the rest of his disguise started to come apart, like a latex mask slipping around the eyes to reveal scales.

The Reptile King of Kingsville.

And perhaps most unnerving of all was that he was completely unchanged from the last time she'd seen him. Like nothing had happened. Like his daughter wasn't missing, off on some quest to find the mother he'd convinced the whole town was dead.

No rumple to his clothes, no odd swoop to his hair, no circles under his eyes or anxious twist to his mouth. Just that same mechanical smile, the same almost-but-not-quite-right practiced flick of the eyebrows as he laughed, the jerky wave of the hand as he explained the source of the incoming snow.

It should have been a relief, if a confusing one, but Winona's rigid posture beside her told her something was off. This was not a win for them.

The weather report was wrapping up, and Lucille fought to

actually interpret his words instead of tuning them out for some kind of self-preservation.

"And while I'd love to complain a bit more with you folks about the injustice of it all . . ."

He looked right into the camera, and for an instant, the mask dropped. His face was lax and dead, like a fish in the icy displays at the market. When he next spoke, the grin flickered back into place with a new intensity.

". . . my lovely daughter would never forgive me if I signed off without saying: *remember, folks, in the Upper Peninsula, a little bit of sunshine goes a long way!*"

The report ended. The video jumped back to the beginning, ready to be replayed.

Feeling chilled, Lucille sunk onto the bed beside Winona. "This is . . ." She cleared her throat, and tried again. "This is good. He's not gunning for us. This is a good thing."

Winona was staring at the wall, looking as ghostly as a starlet in a black-and-white Hitchcock film. "He didn't even mention me being missing."

"That's good," Lucille repeated.

Winona shook her head. "He must have a plan. This has to be part of it. He'd never just let me walk away. Never."

Lucille touched the back of Winona's neck. She meant it to be a comforting gesture, like when her mom played with her hair, but Winona flinched violently, and Lucille jerked her hand back as she realized her mistake. "It'll be okay," she whispered. "We're together, and we'll figure it out. Promise. He's not going to take you from me, Nony."

Winona turned toward her and burst into tears as she threw her arms around her. "Luce, I am so, *so* sorry. About the waitress thing. I don't know what I was thinking!" She tucked her head against her shoulder.

"I know," Lucille said. "It's okay."

"I was so caught up in it, I didn't even realize—but it was shitty, and stupid, and I shouldn't have let him steal from girls like us. People like your mom. That woman needed that money, and I just—I wasn't thinking. It's almost like a bandage has torn off, you know? And the skin under it that I thought was still cut up is like . . . healed. Or like I was supposed to die and I'm *not* now, and it isn't because of Silas, it's because of you. You. You're my priority." She had pulled back and taken Lucille's damp shoulders in her hands. "You're my family, and I promise I'm going to think about you first from now on, like you've done for me. I was caught up and being reckless, and of course I should've left you a note. Honestly, you were so conked out and beautiful and I thought you'd just sleep in forever."

"I know," Lucille said. She usually did, in fact, sleep in forever if she could. "I'm sorry too, Nony. I just got . . . really scared. But nothing happened! Nothing happened, and it's not going to."

"I'm sorry," Winona said again, and Lucille shrugged, and smiled, and they hadn't ever fought before. Now she knew they could do it, that they could sort it through, still be okay. Or maybe she just knew there was no time for fights right now. They couldn't afford to be torn apart because if that happened . . . they'd have nothing.

The vision of Stormy's cold, dead-eyed, fish-face flashed across Lucille's mind, and she shivered.

She had to stop thinking about it. About the wedge Silas could drive between them and the meteorologist with the impossible reach. Worrying wouldn't do her any good. If anything, it would back them into a corner, and that was where she was most likely to make bad decisions.

Winona picked her coffee back up from the bedside table. "There are still donuts. I had to stop eating because I felt kind of sick, so there are like . . . a lot of donuts. And you haven't tried on your angel wings yet."

Leave it to Winona to float right over what had happened and land on something shiny and new.

In the mirror, Lucille ruffled her hair. It was drying as it always did in the heat: electric, wavy, gigantic. On a whim, she dug into her bag and pulled out her tube of Revlon's Cherries in the Snow. Hot, hot pink.

"What do you think about this for today's look, *mon cherie?*" Lucille asked. "This and like, glitter. Like a lot of glitter." Lucille's makeup was mostly glitter.

"Yes," Winona cried. "Exactly! Can you do me first?"

Lucille ran her fingers through Winona's bob. She had taken it out of its topknot. "I still can't believe Stormy did this to you."

"The haircut?" Winona examined it in the mirror.

"It's horrifying. He might as well have just *peed* on you."

Slowly, Winona reached up to tuck a strand behind her ear. "The worst part," she said, "is that he left me pretty. That's the part that makes it a punishment. He knew he wouldn't be able to look at me if I was *ugly*, if I was his definition of ugly . . . and now, when I see myself in the mirror, it's like I can feel him watching. I don't have an opinion on what I look like. It isn't about me. You know—" Winona hesitated.

"What?" Lucille put an encouraging hand on her shoulder.

"I don't know. I was just thinking that . . . that I'd do anything if it meant no one would ever look at me like that again. Like I'm on a platter, being presented to them. Like I've just come out of the hair and makeup department for Stormy's production of *Daddy Dearest*. I'd shave my head. I'd tattoo my face. I'd sew my mouth shut."

"I know," Lucille said, and she did.

"For now," Winona said with an unconvincing airiness, "can you just do something with my hair?"

Lucille put Winona's hair up and away in a crown of braids— Lucille had clever fingers and Winona, a box of 1960s bobby pins—and slathered balm across her lips with a thumb. In the heat, the makeup would slide right off them, so Lucille made it messy on purpose. No foundation, no mascara (Winona's lashes were naturally full and dark, because the world was hideously unfair). Just iridescent highlighter up both cheeks and across her eyelids, cream bronzer in the hollows and around the edges of her face, a dark brow to balance it out. The bright pink wouldn't work with the horns—she opted for an orange-red lip instead, and spun

Winona around to face the mirror like Lucille was a Hairstylist to the Stars.

"Yes!" Winona said again, and there it was, that *squeal* in it that made Lucille's heart seize, the moments she loved best. Like Winona was surprised she was beautiful, like she was surprised that anyone loved her, when all Lucille could think was, *Here it is, here's your confirmation. It's been here all along.*

"I sort of wish I hadn't destroyed my phone," Winona said, adjusting her headband in the mirror. "Isn't that stupid?"

"Selfies?"

"I mean." Winona paused, then fell into a snorting fit of laughter. "I mean, yeah!"

Lucille tossed her phone to Winona, and the other girl spread herself out on their bed, her arm held high above her body like a flag, as she turned her new face left and right for the lens.

Lucille's look was easier, because it was sloppier. She did it all with her fingers: when in doubt, make the hair bigger. Press on rhinestones into the lash line. Overdraw the lips. Sparkly lotion everywhere. The angel wings sat on straps on her shoulders, and she finished it off by taking the piece-y gold glitter from her kit and scattering it over the fake feathers, over her shoulders, over the floor.

"One last thing," Winona said, and Lucille saw in the mirror that she was watching her, that she'd let the phone fall down beside her on the bed.

Lucille was suddenly a little scared to move. Her hands tightened on the dresser.

Her best friend got up, slinky as a cat—Winona didn't move like that—and reached into Lucille's pink plastic kit for the highlighting stick. It was a cheap one that they'd bought on sale at Meijer, and it left a sheen on Winona's fingers. She twisted it up, slowly, her dark eyes on Lucille's neck, and for a minute Lucille had the indistinct sense that Winona was looking for a place to bite her.

Like she was dangerous. Like she was new.

With a finger, Winona traced the line of Lucille's collarbone—the slope above, the slope below, and then she ran her finger down the highlighter. Her palms were sweating. Whose palms? Winona's? Hers?

"You have to move a little," Winona whispered, "so you can see it," and Lucille turned at the waist, looking down to catch the glow. She could only see it in the mirror: a line of light cutting across her body. Winona stood beside her, and the two girls marveled at it—the wings stretching out from her shoulders like a spray of petals, the glitter and sweetness and Winona's dark, dark eyes like a path down into the earth.

It'll always be this way, Lucille thought dizzily, *the two of us forever*—

The door opened. The light flooded in.

"You two look *amazing*," Silas said, in the doorway, as Winona broke free and ran to him. "Do y'all want me to get my camera?"

TWENTY-SEVEN

ONE THOUSAND DOLLARS AND TWELVE CENTS, A CAMERA, SOME BOURBON, AND A MOTEL IN IOWA CITY

Silas had a nice camera, nicer than Lucille expected. He also had a flask, and soon he had to refill it because Lucille had downed the bourbon inside it like it was a wildebeest and she was a really, really thirsty lion.

She'd had a lot of crushes in her life, and things she hadn't really classified as crushes—friendships that ended in fistfights and tears and then the need to be near them again like a hunger, like a sickness; the boys she'd met in the back row of the movie theater, in the break room of the 7-Eleven, in her bedroom when her mother was working late, texting them in her pajamas, saying *come over, come over, come over*. There were, too, the girls she'd kissed on boys' laps at the parties she'd sometimes go to before she met Winona. It was a performance, for the boy, ostensibly, but also for herself, a girl who liked to watch people and to know they were watching her, and though she had always known that ripple had a deeper pool below it, it had always seemed like something she could work out in college, maybe, if she *had* to.

Though, of course, Lucille never expected she'd actually make it to college.

"It is *imperative*," she told them, "that I am not the only one who's drinking." The word "imperative" had unrolled itself in her brain like a carpet; it wasn't something Lucille would usually say. It was a Winona word.

It made Lucille feel really, really lonely.

Winona giggled and swiped the flask, downing a gulp. She turned to Silas and he gave her a sleepy, low-lidded smile, tipped his head back, parted his full lips, and let her pour the whiskey into his mouth. He pulled her in by the waist as he drank, held on to her hip with his hand, her eyes with his. When his lips pressed closed, a tiny rivulet running down the corner, Winona turned back to Lucille, beaming, and reached out her free hand—the one that wasn't tangled in Silas's T-shirt—to draw Lucille in toward their little twosome.

Lucille loved Winona, like something more than a sister—an appendage maybe, or the whole right side of her body—and she hated Silas a whole lot, and this whole situation felt like a one-way train to Terribleville.

"Here." Winona tipped the rest of the flask's contents into Lucille's mouth, and Silas disentangled from them to pick up where he'd left off, photographing them.

Lucille had no idea what Winona was thinking, if Winona was thinking anything at all. Sometime since yesterday, it was like Winona had gone from being a book Lucille knew by heart to being that same book with its ending ripped out.

And Silas just kept taking pictures.

The two of them eating the last of the gummy bears, Winona's horns tipped crazily to the side. Lucille with a vending-machine sucker in her mouth, looking off-camera like a dime-store angel. The girls spread out across the stripped mattress like a display, like a warning. Thank God Lucille insisted they keep their clothes on—even though no one had suggested otherwise, Lucille could feel it coming and it felt *imperative* to lay it out there. Silas reaching down, to move Lucille's hair just so, or gently slide the strap of Winona's shirt down her bare shoulder, lingering so long that even the thick haze of liquor couldn't make the gesture seem casual.

They staged a pillow fight, the feathers in Lucille's hair like the feathers in her cheap angel wings, bent now at the corners from all the rough play. They posed, clothes on, in the shower, in the doorway of the bathroom. Hands in each other's hair, on each other's faces and shoulders, energy racing through the loop the two of them had always formed. Lucille sticking her tongue out, Winona tipping her head to look at Silas through her lashes, and when he finally had to go out for more bourbon—*I think I'm sort of sober*, he'd said, like it was a problem—Lucille thought, *Jesus God, I need to get us out of here before Silas tries to turn this into a porn shoot.*

But Winona was looking out the window like a girl in a different kind of movie, something with a sweeping soundtrack. "This is it," she was marveling. "This is it. This is what having *everything* feels like, being with him. Being with you."

And she didn't know how, but it scooped something out of Lucille, something so vital, so bright, that when Silas came back with a fresh bottle of Jim Beam and a proposition, she found herself saying yes.

"It's simple," Silas said. "My ex and I used to run this con all the time—"

Winona stared him down like she could kill him with a look.

"—and Winona, you are much, *much* prettier than her. Both of you are, of course. We're going to do even better." He flexed his hands, then sat down on the bed. Lucille threw herself down into an armchair and felt the wings bend farther, felt the pinions of the fake feathers dig into her skin.

"We put up an ad. Two teenage girls. Two thousand for one hour. And when they show up, you drug them. You take their money."

Winona was saucer-eyed and nodding when Lucille cast a glance her way. "I don't know," she said. Lucille's cousin was a stripper—sex work wasn't something she had, like, moral hang-ups about—but she didn't want to be near anybody with a little-kid fetish and a wallet full of entitlement. And she didn't want to make a call right now, in these sixty seconds, as Silas stood tapping his foot, about whether she wanted to sleep with those old dudes for cash.

Most importantly, she didn't necessarily trust Silas to keep her—or more importantly, Winona—safe.

"We're robbing them," he said. "Plain and simple, nothing else. These aren't just lonely johns, girls. I'll tell them you're fifteen. They're perverts, we'll take their money, and before you know it, you're up to your ears in—whatever you need that money for."

"My mom," Winona said. "We need it to get to my mom."

"For your mom, then," Silas said, smiling faintly. "What do you say?"

Lucille thought of Ginger Sneakers and how he was probably still on the floor of Room 211 at the King Midas Casino motel. About her brother, selling pills to men who could feed them to girls while he sat, blameless, on the couch in the Pryce house, the police too lazy to do the first part of their job and come get him; she thought about Stormy Olsen, who was probably right now arranging for a SWAT team to break into every hotel between Kingsville and Las Vegas to find his daughter and drag her back by her hair so that he could keep beating her until she would never leave him again.

She tried to think about Winona, but right now, she didn't know where to start.

"I'm in," Lucille said, and coughed. "And I bet you already have that ad up, Silas. Maybe when you were at the liquor store? Yeah?"

He didn't say a word.

"How many takers do you have?"

Silas cleared his throat.

"Our faces weren't in the photos, though, right? *Right*, Silas?"

"No!" he snapped. "I'm not an idiot."

Apparently, central Iowa had enough disgusting scum-bags who were willing to skive off work—and their wives and daughters, and their consciences, and whatever scraps of moral standing they had left—to come to Room 7 of the Easy Go Motel at two in the afternoon to try to have their way with a pair of girls in Halloween costumes.

Lucille didn't know how Silas knew about the drugs. Maybe Winona had told him; maybe he'd glimpsed them sticking out of her duffel bag before the donut run, the coffee run, the liquor run; maybe he'd been cataloging information about them all along. Why on earth had Winona given him her last name?

Because he was gorgeous. Because he made her feel gorgeous. Because, probably, from the moment he'd seen Winona in Patsy's, he'd been making plans on how to get her to trust him.

Lucille's only stipulation, when she laid it all out to Silas, was this: they'd meet each man outside the room, in the parking lot, and when he followed the girls in, they'd pour him a drink and go into the bathroom to "freshen up." Silas would be in there, waiting. And after a few minutes, Silas would go out, and he would take care of the passed-out man while Lucille and Winona barricaded themselves away.

Lucille didn't want to know where he was going to take the men. She'd think about that later, after they'd gotten out of this.

Winona got ready, silently, the Cracker Jack ring on her finger, Lucille's jeans snug around her waist like those were the obvious clothes to run a hooker scam in. She didn't know why that bothered her so much, the jeans.

The room was finally starting to cool down. Silas had figured out how to run the air conditioner. The three of them weren't talking. Not that much, not anymore.

But after they'd met the first man in the parking lot—Lucille couldn't even look at his face—and after he'd been removed, just as she and Silas had planned, there was a stack of bills on the counter next to the man's half-finished bourbon.

Two thousand dollars.

An hour later, they had four.

Time accordioned. It stretched out, it sped up. Lucille was still wearing her wings; she couldn't seem to take them off, to find the energy or even the reason. As she stood in the darkening room, Silas and Winona whispering in the corner, her phone lit up with a message from Chaxton.

Call me.

She didn't think about it. She just did.

"Lucy," Chaxton said, his voice tinny and strange. "Where are you? Your mom is so worried and I went by your house and you weren't there."

Lucille sort of barely knew who Chaxton even was anymore. "I'm in Iowa City," she admitted, "but I'll be gone tomorrow. Don't come looking for me, Chaxton. You've done—you've done a lot"—why was she close to tears?—"but I'm just . . . let me go."

A long, drawn-out pause.

"I'm so sorry," he said, strangled. "I'm so sorry. I'm sorry, Lucy, forgive me, but they said they were going to hurt my mom, and—"

"We're coming to find you," a voice said in the background. Farther away.

Like she was on speakerphone.

"*Marcus?*" Lucille asked, somewhere between a sob and a laugh. "You can't even get off the couch!"

"I'm not coming," he said. "My boss is. Five thousand dollars? Drugging one of his men? The Candy Man is coming for you, Lucille."

"Marcus," Lucille said desperately. "This is insane! You're sending a drug lord after me? I deleted that goddamn app off my phone—"

"You think you're so smart. You think that you can just *run your little games* around me. But you're just my snotty kid sister." Marcus laughed, a hollow sound. "An app? What, the 'Find My iPhone' app? There's a tracker *inside the phone.*"

Lucille punched "end call" and threw the phone into the mattress. It thudded off, ricocheting crazily toward Silas's head, and he ducked. "What the shit?" he said. "What happened?"

"That wasn't Chaxton," Lucille said, and already she was gathering her clothes off the floor and stuffing them into her duffel. "Well. That was Chaxton, *and* my brother, *and* they know about the guy we roofied back at the King Midas. He knows where we are."

"Chaxton?" Silas was asking, but Winona had gone bloodless. She spun to look out the window, as if the Candy Man's car could already be pulling into the lot.

"We have to go," Lucille said.

"*Now*," Winona said. At least someone else understood the urgency here.

Silas scratched his head. "But I have someone else coming— I thought we could make it an even six thousand. Two grand for each of us?"

"Only if you can spend that money from six feet underground," Lucille said. She felt amazing. Why did she feel amazing? It was as though all afternoon, reality had been peeling away from its edges like laminate off a bathroom window. Now she could see clearly again.

"I should destroy my phone," Lucille said.

"That leaves us with no *phone*," Winona said.

Silas, unsurprisingly, was still five steps behind. "I mean— where do we go?" he asked, his handsome face scrunched and confused like someone had asked him what the square root of "idiot" was. But Winona was on it, as always. Already she was swiping a makeup wipe across her face; the glitter streaked down her face like tears. With her other hand, she jammed her things into her bag.

"Denver," Lucille said. She hoisted her duffel over her shoulder. No one knew them in Denver; no one had even heard them say the word.

When Silas didn't move, she groaned and said, "Or feel free to stay here, Silas. These people aren't after you."

After a long moment, Silas sighed. "I mean. If that's what you want . . . I get it. The car *is* a two-seater."

He was doing his best wounded-puppy impression, and Lucille tried not to crow out loud. *A way out!* Her and Winona in the Romeo, Cat Power on the stereo, home free—

But Winona had stopped packing. Her back was to Lucille, her shoulders tensed as a bird's, and Silas gazed over at her like he was a goddamn bird rehabilitator.

Lucille would tear her own face off if Pouty Lips McConMan was going to get her sloppily murdered in an Easy Go Motel.

"Baby doll," Silas said, and Lucille heard herself make a noise that was somewhere in between a grunt and a screech.

He was begging for an invitation, and now, with Winona's eyes welling with tears, Lucille knew she was going to have to give him one.

"Fine! Fine, just come, but *now*, Silas, *now, now, now*—"

They drove south on the back roads. They stopped once, to throw Lucille's phone out the window; they stopped one more time in the morning, to buy a new one at Walmart. Four hundred dollars, gone. But they needed that connection to the outside world. In the parking lot, Silas took the plates off an abandoned-looking RV in the parking lot and put them on the Romeo, tossing Winona's grandpa's plates in their trunk.

Silas drove; he wouldn't have fit squished in the passenger seat with Winona, even if she had draped herself all over him. She didn't have to warn Silas about the risks again: he drove two miles under the speed limit the whole time, and all of it made Lucille want to scream, but it was the only way they could make sure that no one peered into their (stupidly flashy, why-did-we-take-this?) car.

It was the only way. The only way: Winona shivering on her lap, acting like Stormy had already gotten ahold of her again.

It scared Lucille more than anything.

If she was being honest, she'd never really imagined that she was ever going to die. She wasn't one of those fatalists who couldn't picture herself past age thirty; Lucille already knew that, in her later years, she'd dye her white hair purple and leave her vast fortune to her poodle. No, what Lucille had was a kind of Technicolor denial, something that made her smoke with three tattooed busboys in the alley behind the Starlight Diner at midnight, that made her launch herself at Marcus's face like a wildcat when she caught him lining his pockets with her cash. Lucille had lost a *lot* in her eighteen years, but if the stakes were her life, she couldn't imagine not winning. She was lucky in the only way that counted.

But even though Winona felt like an extension of Lucille, she still felt like the most vulnerable part. A limb spun out of glass. A bull's-eye painted over Lucille's heart. As Silas pulled into their new digs—a motel outside of Nowhere Good, Eastern Colorado—Lucille could feel Winona shift in her lap, and all she could think was, *I need to flip this script. This isn't the way it ends.*

Silas went in alone to get a room, and when he returned, he told them that the only one left had one bed, not two. "The rest is under construction," he said, eyes shifting between Winona and Lucille. "Sorry, girls."

Was it true? Who knew. "I'll sleep on the floor," Lucille said, because like *hell* was she going to be the jelly in that sandwich, and she said it again when she saw the room: a king-sized bed like an island in a sea of paisley carpet. In the corner, a pile of something that looked like mouse poop.

Silas went back out to the parking lot to throw a tarp over the car to disguise it. (Winona's grandfather had kept one in the trunk to protect the Romeo from "sun damage," because cars were of course only meant to be driven inside, like, shopping malls.) When the door shut, Winona drifted into the bathroom, still in her dreamlike, terrifying trance, and when Lucille peered in after her, she saw Winona hunched over the sink.

"How are you doing, Nony?" she asked, her voice hoarse from disuse.

"Scared." Winona straightened. "But—maybe good scared?"

"Good," Lucille said. Was it smart to stoke the flames of Winona's recklessness?

Was Lucille the one to ask?

"You'll be safe," she promised.

"No, I won't," Winona said, and she spun around, the awful light above her shadowing out her eyes. All Lucille could see were her lips, the line of her cheekbones.

"You won't?"

"I don't want to be. I don't want to be safe ever again." All in a rush, Winona came out of the bathroom and took Lucille's hands. "Promise me, Luce."

"Your mom," she said. "We're getting you to your mom, not to the circus!"

"What, this isn't a trapeze?" Winona asked. "I'm not holding flaming clubs?"

"Clubs made out of stolen pills and a stolen car and stolen angel wings—"

"I paid good stolen *money* for those wings, Miss Lucille Pryce."

"I wonder where Silas took those men," Lucille said. It was the closest they'd come to talking about what had happened that afternoon.

Winona shrugged. "To a different motel room? Or to a pit somewhere. Does it matter? Did you really want people like that loosed onto the world? Ask Silas. I'm sure he'll tell you."

"No," Lucille said. "I don't want to be able to answer the police's questions about it."

"No one's going to catch us," Winona said—but wasn't that Lucille's line?

She clutched Winona's hands tighter. "There's no going back, is there. Not unless we want to run into the Candy Man's bloody maw."

Winona hooted. "Bloody maw?"

"I heard it in a horror movie," Lucille said, "isn't it amazing?" And Winona hugged her around the waist and pulled her down to the bed, and Lucille wasn't thinking about running. Wasn't making contingency plans, even when Silas came in much later than he should have, wearing a look like maybe he'd met his own ghost out in the parking lot.

Lucille wasn't listening when Silas climbed in next to Winona and took her in his arms and put his mouth against her neck, like Lucille wasn't there, in her boxers and ratty T-shirt, just inches away.

Wasn't listening to the murmurs, the whine of the bedsprings, the wet sound of mouths in the dark. Wasn't sleeping. Even though she tried.

Maybe wasn't ever sleeping again.

TWENTY-EIGHT

THREE THOUSAND DOLLARS AND TWELVE CENTS AND SOME BRUISED LIPS IN OMAHA

Winona awoke still tangled in sheets and warmth. An arm lolled over her hip and hot breath blew an easy rhythm against the back of her head.

She hadn't expected to fall asleep last night. She'd expected to realize that all along, sleep had been another obsolete mandate passed down from her father, the reigning god of her house. But somehow, between the soft touches and fierce heat of colliding mouths, Winona had slipped wholesale into the deepest slumber of her life.

Stormy may not have invented the concept of sleep to keep his daughter locked away for eight more hours each day, but he had certainly misrepresented what sleep was supposed to be.

Not a lockdown, but a release. Winona had come undone in the solid dark of the motel room, and now the light trickling in through the blinds was reassembling her into a better, stronger version of herself.

She slowly shifted away from the press of the body behind her, rolled onto her hip as quietly as she could. Instead of Silas's face, she found Lucille's, and something about it startled her. Her cheeks were pink and full, her thick lashes fanned across their soft curves and a few stray strands of blond floating in front of her lips whenever she exhaled. As usual, she was snoring just a little bit, and the effect was that she looked younger than she had the night they first met.

This, Winona decided, was what had unsettled her. She decided not to think about it anymore and pushed herself up against the headboard, scanning the room for signs of Silas.

Silas. Her heart literally fluttered. It actually sort of hurt. Is that what people meant when they described butterflies? Or was this possibly coincidental, a heart attack she would let kill her after mistaking it for something terribly romantic?

God, how embarrassing.

She slid her bare legs off the bed and stood. She was in Silas's T-shirt. How had that even happened? Everything was hazy. She tiptoed over the mildewed carpet to peer into the bathroom. The light was off, but she bumped the door open just in case.

That was how eager she was to see him after last night. In thirty more seconds, she'd be checking under the bed.

Actually, that was strange: she remembered seeing his bag half-way under the bed the night before, poking out at its foot. But he'd moved it. In fact, the room was *tidy*. He was probably out in the parking lot, loading the car. Which wasn't ideal, given that she was pants-less and thus couldn't run out into his arms and leap into them *The Notebook*–style, a least not without causing a scene. She tripped around the bed and found a pair of Lucille's denim shorts, which she quickly paired with over-the-knee patent leather boots.

Okay, this was sort of a scene-causing outfit anyway, but she didn't care anymore. She was dying to feel his mouth against hers again, to run her fingers through his silky hair. She slipped outside, blinking against the sudden daylight.

God, they really *had* slept. What time was it? She shielded her eyes and gazed across the bleached blacktop. She spotted a beat-up Toyota and a burgundy Ford truck, and nothing else.

He'd probably taken the Romeo to get breakfast. But for once, she didn't feel hungry at all. Or she did, but not in the same way. She hadn't realized you could be hungry for a person and not be a cannibal. Or maybe she *was* a cannibal. Like, how would she even know yet?

The door clicked open behind her, and she spun to find Lucille leaned against the doorframe in her boxers and a T-shirt that read LEBRON. She squinted at Winona for a silent moment. "He's gone," Lucille called across the sunlit lot.

Winona looked over her shoulder again, confirming this. "Must've gone to get some breakfast."

Lucille's expression changed. "Non . . ."

"Huh?"

Lucille folded her arms around herself as if it were cold. It was not. She shook her head. Her voice was quiet, restrained. "He's *gone*," she said again.

"I know," Winona said, feeling both annoyed and confused.

Lucille shook her head again. She disappeared into the room and reappeared seconds later in her slip-ons, trudging over the glass-strewn walkway to stand in the parking spot with Winona. "This was on the dresser," Lucille said, and handed her a ten-dollar bill.

Winona blinked down at it as if it were covered in ancient runes instead of plain-old English. She recognized the handwriting immediately—though she'd seen it only once, on a bar receipt in a stolen wallet.

SORRY, GIRLS, the ten-dollar bill said. He'd written it with a Sharpie.

Winona read it rapidly, read it twenty-five times, and still it didn't make sense.

"Everything's gone," Lucille said. "The money, the stash, your clothes. He left mine. Guess that's not much of a shock . . ."

Winona finally looked up. Lucille was smiling faintly, but her eyes were glazed.

"I'm sorry, Non," she said. "I really thought . . . oh God, I'm just sorry."

Winona couldn't comprehend what Lucille was saying. Her mind was an icy landscape that all her thoughts kept slipping over.

She brushed past Lucille and hurried into the room. She stalked to the bathroom, gaze sweeping back and forth like a metal detector on a beach. Nothing, nothing, nothing. Nothing but towels on the bathroom floor. Nothing but Winona's makeup bag and Lucille's bowie knife on the sink. Nothing at all on the TV stand, or the bed, or the laminate desk pushed up under the window.

She jerked the chair out from it and scoured the dirty carpet for so much as a dropped quarter. She tossed the bedding off the mattress, threw open the drawers of the bedside table.

"Winona," Lucille said gently from the doorway. "It's gone. He's gone."

"I know he's gone!" Winona spun back, and Lucille flinched so badly Winona wondered whether she was frothing at the mouth. "I know he's gone, but I can't figure out why!"

Lucille gave a gruff, humorless laugh. "Because he's a fucking con man! Because we were idiots to ever trust him!"

"Oh my God." Winona couldn't really breathe. She started to pace in front of the bed. "Oh my God. Oh my God. Oh my—"

And now she understood Lucille's apology in the parking lot.

Stupid, stupid Winona—it was obvious.

They had no money. They had no car. Lucille wasn't apologizing because Silas had cleaned them out hours after giving Winona her first (and second and third and fifteenth and fortieth) kiss. She was apologizing because they were out of options.

"No," Winona said hoarsely, stumbling backward until she hit the desk. "No. No."

They couldn't go back. Stormy would kill her.

They couldn't go back.

Her stomach gurgled once and then again, this time louder, like it was angry. Lucille slumped onto the edge of the bed and buried her face in her hands. "What do we do," she whispered to herself a handful of times.

Winona's stomach groaned again. "I'm starving," she said pathetically, and then she broke down into tears.

"*Nony.*" Lucille crossed the room and pulled Winona into her arms, but Winona just cried harder, until it was something forceful and hideous and angry.

Until it couldn't stand to be contained any longer.

Winona ripped free and ran into the bathroom, grabbing Lucille's bowie knife as she went. She slammed the door behind her, and within seconds, Lucille was calling her name through it, but Winona ignored her.

She stared at her puffy, tear-streaked face in the mirror.

Her high cheekbones and full cheeks. Her doe eyes. The smattering of freckles over her button nose. She knew she should feel lucky that she was part of that slim subset of girls the world wasn't hell-bent on brainwashing into hating themselves, but when she looked at herself now, all she could think was, *This is what Silas saw from across the casino bar.*

This is the girl he stole from.

He looked right at you and saw a lamb.

Lucille was really pounding on the bathroom door now, screaming herself hoarse, but Winona kept ignoring her. She lifted a tendril of hair between her thumb and forefinger.

She'd thought all she wanted was freedom, to not be the girl sitting stock-still while her father snipped her curls off one by one.

Now she knew the truth.

She wanted to be the person holding the blade.

She lifted the hair straight up from the top of her head and drew the bowie knife across it like a bow against violin strings, sawing it back and forth across the hair, hacking it away from the root until it came away in her hand.

She didn't cry or shiver or sniff. She was floating outside her body, only dimly aware of the hunger burning in her stomach or the soft tickle of auburn hair falling loose on her shoulders with each new slice of the knife, barely aware of Lucille *swearing to God if you don't open up!*

Finally, Lucille made progress with the door. Its cheap lock gave out, the door flung inward, and Lucille tripped into the bathroom, eyes wide, to stop short at the sight of the bowie knife.

Relief hit her face first. "Thank *God*, I saw you took my knife and thought you'd gone all . . ." Her words trailed off as she took in this new and improved Winona.

She cupped her hand over her mouth. "Your hair . . ."

"It's horrible, isn't it?" Winona whispered.

"What? No! I mean . . . It's just . . . Wow." Lucille studied her for a few more seconds as she searched for words, mouth opening and closing.

Winona looked at herself in the mirror, the random tufts of reddish brown sticking up at odd, uneven angles. "Horrible! I look like Hungover Peter Pan!"

Lucille fought to keep a chortle in. "Oh my God. I mean, what the hell were you thinking, Nony? You gave yourself a bowie-knife chop-job!"

"It was an Angry Haircut!" she explained. "A Hangcrut."

"That's not a thing!" Lucille said through gasps of laughter.

"A revenge haircut!" Winona cried.

"Shouldn't you have done that to *Silas*, not yourself?" she demanded in a breathless squeal.

Laughter was bubbling up in Winona now too. Why was it that, the worse things got, the thinner the line that separated emotions seemed to be?

Winona studied herself in the mirror, then turned her face side to side, retracting her chin into her neck. "Oh my God. Look. I look like a thumb!"

"I never realized how much of a chin you *don't* have. I swear, if you'd told me you were going to shave your head, I would have assumed you'd look full Natalie Portman in *V for Vendetta*! This doesn't even make sense!"

"I look like a not-hot Tom Hiddleston! It's amazing!"

Now they really lost it. The giggling dissolved under the weight of something bigger. This was gut-out, nose-dripping, stomach-aching, falling-into-the-sink laughter. They tried for a while to stay on their feet. They tried to keep the joke going too, but neither of them could get words out, so it was mostly a lot of slapping each other like, *Wait, wait, I've got something to say!*

They slumped onto the bathroom floor together, still laughing. Lucille flopped onto her back, rocking back and forth as she clutched her ribs, and Winona crawled over, wheezing, and propped her head on Lucille's stomach, endlessly wiping the tears from her cheeks as the two of them shook with laughter.

It took a while, but finally they settled, soothing the monsters that lived in their skin back to sleep. They were nothing but two girls. Two seriously screwed girls.

"Maybe if he'd seen me like this," Winona said, "then he would've known not to fuck with me."

"Who?" Lucille asked. "Stormy or Silas?"

"Et al," Winona said. Her stomach gurgled.

"There's a McDonald's across the street," Lucille offered quietly, her hands running back and forth over the mangled terrain of Winona's hair. "You need to eat something, okay?"

As the girls sat up, Winona wiped away the last of her tears. She was suddenly embarrassed to speak. The only thing there really was to say was, *All this is all my fault*. Lucille had been suspicious of Silas and she'd brushed those worries aside because Winona wanted her to.

"You'll feel better after a McGriddle," Lucille promised.

Winona said nothing. She wasn't ready to go back to a world of lies, and pretending a rubbery fast-food breakfast sandwich would make things peachy was the first step on the long road back to life under Stormy Olsen's thumb. Performing for him and his audience.

Maybe that was why she'd given herself the haircut. Not so she wouldn't be the girl Silas had chosen as his mark, but so she would be too damaged for Stormy to take back. Too ugly to sit on his shelf.

She stood in the middle of the room as Lucille gathered their room keys and the ten bucks and Winona's makeup bag. She gave Winona a tentative smile like, *A fresh coat of lip gloss and a slab of low-grade sausage and you'll feel good as new?*

She wordlessly followed Lucille out the door and back into

the sunlight. Her brain had gone oddly calm, emptied itself out of self-preservation, and she followed Lucille (who kept casting her frantic, worried glances whenever she thought Winona wasn't looking) through the crosswalk to the McDonald's on the far side of the street.

"Why don't you go find a seat and I'll order?" Lucille said, which Winona took to mean, *I understand that you may never speak again and that could make ordering from a stoned fifteen-year-old cashier rather challenging.*

Winona drifted to the back corner, floated into a booth.

A few minutes later, Lucille joined her, carefully unloading the paper-wrapped contents of the tray between the two of them. "*And* we have two bucks left," she said with impressive cheer.

Winona unwrapped her sandwich and started eating. She couldn't taste it. It might as well be sand.

She wondered dully if she was having some kind of stroke, if that was why her senses seemed to be functioning as if through a layer (or several) of cling wrap.

When the sandwich was gone, she opened her makeup bag out of habit to reapply her lip gloss, and felt a pang of resentment that Lucille had been right about her.

Winona wanted to be someone else. She wanted to be anyone other than who she was, the girl who still was going to put on Laura Mercier after her meal, even if she was being ferried directly from it to the electric chair.

She unzipped the bag and fumbled through it without looking. She put on a coat of the faint pink shine, then handed it over to

Lucille, who looked way too grateful for the gesture. She applied and passed the gloss back. Winona thrust it back in and her hand hit on something unfamiliar. Cool metal. She looked down into the bag, and her jaw dropped.

"Non?" Lucille said. "What's wrong?"

Winona slowly lifted the watch from the bag, and her heart began to race. She dropped the diamond-encrusted Rolex on the table and met Lucille's saucer eyes.

"Shit," Lucille said, "that is . . . a watch."

"The watch to end all watches," Winona agreed.

"The love child of a watch and a mobster's wife," Lucille said. "Do you have any idea how much that monstrosity is worth?"

Winona glanced at the menu at the front of the store, debating ordering a second sandwich. The taste of maple syrup flooded her mouth. "A lot, Luce," she hissed. "Thousands, easily."

She had the engagement ring and wedding band in there too, but Stormy had bought those before marrying into the Pernet fortune, and they were more sentimental (or an impression of sentimentality) than actually valuable.

Lucille stared at the watch for a few seconds. "Enough thousands to get us to Vegas? Enough to get us . . . wherever after that?"

"Possibly," Winona said. "But before we can even consider that, we'll need enough to get the world's worst used car and a tank of gas."

Lucille made the face that meant she was doing math and not liking the results. "That doesn't seem promising."

"It doesn't, but we don't necessarily need enough to get an

apartment." Winona leaned across the table. "Denver," she hissed. "We just need to get a car and get to Denver."

Lucille made a face, but Winona went on. "We get to Denver, we find Silas, we take back our stuff, and whatever else he's got. *Then* we go to Vegas. With a cushion."

Lucille's head tilted uncertainly. "Winona, we've got to be realistic."

"Since when?" she bit out.

"Since we woke up to the world's emptiest hotel room! No, scratch that—since we robbed a gas station. I mean, how are we even going to find Silas?"

"Armie Quinhole," Winona said.

"Excuse you," Lucille panned.

"His cousin. He runs a chop shop," she explained. "I mean, how many Armie Quinholes can there be in Denver?"

"Surely no more than ten or eleven."

"Lucille," Winona said evenly, channeling every ounce of composure she usually reserved for Stormy's coterie of Important Friends. For once, *she* needed to convince Lucille to do something, something definitely very stupid but highly important. "Think about what he did to us," she went on. "Silas *preyed* on us. He used us, just like Marcus used you to buy him dumb shit, like my dad used me as Sculpture Number 4 in his fucking display case."

"We're not exactly Mother Teresa and the Virgin Mary," Lucille pointed out.

"No," Winona said sharply. "Exactly." She reached out and slid the Cracker Jack ring off Lucille's finger and popped it onto her own, admiring it as if it were the Wittelsbach Diamond. To her, it was. "We're *not* the Virgin Mary, but we're not the Whores, either. They tried to make us into them, to box us in, and maybe at some point we fit where they wanted us, but they pushed too hard and we're not those girls anymore. I'm not. God, Lucille, people like Stormy and Silas and Marcus take whatever they want, and for years—for our whole lives!—we've just let them. Well, guess what? *I* want things. I want something that's just *mine*, that I took and kept. Don't you? I mean, honestly, Lucille, don't *you*?"

Lucille stared back at her, and Winona's hummingbird heart rose through her throat. She needed to be right about this. She needed Lucille to understand, because if she didn't, Winona would be alone again, like she had before that night in front of the police station.

Lucille's eyes dipped to the Rolex. She chewed her lip. "Craigslist?" she asked, arching an eyebrow.

"No way. We're done *trying* to get ourselves murdered," Winona said. "Pawn shop."

Lucille gasped, and a cloud of excitement puffed off her. "Pawn shop." She stood and marched back to the cash register and returned with two more ninety-nine-cent hash browns. "Spent our last two dollars," she said. "Cashier says there's a pawn shop four blocks from here."

Winona stuffed her hash brown into her mouth and stood. "What are we waiting for?"

Lucille laughed at the spray of crumbs from Winona's mouth. "Literally nothing."

TWENTY-NINE

ZERO DOLLARS AND ONE HIDEOUS WATCH

The pawn shop was called Ric's, but the man working there was not. He wore a '70s polo whose color sat halfway between Bruised-Banana Yellow and Barbie-Skin Pink. His skin was sun-mottled and drooped at the elbows, and little white curls of arm hair caught between the links of his yellow-gold bracelet.

When Winona handed him the Rolex, he first held it as far from his eyes as he could, then spun on his stool and slid it under a microscope behind the glass counter. When he saw the inscription behind the watch face, his eyes sliced up to Winona. "This really yours, girls?"

Winona nodded. It had belonged to her mother, so of course it was hers. Just like the house. Just like the sculptures and paintings. Just like the Romeo and the luggage and the pink lace Trina Turk dress inside it, the Coach bag.

"My mother died," she told Not Ric. "She left that to me."

Not Ric's lip curled. He shook his head. "And now you want to trade it for a quick buck." He laughed and set the watch down.

Winona felt an unfamiliar urge to verbally disembowel the man. Lucille must've sensed it: she grabbed Winona's arm and bumped between her and the counter. "How much can we get?"

Not Ric crossed his Italian-sausage arms and leaned back on his stool. "Three thousand."

"Three thousand?" Winona fumed. "It's got to be worth more than that."

"Oh, it's worth a lot more than that," Not Ric agreed. "But this is a pawn shop. If you think I'm shelling out eleven thousand bucks for a—"

"Fine," Winona interrupted. "Three thousand."

"Non," Lucille said gently, touching her arm again. "Are you sure? I mean, that was your mom's and—"

Winona cut her off. "Three thousand, but you throw in *that*."

She pointed up the wall behind him, and Not Ric slowly turned, his gaze traveling up. He spun back, confused. "*That?*" he said at the same time Lucille said brightly, "That!"

Winona nodded. "Three thousand and the mounted muskie in exchange for the Rolex."

They owed Glenn, for the one creep-turned-cop Jay Algren had torn off his wall.

They owed the Cliffside for giving them their first taste of home, of a place that was theirs, where *they* were *them*. That gift had been priceless, but that wasn't going to stop Winona from trying to repay it.

She and Lucille had been shown so few true, no-strings-attached, nothing-to-gain kindnesses in this world that each was a treasure, a memory she wished she could store on a shelf. Now Glenn would have one to hang over his bar.

Not Ric's brow crumpled, and now he really looked like a mushed banana. "That's not a musky, sugar. It's a trout."

"And I'm not a sweet-tasting, soluble carbohydrate, I'm a human person, but you don't see me throwing a fucking fit."

Lucille turned a chortle into a cough. Winona beamed; she knew she'd sounded more like her friend than herself. Or maybe this *was* how Winona sounded after a few days off leash.

Not Ric sighed as he spun back and labored to his feet to fish the Not Muskie off the wall. "You got yourselves a deal."

Lucille squeezed Winona's arm and whispered so Not Ric couldn't hear, "Are you sure you won't miss the watch?"

Winona nodded.

She still had the engagement ring. She still had the hope of seeing her mother. But right now she had to focus on Lucille and herself, and Winona would have cut off a limb and sold it to get the two of them out of danger if that was what it took.

Not Ric slammed the trophy fish down on the counter, then turned and disappeared into the back room, probably to visit the safe. A moment later, he returned with a handwritten receipt and a very full envelope. When Winona reached out to take it, Not Ric held tight for a second, eyes locked on hers.

"I don't know what you two are mixed up in," he said, "but you girls had better be careful."

Winona pulled it free and stared right back at him.

"No," she said, and they turned and left the store.

Two hours later, after stopping into FedEx to send a special delivery back to Glenn at the Cliffside, they found the maroon Oldsmobile in a Walmart parking lot.

"Fifteen hundred bucks," Lucille said soberly. It was written in neon green paint on the window. Not *$1500.00*, literally *1500 BUCKS*.

"Worth every penny."

Lucille snorted. "Remember you said that when we're pushing this to the side of the highway in two hours."

"We don't have any other choice," Winona snapped.

Lucille drew back, lifting her arms in surrender. "I know, okay," she said. "Sorry."

Winona tried to shake it off. The apology, her outburst. It wasn't them. She let out a long breath. "I'm sorry," she replied. "God, Lucille, I'm sorry. I know none of this is your fault. It's mine, and maybe that's why I'm so angry."

Lucille's brow furrowed. She took Winona's hand. "It's not your fault. It's Silas's. Or maybe it's mine. I'm the one who took Marcus's drugs. If we hadn't done that . . ."

"If Marcus hadn't had them," Winona said. "If Stormy hadn't hurt me . . ."

"If the Sperm Donor had sent one single child-support check," Lucille said. "If I hadn't kept my money where Marcus could find it."

"If the meteor had never hit earth," Winona added, threading her fingers through Lucille's. "If the Ice Age hadn't happened and dinosaurs had prevented the evolution of mankind."

Lucille dissolved into laughter. "Oh God, wouldn't that be nice?"

"Some days," Winona agreed. "But not always."

"Yeah." Lucille smiled faintly. "Sometimes it's worth it, isn't it?"

"It is," Winona said. When she was with Lucille, it was worth it.

They called the number scribbled on the window under *1500 BUCKS*. Forty-five minutes later, they were pulling off into the sunset in their Oldsmobile, and it was worth it.

THIRTY

FIFTEEN HUNDRED BUCKS AND AN OLDSMOBILE THAT APPEARS TO BE CAPABLE OF FARTING

The car reeked, but here was the kicker: the smell was inconsistent. They'd go twenty minutes stench-free and then suddenly it was like a portal to hell had opened up in the brown-stained back seat.

They'd willfully decided to believe the splatter was the result of coffee, or a sun-melted chocolate bar, but as they cut west toward Denver, it became increasingly easy to believe that the car was haunted by whoever, or whatever, had shat its back seat.

They didn't talk about where they'd come from or what was following them, and they didn't talk about where they were heading or what they might find there.

They didn't really talk about anything but how their farting ghost might've died.

"Held it too long," Lucille suggested. "You know how parents are always like, *Don't hold it too long! Blah, blah, blah, your bladder will explode.* That's what our ghost did. He held it."

"If that substance came from his bladder," Winona said, "he already had bigger problems."

They had all the windows down, Taylor Swift's newest album blasting at full volume, and they took turns singing along passionately and screaming new ghost theories over their least favorite songs.

All the passenger-side speakers were blown, but they could make out the crunchy bass line, and that was enough.

The light had gone golden, painting the scrubby woods on either side of them in sepia tones. Winona had never noticed the coppery undertones to Lucille's hair, but as the wind whipped it around her face, the highlights caught and flashed. She looked like fire.

Like a torched gasoline spill on the surface of a lake.

Winona kept looking away from the road to watch her sing, to laugh with her. At one point Winona found herself in tears, and she told herself it was because of the wind tugging at her eyes, but the knot in her chest had been loosened too much to hold the truth in.

Winona was furiously happy to be in *this* Oldsmobile, on *this* road, under *this* sunset, with *this* person, and it had just occurred to her that she would never again be in this exact moment.

Lucille looked over then—she had probably heard Winona's thoughts—and her teeth glinted from behind the feathery curtain of her windblown hair. She gave her hand to Winona, and Winona held it tight and turned her eyes back to the road. She hated that they had to keep going, but as long as they went together, it would be okay.

After that, they barely spoke, except for when Lucille regarded the map they'd bought at the last gas station and murmured directions. They'd left the highway ages ago, after deciding back roads were more discreet. "Discreet" was an understatement. They hadn't passed another car in twenty-five minutes.

For all they knew, the world had ended. They were the lone survivors, driving over a severely potholed road through Butthole, Colorado.

But even though there was no one there to see or hear them, the girls didn't make a peep for miles. Not to speak, not to sing.

They gripped each other's hands and drove until the sky turned periwinkle, violet, deep blue, star-sprinkled black. If they let go, Winona worried time would come apart. The car would rip in half. One of them would be sucked out through the window and into space, and the other would fray apart like an unwound sweater.

The ground jutted up into hills, and then into mountains, and the trees got thicker and thicker. The black of the night sky devoured the world bit by bit as they drove and the glow of streetlamps and glass-fronted businesses came fewer and farther between as they hit a sort of dead zone preceding the suburbs of Denver.

The longer they went without spotting a convenience store, the more persistently Winona's stomach grumbled and ached. Once, she thought she'd spotted one: a few whitewashed posts and a corrugated tin roof over a handful of pumps, but as they neared, she realized her mistake. The shop was dark, the parking lot empty and full of trash, the building heavily graffitied, and a few gas hoses ripped off and coiled on the ground like shriveled snakes.

Lucille told Winona to turn left. Five miles later another building sprung up, this one huge and charred. The old-fashioned paint job on the side was mostly illegible. All Winona could make out was "ITOE'S SHOE FACTORY."

"That place is haunted," Lucille whispered.

"Super," Winona agreed, and they kept on in silence for another fifty minutes.

"There," Lucille said finally, and pointed to the green glow of the low-squatting motel ahead on the right. The only other structure in sight was the gravel-lotted preschool across the street.

They were still an hour outside of Denver.

"We have to sleep," Lucille said, anticipating Winona's thought. "I doubt we can find Armie Douchehole in the middle of the night."

"He's probably nocturnal," Winona argued.

"Well, I'm not."

Winona pulled over.

"I'll get the room—more subtle if it's just one of us," Lucille said, and slipped out of the car to go check in. Winona watched from the car. She hated the way the fluorescents made Lucille go sallow.

Her chest ached. The memory of the coppery light splashing over the crown of Lucille's head was already fading. She could think of the words she would've used to describe the image but couldn't conjure up the moment exactly as it had been.

Lucille stepped out of the registration office and lifted a finger, pointing down the sidewalk toward their room. Winona gathered the Snickers bars, Goldfish crackers, and gummy worms they'd gotten at the gas station, and climbed out of the car. The day had been surprisingly warm but without any of the summer's humidity; there was nothing to trap it there when the sun went down.

Winona shivered as she jogged across the parking lot.

Inside the room, Lucille splashed her face with water and Winona checked the mattresses for bedbugs. Only a couple days ago, she wouldn't have thought to do this, but a couple days ago, Winona also hadn't known you could get a motel room for thirty-nine dollars a night, and that explained the lack of complimentary Perrier as well as the long black hair stuck right in the middle of the sheets when Winona threw the comforter back.

"Ugh," Lucille said.

"Ugh," Winona agreed.

Lucille threw the comforter back up, and the two of them flopped down on top of it, side by side. Winona spread the "food" on the bed between them, and they lay on their backs, silent except their chewing.

Then Lucille's new phone buzzed on the side table. They both went rigid, a gummy worm still caught in the corner of Winona's mouth.

"Chaxton?" she said with her mouth full.

Lucille sat up and grabbed the phone. "Amber Alert," she said. Her brow furrowed, then shot up. "Oh my God."

"What?" Winona slid her legs over the edge of the bed and scooted up to Lucille, reading over her shoulder. She swallowed the gummy bear. "That's Grandfather's car! The Romeo."

"Guess he opened the garage after all." Lucille started gnawing on her lip. "Shit. Shit. We should check the news. See if we're on milk cartons yet."

"I'm willing to get a nose job," Winona offered helpfully. She barely knew what she was saying, she was so tired.

"Maybe you should just cut your hair off with a bowie knife," Lucille deadpanned. She snapped up the remote and flicked the TV on. It took a few minutes to find the local news, and only a few more to confirm Winona's greatest fear.

She should have been prepared when the local anchor chirped, "Daughter of beloved weatherman Stormy Olsen!" but she'd said his name so much in the past few days, it had lost its power.

His face, though—that was different.

Different from when she'd been home, and different from the man she'd watched grin and wink on the Channel 5 website.

When the camera cut to prerecorded footage of her father in front of a podium on the steps to the Channel 5 studio, Winona's teeth glanced off the candy in her mouth and clamped down on the side of her tongue.

Lucille's eyes flashed to Winona's. "He's not here," she said in a low voice. "Remember he's not in the room with us."

But Winona's heart was racing as if the TV had opened a wormhole and he could see her through it. He was dressed more casually than he ever did at home: a soft gray button-up, hastily (or painstakingly) halfway tucked into his pressed navy trousers. He wore no tie, and his sleeves were rolled to his elbows.

He was crying. His voice had dropped to a lower register, but there was a faint quiver to it.

"Just want my baby girl home," he said. "*Please, please*, whoever's doing this, don't hurt her. This is the light of my life. She's my everything." His chin dropped. A tear slid down his nose and dripped onto the statement he was reading from.

"Who the fuck is he impersonating? I mean, seriously!" Lucille growled. She hurled a gummy worm at the screen. "Unroll your sleeves and put on your tie, asshole! You're not fucking Liam Neeson!"

He shook his head, as if in direct response, and lifted his gaze. "I'm offering ten thousand dollars to anyone who can bring my girl home. Any tip, any piece of information—no matter how small could—could be the difference between life and death for my sweet Winona Lorraine."

Lucille made an inhuman snort, but Winona was hypnotized by the display. She really couldn't tell if it was all a ruse or if he really was worried for her. He had to have known she wasn't kidnapped—that the Romeo's keys had been taken from Grandfather Pernet's house with the help of its own spare key, on the same night she'd mysteriously vanished—but did that mean the tears were all for show?

She'd seen him choked up before, and nine times out of ten a podium and/or video camera were involved, but something about this was different.

Maybe.

"Wow," the local anchor was saying, when they cut back to her desk in the studio. She splayed her hands on her notes and radiated aggressive sympathy straight into the camera. "For those just tuning in, what you heard was a father's tearful plea. Sturgis 'Stormy' Olsen is the meteorologist for our neighbors to the nor—"

The sound cut out; Lucille had muted it. She jumped up to pace like a mountain lion in a zoo's glass display. "I don't believe him," she fumed. "Well, I do. I absolutely do. But you know what I mean. Where does he get off? I mean, where. The hell. Does he get off? And he didn't even mention me! I guarantee he knows we're together, and saying so could only help them find you." She scoffed angrily. "He couldn't even say my name. If you'd *really* been kidnapped, and I'd been taken too, he'd probably hire a private militia to extract you and put me out of my misery."

"Are you kidding? Do you *want* him after you?"

Lucille chewed her lip. "I mean. A little recognition would be nice." She huffed as she sat at the foot of the bed. Winona had gone back to watching the muted screen in a daze, but in her peripheral vision, she caught Lucille looking at her, waiting for some kind of reaction.

Probably expecting Winona to crumble at any moment.

A staccato laugh jumped out of her. Lucille's expression shifted to ask, *Are you okay? Are you in need of hospitalization?*

Winona tried to explain, but the laughter overtook her. She flopped back and clutched her stomach as the laughter shook out of her. Lucille gave an uneasy giggle. "What?" she demanded. "What is it?"

Winona shook her head. There were tears streaming down her cheeks. Lucille jumped up onto the mattress and bounced. "Come on!" she yelped. "Tell me what's happening in that gorgeous GI Jane'd head!"

Winona still couldn't get the words out. She just kept shaking her head through the laughter. Lucille hoisted her onto her feet and they jumped, Winona still half doubled over in squeals as she forced it out syllable by syllable. "It's just so funny. They're so stupid!"

"He. Is. Stupid!" Lucille said, in time with her jumps. "But. What. Exactly. Are we. Talking about?"

"Silas," Winona answered, still in hysterics. "Silas stole my father's car. If we get caught, we can just say he kidnapped us!"

Lucille's laughter faltered, but she kept jumping, smile frozen in place on her lips.

Winona wished she could explain why it was so funny. She wasn't explaining it right. If she could explain it right, Lucille would see how funny it was. Lucille would laugh.

It really was hilarious.

THIRTY-ONE

FOURTEEN HUNDRED TWENTY-TWO DOLLARS AND A CHOP SHOP IN DENVER

Lucille woke up at dawn to a text from Chaxton: *They're going to find u Lucille they're going to find u. they want five thousand dollars for the drugs and for damages.*

Lucille the Candy Man is going to get you

Lucille

Lucille

Lucille regretted ever texting him from this number to tell him she was okay. She wrote, *This is Martina Von Engelhoven and I am blocking this number.* Then she turned her phone off and went back to sleep.

If the Candy Man caught up to them, she'd have bigger problems than owing them money. And Lucille needed at least another hour of sleep if she and Winona were going to make it to downtown Denver by nine in the morning. Enough time to find Armie, find Silas, shake him down, and still get to Vegas by nightfall the next day.

She and Winona pulled out of the motel at 8:45 a.m., the Cracker Jack ring on Lucille's hand on the steering wheel.

"The worst thing about this Amber Alert is that we can't even get an iced coffee without someone calling the cops or, like, Nancy Grace," Lucille said as they passed yet another Dunkin' Donuts. She gazed after it with lust in her heart.

She had so much to freak out about right now, she didn't know where to start. How about: Winona was still seventeen, so Stormy Olsen could still call the cavalry after her since she wasn't an adult. Why hadn't Lucille thought of that? How about: Winona went from seeing Silas as her Rat Prince Charming to, two seconds later, wanting to shove him into a meat grinder so she could make him into chum for the sharks. How about: Lucille hadn't really slept since she started worrying she was losing her best friend, who was (a) a fugitive (b) possibly now running the show (c) revealing herself to be folie-à-deux-midnight-screaming-unhinged, and she was running on two hours of sleep and a major burst of electric panic.

There was not enough coffee in the world.

"Wait, I know," Winona said, and she took a sharp turn into the gas station across the street from the Dunkin', pulling into the back. There were bathrooms there, with external doors—they wouldn't have to go through the minimart. "We still have those wigs in the back seat. I bought them to go with the devil horns and the wings—but then you braided my hair, and, well."

"And it looked amazing," Lucille said. "You were like an evil Disney princess."

Winona preened a little. "Wigs, then. If you don't mind going into a donut shop in sunglasses and purple hair."

"I think it's pink," Lucille said, digging it out of the back seat. She'd seen a pair of aviators in the glove box when they'd inspected this trash heap of a car, and she pulled them out now. "What do you think?" she asked, assembling her outfit. "Budget Xtina? Or stripper at a kid's birthday party?"

"I feel like you need a pillbox hat and a pair of little kid gloves," Winona said. "Class it up a little."

"I left those back in Stormy Olsen's torture chamber, with your Kate Spade rubber ducky purse."

"My minaudière," Winona moaned. "I miss that minaudière."

"See, I told you," Lucille said as Winona adjusted her blond Bond Girl wig, "it's not even a purse."

Lucille took over driving; Winona hid in the back seat. "No one's slathering *my* face on the television," Lucille said as the Oldsmobile trundled through the Dunkin' drive-thru. "It's better if they think I'm just some girl coming home from clubbing."

"Where did you go clubbing that you drove an *Oldsmobile?*" Winona asked miserably, crouched behind the driver's seat with the Ghost of Farting Past. "A nursing home?"

They bought half a dozen donuts and two giant iced coffees, and Lucille did some math in her head. After gas and the motel, their finances were dwindling. They needed the money that Silas had almost as badly as Lucille needed to dismember his body. If Winona didn't get to him first.

But to do that, they had to find Armie Quinhole's chop shop.

"Can you just Google it?" Winona slurped her coffee. Lucille could hear it more than see it from the driver's seat.

"Chop shops? I'm sure they'll list it next to 'dog-fighting rings' in the yellow pages."

"Isn't it just like a garage? I thought it was slang for 'mechanic.'"

"Chop shops," Lucille said, making a left-hand turn, "are the places you take Alfa Romeos after you boost them from fine young ladies and need them taken apart before the cops track you down. They do paint jobs. They swap parts. That kind of thing. Even if Armie wasn't Silas's cousin, Silas would be looking for a place like that right now if he has any brains at all."

"Huh," Winona said. "How do you know all that?"

"I'm half Pryce, half Folgarelli. Nobody in my family has paid for car repairs in like, millennia. My cousin Tony went to jail for grand theft auto. My cousin Mikey taught me to fix my mom's car when I was twelve."

"How did I not know this about you?"

"Because, despite our soul-bond, I've only known you for like, one-eighteenth of my life."

"Hold on," Winona said, popping her head between the seats. "Does this mean you're going to, like, woo Armie Quinhole with your car knowledge? Before challenging him to a dance-off?"

Lucille cackled. "Hold on," she said, slowing down. "I think this is a good place to start looking."

It was a strip club called OPTICAL ILLUSIONS.

"For strippers who need glasses?" Winona asked.

"Get down!"

"It smells like fertilizer!" Winona whined, but did it anyway.

Lucille pulled the Oldsmobile into the parking lot. "I'll make it up to you. Are you hungry? The sign says 'lunch buffet all you can eat.' Do you think they have steak?"

Winona was snorting too hard to talk for a minute. "Hold on. I honestly don't get it. How is this going to help you find Armie Quinhole?"

"Five minutes," Lucille said. Then paused. "Maybe ten."

Lucille had a smorgasbord of unexpected skills, though they expressed themselves in unusual ways. Like: Lucille liked to eat popcorn and read about New York Fashion Week, but while dressed like the love child of a grandmother and a six-year-old high on Pixy Stix. Like: despite what she'd just told Winona, though Lucille could usually figure out what was wrong with her mom's car, she could only fix it half the time. The other half, things happened like a tire coming clean off when you hit sixty on the highway, or the trunk popping open at every red light. Like: Lucille was a really good liar, but she could never remember who she'd told what, and so she tried not to risk it. Not after Miss Bender had called home in kindergarten to say that Lucille claimed she had not one, but two wooden legs. (Lucille had been wearing shorts at the time.)

No, it was a skill best used in situations like these. Lucille checked her wig and makeup in the rearview mirror, then went in.

The first strip club didn't yield results. Or the second. Or the third. But at the fourth—ANIMAL HOUSE, it was called; Winona was on her fourth donut by then—she struck gold.

Within five minutes, she'd charmed her way into the dressing room in the back. (Thank God the lunch shift was slow.) There, she told Rainbow and Destiny that her brother got high and stole her car and he was probably taking it somewhere to get rid of it. "I'm supposed to start working here tonight," Lucille said through tears. "My mom's waiting out front, I told her I had an interview as a *waitress*, but she's going to know something's up if she needs to give me rides here every night. She'll throw me out. Where could he have taken it?"

"I'm from Cherry Creek," Destiny said, scrolling through her phone in a director's chair. "I seriously have no idea how to help you."

Rainbow rolled her eyes. "Let me give you an address," she said. "If it's not the right one, they'll know it. Tell them Maryann sent you."

Lucille nodded. "Thanks. I really appreciate it."

"Maryann?" Destiny said, finally looking up. "Really?"

"Shut up, Patricia."

Lucille took that as her cue to leave.

"But why strip clubs?" Winona asked as they got onto the highway. The address that Rainbow had given her was thirty minutes away in traffic. "I don't get it."

"Tammy was a stripper," Lucille said. "I used to go hang out with her sometimes after dinner, if my mom was working late. Like, back when I was twelve, thirteen. The club owner had been friends with the Sperm Donor, so he let me, as long as I stayed in the dressing room. The girls there were always really nice, and they liked to talk. Some of them worked there because they loved it—the money, or the dancing, or the attention. Some of them were there because they didn't have any other options. Either way, they heard things. I figured it wasn't a bad place to start asking questions."

Winona was quiet for a long time.

"What are you thinking about?" Lucille asked finally, a little worried that Winona was going to come at her with something like "would you ever do something like that for money" (probably) or "I feel so bad for Tammy" (Tammy felt fine about it).

"Sweet revenge," Winona said at last.

Or that.

Lucille had never seen mountains before, and it was increasingly hard for her not to gape over the steering wheel. There was a weird poetry to it, how the usual nail salons and Dress Barns and Save-A-Lots still existed despite the evidence of actual smashed tectonic plates behind them. There was a bite in the air she didn't associate with summer; summer meant mosquitos by the lake and trying to breathe through the pea-soup humidity.

Not purple mountain majesty with a side of CHECK CASH-ING DELUX.

Winona hummed to the radio as Lucille watched her maps app. When they finally got to the address, the gate was bolted and no one was inside. A piece of printer paper was duct-taped unnecessarily to the combination lock: AT LUNCH, BACK AT SIX.

"Seriously?" Winona asked.

"Whatever," Lucille said, and they parked across the street, jacked the seats back, and took a long, long nap.

When the two of them finally climbed out of the car, the gate was open. Inside, the chop shop was as described: sprawling, covered in the cut-up bodies of cars, their parts strewn around like organs or something. (*Dark*, Lucille told herself. *Too dark*.) Lucille and Winona kept their wigs on, but Lucille threw on a jean jacket as they stepped out of the car.

"My legs are killing me," Winona said, stretching them out, "and my nose is never going to recover. Luce. Are you trying to look like a greaser? Like, someone from *Grease*?"

Lucille rolled up the sleeves. "Yes," she decided. "That's it exactly."

"Cool," Winona said.

Two girls in candy-colored wigs in a glorified junkyard?

It wasn't hard to get some attention.

The first man they talked to played dumb. The second appeared to be a legitimate mechanic who said "bless you" when Lucille asked for Armie Quinhole.

The third?

The third was a different story.

"His office is in here," the girl said, crossing her arms below her buzz cut. She'd led them through a warren of jacked-up cars in various states of disrepair. The Volvo lofted above them was missing its doors.

"Who boosts a Volvo?" Lucille asked under her breath.

"Someone looking for reliability," the girl replied, without missing a beat. "Not that that wagon's stolen. Belongs to a nice family of four."

"Do they also have one point five dogs?" Winona asked.

"Listen," the girl said. The door behind her said MANAGER.

KEEP OUT, but she was blocking it with her shoulders. Her T-shirt said ZILDJIAN, which meant she was a drummer. (Lucille had dated a lot of drummers.) "I came out to get you guys because you looked like My Little Ponies auditioning at a glue factory. My brother might do the books, but I run the floor, and the last thing I want to have to do is fire some perfectly capable mechanic for groping an idiot girl."

"Oh yeah," Winona huffed, "poor men. Can't control themselves. So much for female solidarity."

But Lucille was fascinated. "You're his sister? What's your name?"

"Marla," the girl said with dignity.

"Marla Quinhole." Lucille shook her head, amazed. "We need to get you two a reality show. Next up: QUINHOLE MOTORS. *Don't mess with the best*. Vroom, vroom—"

"I desperately need you to shut up," Marla said, and pushed the door open behind her. "Armie! There are some brats here to see you!" She stalked back out onto the floor.

"Good luck with your drums!" Lucille called after her, because when you'd destroyed reality as thoroughly as she had, these past few days, you might as well just go for the punch line.

"Wigs off," the voice inside the office said. "Or you can't come in."

Winona looked at Lucille. Lucille looked at Winona.

"Fine," Winona said, and pulled hers off and grinned victoriously.

Armie Quinhole was . . . not what Lucille was expecting. He

was mid-twenties, maybe even a little younger, and he had that kind of gorgeous Sicilian look to him—*real* eyebrows, and full lips, and he had on jeans and a white T-shirt with an honest-to-God pack of cigarettes rolled into the sleeve.

The office was bare-bones: a television, a set of security monitors, a desk that was empty except for, improbably, a wrench. There wasn't anywhere for them to sit, so Lucille shifted her weight and studied Armie's Adam's apple. *Silas sucks,* she thought, *but his family's got good genes.*

Armie Quinhole was not impressed by Winona's shaved head. "You can," he said, "put the wig back on."

With an eye roll, Lucille tossed hers to the floor. "Armie Quinhole, I presume?"

"It's Italian," he said. "They fucked it up at Ellis Island. We used to be the Cinchettos. Get that dumb look off your face. You were looking for me? Here I am."

Before Lucille could unfold the next phase of her plan—bat her eyelashes, talk about carburetors, drape herself all over his desk chair if she needed to (she sort of even *wanted* to now)—Winona was striding forward. "We're looking for Silas," she said in an I-need-to-talk-to-the-manager voice. "Where is he?"

Armie whistled. "That's a good question. Why? Who wants to know?"

"I do," Winona said, nodding her head. "Me. Juliet Simmonds."

He squinted at her. "No," he said. "I'm pretty sure I had you clocked as that missing girl the second I saw you on my security feed." He pointed to the black-and-white monitors. "I keep seeing your picture on Twitter. Winona. Like the actress. Not Britney-post-breakdown, like you are here. According to the video clip, you got a dad who's a pretty crier."

Lucille dragged her hands over her face.

"Oh," Winona said faintly. "I hate Twitter."

"Me too," Armie said, "but I have to be on there for work. Look—there's a major cash reward for you out there. Ten thousand bucks. I wouldn't just take off your wig when any old guy says *take off your wig*. Maybe keep your sunglasses on too."

"Is that a threat?" Lucille said. "Bullshit."

"I'm not turning her in," Armie said.

"I don't buy that. We're sitting here, an easy opportunity—"

"I'm not going to turn *her* in," Armie said. "I haven't heard anything about you. What are you worth to them? What's the reward? Nothing I've heard."

That was the part that broke Lucille a little bit more each time she remembered it—sure, she was eighteen, a legal adult, and yes, okay, sometimes people in her family just *left* and no one ever did anything about it, but she had thought that her mother would at least call her in missing. Would at least call Lucille's *phone* and say, *Lucy, where did you go, why didn't you say goodbye—*

Maybe she thought that Lucille had kidnapped Winona. Maybe she was afraid to tie her daughter's fate to Winona's. Lucille had hinted, darkly, at the realities of her best friend's home life, and Mrs. Pryce wasn't stupid. Maybe she didn't want the Sauron eye of Stormy Olsen casting its shadow on Lucille, too.

Maybe she was just happy she had one less mouth to feed.

"Anyway," Armie was saying as Lucille tuned back in, "I'm not going to call you in. I don't want cops in my shop. But also, who am I to give up my cousin to a pair of strange girls?" He picked up the wrench that was sitting on his desk. "But also . . ."

"But also?" Lucille echoed hopefully, because she couldn't help herself.

"Also," he said, glaring at her, "he hasn't been into work for the last week and he owes me five thousand bucks, meaning, for now, I own his ass. I'm fine sending a problem like you two, gift-wrapped, to his front door."

"A problem?" Winona asked. She looked weirdly like she belonged there, across from Armie Quinhole, with her shaved head and her thumbs in her belt loops. There was an easiness to her that was crazy, given their situation, and still Lucille admired it.

"Oh yeah." Armie took a Sharpie from his pocket and motioned Lucille over, then scrawled the address on her arm. He smelled like motor oil; his handwriting looked like a toddler's. "I don't know you or your business, honey, but I can tell you this—you two are the Lamborghini of problems."

Lucille snorted.

"Glad you think that's funny," Armie Quinhole said. "Now get the fuck out of my shop."

THIRTY-TWO

FOURTEEN HUNDRED AND TWO DOLLARS AND A HOT TIP FROM ONE ARMIE QUINHOLE

Admittedly, there was a part of Winona that hoped they'd pull up to an orphanage. She'd find Silas on the front porch, doting on children who clearly adored him. *I didn't want to steal from you*, he'd say, *I had to. I traded the Romeo for vaccinations for these uninsured babies!*

He'd be the kind of person Winona had mistaken him for. He'd be like Lucille. A giver who lived in the moral gray zone. Someone who did bad things for good reasons, who could only hurt one person if it meant saving another.

Instead, she spotted the burst of cherry red the second they turned onto Silas's street. It was parked in a lineup of indistinct junkers in front of a sensible brick apartment building that backed up to woods. The building was a squared-off U-shape with a courtyard in its center, empty apart from a drained fountain, a few metal benches, and a pair of overflowing ashtrays balanced on an overflowing trash can. Everything except the Alfa Romeo was cast in dreary neutral. It was a pretty bold move, both show-offy and stupid, to park a car like that in a place like this—especially a stolen one, whose make and model had been broadcast via Amber Alert, even if he *had* changed the plates—and Silas's decision to do so sent a flare of disgust through Winona's chest.

Was there anything worse than parading one's belongings around? Especially when the *belonging* in question didn't truly belong to you. Especially when all the red paint and purring engines in the world wouldn't change who you *really* were. A sack of shit painted gold would only fool people for so long.

Someday Silas's beautiful face would spot and wrinkle. Probably his teeth would fall out and his bladder would loosen, and this thought delighted her. It didn't matter that it would happen to her someday too; now she wasn't pretending to be anything but what she really was, so when the rest of her superficially pretty exterior fell away, like her hair had, and she looked more monster than human, she wouldn't have lost anything. If her haircut was any indication, she'd feel freer when she wasn't burdened by being a pretty object.

"You ready?" Lucille asked with an arched eyebrow.

Winona took a deep breath. She decided to use her Stormy-approved Composed Face. Her face muscles struggled to find it. She flipped the visor down and checked herself in the mirror. She and Lucille had decided she could stay in the passenger seat as long as she kept her wig and sunglasses on.

"What's going on?" Lucille said. "Are you about to have diarrhea or something?"

Winona frowned at her. "I don't remember how to lie."

Lucille's eyes crinkled with a half-realized smile. "Why do you need to?"

"I don't want him to think I fell for his shtick," she explained. "I'd rather he *didn't* think I was an idiot."

Lucille rolled her eyes and pushed the car door open. "Nony. You could somersault through his door wearing your pants on your head, and this shithead's still going to take one look at you and know *he's* the idiot here. At least until you take the wig off."

Winona cackled. She wanted him to be sorry, but not because Silas Fucknut was mourning her perfect Rodin tresses, but because he'd missed the monster underneath it, waiting to be truly seen.

She thought about the gun in Stormy's valet box. She imagined how its weight would feel against her hip as she walked into Silas's apartment. Not to use! Just to have. Then he would really feel like an idiot. He would understand that he'd messed with the wrong girls, that Winona was more dangerous for him than he could ever be for her, because hadn't truly *seen* her.

She craved the moment he would.

Lucille reached over the console for Winona's hand and seamlessly slid the red plastic ring onto her finger before giving her a little squeeze. "You're ready, Non." This time, it wasn't a question.

She was. The girls got out of the car and passed through the courtyard to cross a threshold of cigarette butts and empty soda bottles to get to the door. Winona expected to have to wait until someone was leaving to get inside, but the door was unlocked.

Inside the drab hallway, Lucille examined the numbers on the door. "They all start with two," she pointed out.

"He must be in the basement," Winona suggested.

"How fitting."

They followed the hall to its dead end, an echoey stairwell that looked like it had been re-spackled a dozen times without any sanding in between until it resembled the inside of a child's (and not a particularly gifted one's) papier-mâché project.

On the basement level, they followed the numbers right to Silas's door. They hesitated there, staring at the bronze numbers mounted beneath the peephole of the blue-gray door. Winona could hear voices through it, and Lucille shot her a narrowed look.

"He's not alone," she whispered. "We'll have to come back."

Winona's stomach clenched stubbornly. She was about to argue that they could handle *five* Silases, easy, when the sudden uproar of laughter sounded behind the door, and her mood instantly lightened. "Laugh track!" she hissed.

Lucille angled her ear against the door, waiting for it to happen again. "I think you're right!"

Winona pressed her ear to the door too, and the two of them fought a sudden wave of laughter as they listened in.

"You think he's in his underwear with a forty watching, like, *Big Bang Theory*?" Lucille whispered.

"God, the way he talked, I would've expected to find him

spinning Glen Campbell on his record player while he smoked a cigarette and made an abstract painting."

"Definitely underwear sitcoms," Lucille concluded.

A door down the hall opened, and the girls jumped, then did an impressive imitation of someone casually loitering for definitely no real reason in a basement hallway as the goateed man carrying his garbage bag past them to the stairwell did a stunning rendition of Man Who Does Not Give One Flying Shit Who You Are Or Why You're Here.

Of course, that was what they'd always thought about Glenn back at the Cliffside, and now they were FedEx-ing him a mounted trout.

They waited until the goateed neighbor had returned from dumping his trash and his door had kicked closed behind him, and then they turned their focus back to the reason they'd come here.

Lucille covered the peephole; Winona knocked.

The TV went silent. They waited.

Winona knocked again, every hair on her body prickling with expectation, her heart in her throat. She hadn't decided what she was going to say. Maybe something sassy like, *Did you miss me, bitch?*

Was calling him a *bitch* somehow degrading to women? To female dogs? She'd never had a dog. As badly as Stormy Olsen would have liked to appear to be the kind of a man who loves dogs, he couldn't stand the mess.

Maybe Lucille and Winona would get a dog when they got to Las Vegas. They would take such good care of it. It would be so happy in their home.

Lucille huffed and pounded the door. "Hey, ass-face! We know you're in there! Open *up*, Silas!"

Inside there was movement. Finally, the door swung open.

"Did you miss me, b——" Winona's voice dropped off at the round face and shoulder-length brown hair that greeted her.

Not Silas. Not even a man. Winona's eyes slid to the bulge of the belly protruding between the open door and the jamb. The girl's powder-blue T-shirt was stretched so tight over her pregnant stomach that Winona could make out the outline of her belly button.

"Oh," Winona said. Her fist was still hovering, prepared to knock again. She dropped it. "Sorry. We thought you were . . . we must be . . ."

The girl's eyes juddered between them. "What do you want with Silas?"

Winona was so confused by the question that she just said, "What."

Lucille cleared her throat and looked at the pregnant girl. "Is he . . . does he live here?"

"He's in the shower," the girl said. She shifted between her bare feet, then pressed the sole of one against her shin. "Can I help you?"

"Who are you?" Winona blurted.

"I'm Sandy."

So? Winona wanted to say. *What is that supposed to mean to me?*

"The girlfriend!" Lucille said without missing a beat. "Great to meet you!"

Sandy, Winona realized, was holding a pint of Ben & Jerry's ice cream. She shifted it to her other hand as she stared at Lucille like she was an alien. "How do you know Si?"

"We work with him," Lucille said quickly, probably because she sensed Winona was about to answer the question a bit too honestly.

Sandy seemed dubious. "At the chop shop?"

Winona laughed once before Lucille gave her a warning look. She clamped her mouth shut. *Sorry*, she thought at Lucille, *It's just so funny*.

Of course his girlfriend thought he still worked at the chop shop. What did he tell her when he disappeared for the last couple weeks? It wasn't like he was a freaking US ambassador.

"Yes," Lucille answered Sandy. "Juliet and I are *really* into cars. Aren't we, babe?" She threaded her fingers through Winona's, clearly trying to drown out any *I made out with your boyfriend for literally one whole night* vibes Winona might be putting off.

Winona felt sick. She didn't want to lie anymore. Shouldn't they just tell her? Shouldn't Silas get what he had coming to him?

"Look," Lucille said. "We really need to talk to—"

"Babe?" A familiar lilting voice sounded over Sandy's shoulder and she looked back toward its source.

"Some girls are here to see you," she said with distaste. "From the shop."

And then there he was, moving into the harsh light of the hallway. Damp hair slicked back, face pale, split lip starting to heal, and an expression of panic every bit as delicious as Winona had hoped.

He cleared it away in one clean swipe, like chalk from a

blackboard. It was hard to pick his face out of the blank slate in front of her. Like she was looking at a bar of soap in which she'd seen the form of Christ a minute ago, only now the light had changed and there was nothing but two scratches and a divot.

"Hello, girls," he said lightly, and slung an arm low around Sandy's hips. He turned his nose in against her temple and kissed it lightly. "Babe, why don't you go start on dinner."

She gave him a pout, and he smiled down at her. "I'm sure this will just take a minute. Winona probably has a question about a carburetor, right?"

"Who's Winona?" the girl asked.

"I am," Lucille said quickly, flashing a smile. She lifted their tangled hands and gestured toward Winona. "That's Juliet," she reaffirmed, "and I'm Winona."

Silas's face had paled just a little and Winona didn't bother fighting the evil, toothy smile she felt unfurling across her face.

"Babe," Silas said again. "Dinner?"

She cast the girls a mildly suspicious gaze, then shrugged and shuffled off, spooning more Chunky Monkey into her mouth. Silas looked over his shoulder before he tried to step into the hallway, but Winona caught the door and pushed her way in.

"Nice place you have here," she said. "Isn't it nice, Lucille?"

"I don't know who Lucille is," Lucille played along, brushing past Silas to stand inside the foyer. "I'm Winona, Juliet."

"Right, Winona," Winona said. "But what do you think of Silas's place?"

She looked around, appraising it with all the care of an art collector in a Chelsea gallery. "Well, it *imitates* life, at least."

"This isn't funny," Silas hissed. "Get out of my apartment."

"No thanks," Winona said. "But would you like to come?" She turned and led the way down the hallway. She felt lightheaded. She didn't hate it, but it was strange.

There were framed photos on the wall. She couldn't picture Silas hanging them. Sandy must've done it.

Winona stopped beside a prom photo. Sandy was in shiny satin, hot pink and ruched down the bodice, and Silas was in approximately the same outfit he was wearing right now, that he wore all the time, like he was just some iconic cartoon character and not even a real-life human.

Winona snapped her fingers. "Indiana Jones!" she said brightly. He'd followed her down the hall, and she spun to face him, pointing one finger his way as Lucille sidled up to examine the picture. "That's what your costume is," Winona said. "Off-brand Indiana Jones."

He threw a nervous look over his shoulder. "You want the car back?" he whispered. "Is that what this is about?"

Lucille and Winona exchanged a look. Was it about that?

Not really, Winona didn't think, but she was having trouble remembering. She was having trouble thinking clearly about what came before this moment or what would follow it. She turned and pushed open the door on her left into the master bedroom. The mattress, a queen, sat on the floor, and a half-empty (definitely

251

half-empty, definitely not half-full) water glass rested on a stack of Jack Kerouac hardcovers. Next to it, the bag holding Marcus's stash. Winona lifted one foot and gently toppled the stack of novels. "Those books are bullshit," she said, and flopped down onto the bed, spread-eagled.

She nestled into the comforter, rolled over, and buried her face in the pillow, mouth open so that it left wet marks on the pillowcase. She flipped onto her back again and propped herself up on her forearms and pulled her wig off, tossing it at Silas's face.

He yelped as it hit him and slid to the floor, and then he stared at her as if she'd just lit herself on fire. Lucille covered her mouth to hold in laughter.

"Oh come on, Silas," Winona said. "Lighten up. It's not like we're here to kill you . . . ha . . . ha."

"What happened to your head?"

"Whatever do you mean?" She reached down beside the bed and picked up the topmost book from the toppled tower. She opened it and took the gum she'd been chewing and stuck it there, in the middle of the page.

Somehow, that was the thing that snapped Silas out of his daze. He shut the door and crossed the room to her. "Winona," he said in a low, husky voice, crouched in front of where she sat on the bed. He pulled the book from her hands and set it aside, then took her palms between his. His featureless Mr. Potato Head face was rearranging to emote Sad, Sexy Regret. "I'm sorry," he said. "God, honey, I really am so sorry. I wish it could have been different, but I had no choice. Honest, I didn't."

Anger, like a bolt of lightning branching out through her limbs, a red-hot urge to destroy the beautiful mask of his face. Instead, she pulled her hands free, cradled the book to her chest, and asked, "You had no choice?"

He nodded furiously. "Honest, I didn't. Everything I told you was true—I just didn't tell you everything. There *were* people I was running from. Dangerous people, Non."

She flinched at the sound of Lucille's nickname for her spoken in his voice. "Don't call me that."

She couldn't tell whether the look of hurt on his face was real or manufactured. God, why couldn't she ever tell?

Why did people lie? With their words, with their voices, with their bodies, with their beautiful houses and beautiful clothes and sometimes even their faces? Why couldn't everyone just be what they were?

Monsters should look like monsters.

"I owed people money," Silas went on, a little wild-eyed now. His gaze flickered between Lucille, standing against the door, and Winona, perched on the bed in front of him. "Dangerous people, Winona. Horrible people! And I have a kid coming! Sandy's pregnant."

Lucille mock-gasped. "Really? We didn't notice when *your pregnant girlfriend* answered the door five minutes ago, asshat! Where's our money, dirtbag?"

He seemed to barely have heard her. He was looking up at Winona again, Winona only, pleading. "I had to watch out for my kid!" he hissed. "This was the only way I could come home.

The only way my family could be okay. I didn't want to hurt you, Winona. I *liked* you! If things were different—"

Winona broke free from him and jumped up to pace in front of his open-drawered dresser. God, she was angry now, really angry and also *seriously* lightheaded. She wondered if she'd been forgetting to breathe. She tried to take a long drag of air, but not much went into her lungs.

"I needed that money!" he said.

She spun back on him and screamed right into his face, so hard spit hit his forehead, "*I* needed that money."

He flinched back from her, and she thought, *Good*, and went on: she flung his copy of *The Dharma Bums* directly at his forehead, right where the spit had landed.

He winced as it hit and rebounded onto the bed. One hand clutched the red mark it left behind, and he stared at her like she'd just removed her black robes and revealed herself to be Death Incarnate, calling his number.

GOOD, she thought again.

She shoved the burn scar on her wrist into his face. "*I* NEEDED THAT MONEY."

"Winona," Lucille said gently from beside the door, but Winona ignored her.

"I needed that money, Silas," she raged, "and you knew it! You saw what he did to me. I told you what he did to me."

"Non," Lucille said again, but she was background noise, sort of like the high-pitched ringing that had taken up residence in Winona's skull.

"I know!" Silas was yelling back, teary-eyed and convincing. "Christ, Winona! I'm sorry! I know! I didn't know what to do! I was just trying to save myself! I was just trying to save my family. It's gone, okay? I'd give it back if I could, but it's *gone* now—that's the only reason I can be here right now! Alive, talking to you!"

"*Winona*," Lucille said, louder and firmer this time, and Winona reeled around, ready to release all her anger on the next face she saw, regardless of whether that person deserved it.

But then she saw Lucille's face.

Mouth open. Eyes wide and wet. Face pale as a lily.

"Do you hear that?" she whispered shakily.

The high-pitched ringing. It wasn't in Winona's skull after all.

It was police sirens. A lot of them. And they were getting louder every second.

"No," she choked out, and shook her head. She looked into those boyish blue eyes she'd been so dazzled by. "This isn't how it ends."

He didn't get to be a dad. He didn't get to have the family and the house and the life that was supposed to be hers. That she and Lucille had fought tooth and nail for.

He didn't get to have it all while she and Lucille got dragged back to their cages in Kingsville.

She didn't care about his kid, or his girlfriend, or anyone else. She cared about herself. Herself and Lucille.

If they couldn't have anything, neither would he.

THIRTY-THREE

FOURTEEN HUNDRED AND TWO DOLLARS AND A BRAND-NEW PLAN

Winona's hands were clenching and unclenching by her sides like she was a cartoon, like she was about to whip into an animated tornado and rip this basement apartment down. "I am not getting taken down because you decided to park Stormy Olsen's car on the street like a *goddamn trophy*. A car that you *stole from us* and parked outside of your shithole apartment so you can keep living your shithole life here like the shitmouse you are—"

Ninety percent of Lucille was cycling through their options: *How do we run, how do we hide, how do we not get hauled away back home?* She was marking the exits. She was figuring out if she could take Silas down—physically down—if she had to, if she could haul Winona out in a fireman's carry if she went ahead and lost it in the way she was promising to.

That was ninety percent of her. The practical part, the pragmatic part, the part that got them into this mess and would damn well get them out.

The other ten percent was thinking, *What have I done?*

Because Silas and Sandy's apartment wasn't a shithole. Despite the lack of light, they had almost as much room as the Pryces did in their house. And yeah, okay, the courtyard needed a good cleaning, and someone should probably vacuum the hallway outside, but—

But it was way nicer than any place Lucille had ever lived. And she had never been in this to hurt a pregnant girl she didn't know.

The sirens were deafening now. *Why is this what I'm thinking about?* Lucille tried to drag her head back to the present moment, but couldn't.

"You're *trash*," Winona was telling Silas, and no one would deny that he was a garbage human, but what Lucille heard was *The Pryces are trash, Winona*, and she needed to take a shower.

"Nony," Lucille said, inching toward her. "Nony, we don't have time for this—"

"No," she said, whipping around, and there was something almost reptilian in her eyes. "No. We have *plenty* of time. Because Silas here is going to get us out of this."

Silas crossed his arms. "I told you I was sorry, but I'm not going to lie for y'all."

"Oh no," Winona said, and there was that *laugh* again, bubbling up and out of her like from the depths of a tar pit. "Oh, you are. You are going to march to that front door and tell them that you found the Alfa Romeo abandoned back in Kingsville, and you're so *so* sorry, you haven't seen *any* girls, *any* Winona Olsens, you don't even *know who that is.*" With every word, she took a step forward, crowding Silas back against the door.

"Baby?" Sandy said, from the other side. "Why are the cops outside? Do you think the neighbors were fighting again? Usually we can hear them——"

"Winona," Silas said, his hands up now like he was training her to box, "I have a *family* to protect——"

"And you will protect them," she said with satisfaction. "Because if you give that story to the cops, I won't call the drug lord hunting us and tell him that you have his stash."

Silas's eyes darted over her head to the baggie of pills (and coke, and God knew what else) next to his stack of books.

Lucille, at this point, had caught on. "And give him your address," she said.

"And the place that you work."

Silas sucked in a breath. "Y'all want me to lie to the police." He leaned against the door. "Oh my God——"

Now he had moral compunctions.

"It's not just the police," Winona said. "Don't worry about them. You think my father's going to be mad when I tell him you kidnapped me? That will be nothing compared to when he finds out you shaved my head!"

Silas's perma-sleepy eyes widened. "Shaved your head? What the——"

There was a slamming noise on the other side of the door; he jumped, then turned to swing it open.

To find Sandy, one hand on her globe of a belly, an oven mitt tucked under her arm. "I have," she said, "so many questions."

"Baby—"

"And you are going to answer them *all*," she said, and that was when the banging on the front door started. *Police!* "But first I am going to get your ass out of this so that our child doesn't grow up without a father."

"He isn't much of one," Winona said, and Sandy whirled. "Don't get me started on *you*, whoever you are—"

For a hard second, Lucille thought about the Sperm Donor. About her mother, overwhelmed and, yes, fine, *useless* sometimes, useless in the ways that really counted. About how Marcus could ride roughshod all over her from his seat on the couch. About Sandy and Silas's kid, about Sandy alone, about the chicken fingers she could smell burning in the other room.

About how, despite all her failings, Lucille's mom would've lied through her teeth to keep her out of jail.

Lucille turned from Silas. It didn't matter anyway. He and Winona were still staring each other down like a pair of dogs.

"You a good liar?" Lucille asked Sandy.

Sandy nodded grimly. "I'm a better one than he is. And I'm also pretty good at hearing what people say when they think no one's listening."

Police! We are going to BREAK DOWN THIS DOOR!

"Then you know what to say."

"I got it," Sandy said.

Lucille gave her a sharp nod. "How do we get out of here?"

Silas pulled a hand through his hair. "We're in the basement—"

"There's a high window in the kitchen," Sandy said right over him. "You can climb up on the counter and then push out."

"We're gone," Lucille said, and squeezed past Sandy into the hallway, pulling Winona along by her wrist.

"Hey, shithead," Winona called to Silas. "We know where you live."

"Obviously," Lucille added, and then they were scrambling out down the hall and into the kitchen, through the smoke billowing from the oven, up and onto the counter—their shoes in the sink— and through the small window and out into the night.

The red and blue lights made the world into a Fourth of July parade. As they darted into the woods, Lucille pulled Winona along behind her, still by the wrist, and she tried to be gentle but she still had this horrible vision of her yanking Winona hard enough that she pulled her arm clean off. *Would that really be that weird*, Lucille thought, *after everything that's happened—*

They ran through the scrubby patch of forest that backed up to what felt like a patch of national park. *This apartment must cost a lot more than I thought, all this green*, and then Lucille was doing math again in that part of her brain that was always doing math, even if (as she now knew) the hounds of hell were after her. *They might be paying five, six hundred a month—*

She let go of Winona's wrist, and the other girl stumbled, went down to her knees in the dirt.

Lucille skidded to a stop, bent over, panting. "Are you okay?" she asked.

It was a dumb question.

Winona stared up at her, her fingers planted in the ground. "I wanted to kill him," she marveled.

"Yeah," Lucille said. "Pretty much."

"No. I wanted to—like I thought for a moment that I was going to just tear his throat out with my *nails*."

Lucille took a physical step backward. "Okay," she said uncertainly. "I mean. It's good that he's alive? Because he's taking care of the car thing? With the police?"

Winona's eyes weren't focusing. She was on all fours on the ground, her fingers seizing in the dirt, and her gaze was somewhere straight through the center of Lucille like she was part of the woods. Like she wasn't something Winona could eat, and so she didn't exist at all.

"Nony," Lucille said, crouching down, and even though Winona might be losing it, might see Lucille as second-class, low-rent, just a ride out of Dodge into the great wild unhinged unknown, she was still the only good thing that Lucille had. Gingerly, she reached out to put a hand against Winona's face.

Despite everything, Winona was still beautiful.

Or, at least, she was still Winona, which was better.

"We have to go home now," she said gently. "It was a good call with the car—but I'm at the end. I'm out of ideas."

"Go home?" Winona asked like a child.

"Yeah," Lucille said, and she helped her up to her feet. "I'll work off the money for the Candy Man. You only have three months left until college—we can make another break for it in August—"

Stormy will kill her, the voice in her head said. *Or, worse, he'll haul her off to Chicago to his little condominium jail. Marcus will kill you. Or, worse, you'll be working your fingers to the bone so that your brother can sell date rape drugs—*

And they were standing in the middle of some scrub woods outside of Denver and the whole damn country was looking for them.

For Winona.

Lucille was so tired.

"All Stormy wants is you," she reminded Winona, and her voice sounded heavy even to her. "That's all. Maybe—maybe it'll be okay. It *has* to be okay. Because I don't know what comes next."

Winona calmly wiped her hands off on her jeans. "That's okay," she said. "I do."

THIRTY-FOUR

FOURTEEN HUNDRED AND TWO DOLLARS AND A HAIL MARY PASS

A deathly calm came over Winona. It made perfect sense.

In Silas's apartment, she'd been backed into a corner and any plan she could have come up with would only have been a reaction to that, but out here, in the blue-glazed woods, she could taste the world, and she understood.

They'd run away to be free, but as long as Stormy or the Candy Man was looking for them, they wouldn't be.

She had to make them stop.

"We have to give them what they want," Winona said.

"Nony," Lucille repeated. "We don't *have* the money for the Candy Man, and all Stormy wants is you, back on your spit-polished shelf."

"Exactly," Winona said. "But *he* has the money, and as far as he knows, the Candy Man has *me*."

Lucille's head tilted. "I'm not following."

Winona grabbed for her hands in the dark. They were cold and her fingernails were bitten down from the stress of the last few days. "My father doesn't just want me home. He wants a world where I never wanted to leave. He wants me to have been *taken* so his tearful pleas with his fucking rumpled shirt add up to something, so it all means something—something *good*—about him. So we give him that."

Lucille's head cocked the other direction and her lips parted, as if to exhale a wisp of her dawning realization. "So what, we tell him the Candy Man took you, and the dude gets arrested, but then we just wind up back in Kingsville, with no guarantee he won't be cleared."

Winona shook her head furiously. "That's not what I mean. We have to give them *both* what they want. We call my father and tell him I'm in trouble, that the only way I can come home is if he pays up. We send him, with the money, to meet my captor, to trade the money for my safe return."

"Your captor?" Lucille snorted. "Is that supposed to be me? Because I'm *not* facing a pissed-off, sociopathic weatherman, Nony."

Winona gave an impatient huff. "No. We send him to meet 'my captor,' who doesn't exist. And meanwhile, we send the *Candy Man* to collect the money we owe him. We tell him stealing from him was never our idea, that we're working for someone else, and *that* person is going to meet him with the money he wants. Stormy shows up, guns blazing, to get me back. The Candy Man shows up guns blazing-er to get his money and revenge. Two birds, one stone."

"Oh my God," Lucille blurted. "You're describing a fake ransom, Non! I'm pretty sure faking your own kidnapping is frowned upon by law enforcement, if not downright felonious. We can*not* do that."

"Of course we can," Winona disagreed. "We have to. It's the only way out of this."

"Your dad could . . ." Lucille trailed off. "We don't know what will happen if we set this in motion. Even if they wind up killing each other, we're still broke, and it's over anyway. Unless you think we're going to tiptoe into the middle of their standoff, grab the burlap bags of money, and take off into the sunset. In which case, by the way, whoever survives this little blind-date setup is going to be *right back* on us, and more pissed than ever."

Winona shook her head again, excitement brimming to the surface of her skin, hot and shivery at the same time. "They're not going to have a sit-down conversation," she said. "They'll never know we played them against each other, *and* there's a way to get the money. We tell my dad the Candy Man wants *twice* the amount he actually wants. We have him drop half the money someplace secret, where we can go get it once he leaves." Her voice came out as an unfamiliar rasp. Actually, it wasn't all that unfamiliar. It sounded like Lucille, Lucille when she had an idea. Lucille when she was about to coax Winona into something. "Then we have him take the second half—the Candy Man's cut—to the *real* rendezvous point."

"And why," Lucille pressed, "would your pretend-kidnapper have your father make two different pit stops with his bags-o'-cash?"

Winona's lips curled into a smile. "Insurance. They're not going to release me until they're sure they're getting their money. They want him to leave half at one drop point, then drive to the next. When they've confirmed the first delivery, they'll come meet him at the second predetermined point, and trade me for the rest of the cash. Except of course, we'll just send Marcus's ghouls straight to the second drop point. They'll already be there, waiting to collect what we owe them when Stormy shows up, and meanwhile, we *will* be riding off into the sunset with a hefty bag of dollar bills. Well, hopefully not dollar bills, but like, you know, *hundreds*."

Lucille was gnawing on her lip when Winona finished. She looked through the copse of shagbark hickories to the apartment complex in the distance. The sirens had long since fallen silent, but the flicker of red and blue lights was still glancing off the building's sides.

"What about the police?" Lucille asked.

"No police," Winona said. "No police or they'll ditch, and he'll never see me again."

"Does that *work*?" Lucille pressed. "I mean, do people ever *really* show up without police? Winona, this could seriously backfire."

"Everything we've done this week has seriously backfired," Winona growled. "There's no way out now, and I'm not going back to Kingsville. It's either deeper in or dead at this point, Lucille, and I don't know about you, but I choose deeper in."

She sighed and glanced toward the apartments again. Winona followed her gaze. "They'll search the whole building for us," she said. "Hopefully that neighbor with the goatee isn't feeling chatty. Or was fooled by our *Blade Runner* sex-worker wigs."

"For you," Lucille corrected her. "They'll search for *you*."

"What, are you thinking of ditching me?" Winona teased, and Lucille gave her a sour-faced frown.

"That's not funny. I would never do that."

"I know," Winona said.

Lucille stared at her through the dark for a long, laden moment. "Deeper in or dead," she whispered.

Winona wrapped her arms around Lucille's shoulders, pressing a kiss to her forehead. "Deeper in or dead," she agreed.

They settled into the cold mud, backs against rough bark, and waited for the police lights to vanish, the yellow lights of the apartment complex to pop off one by one as people shuffled back to bed, wondering what had become of the daughter who vanished from right under that handsome meteorologist's nose.

THIRTY-FIVE

FOURTEEN HUNDRED AND TWO DOLLARS AND AN OSCAR FOR WINONA

They decided Lucille should go back for the Oldsmobile, in case the whole neighborhood was still on high alert for Winona's face.

"Are you sure you're okay to go alone?" Winona asked again, and Lucille waved her off.

"Babe," she said, "I was basically *born* alone."

Winona smiled weakly. Truthfully, she knew Lucille would be fine. It was Winona who wasn't crazy about being separated. They only had one phone, and if Lucille walked out of her sight right now, there was no guaranteeing that something wouldn't happen to permanently rip her away.

"It'll just be a few minutes," Lucille reminded her, but Winona still pulled her into a tight hug before Lucille set off toward the apartment and Winona headed to their right, where they'd determined a cross street interrupted the woods in a mile or so.

As she walked, she looked up flights. If their plan had any chance at succeeding, she needed to make sure both the Candy Man and Stormy could actually make it to their rendezvous points in time.

Luck was in their corner. There was a red-eye tonight. Stormy wasn't a *patient* man. He'd want to take action right away, so this worked in their favor. Assuming the Candy Man was willing to play.

As it turned out, Winona and Lucille had run pretty far in their initial escape from Silas's apartment building, and Winona made it to the forest's edge and the empty road a full ten minutes before Lucille pulled up in the Oldsmobile, leaned over, and pushed the door open.

Winona leaped out of the forest and jumped in, and then they were off, back the way they'd come.

Back in the woods, they'd chosen their two drop points—the abandoned gas station and the empty shoe factory they'd passed on their way into town. It would take an hour or two to get back there, but they'd set the meet time for the next afternoon so both Stormy and the Candy Man would have time to drive down. All that was left to do was make the calls.

"You should be crying," Lucille coached as she drove through the light-polluted streets of outer Denver.

"Right," Winona agreed. She flipped the passenger-side visor down and eyed herself in the mirror. She was trembling at the prospect of hearing her father's voice, but even so, she couldn't summon tears. "Shit! How do I make myself cry?"

"I don't know!" Lucille said. "How does Jennifer Lawrence do it?"

"Probably just thinks about Hollywood pay discrepancies?" Winona said. "I don't think that will work for me." She took a deep breath and closed her eyes. "I've just got to do it. I can do it."

She was almost done acting. She was almost free.

She imagined herself shedding her skin, her skeleton crawling out of it, her insides made visible. All she had to do was make one little phone call.

She opened her eyes and grabbed Lucille's phone from the dashboard. If she waited any longer, she would only panic. She dialed his number as quickly as she could and pressed the phone to her ear, feeling her eyes fill with tears at the first ring back.

Her throat tightened; phlegm rushed into it and her nose stuffed. She felt nothing. She was simply losing herself in the role like she'd been taught.

She let out a sniffle. The phone rang again. A pathetic squeak eked from her throat. It rang again.

"Hello?"

The voice was thick, laced with sleep, but unquestionably his. More his than when he'd accepted his Changemaker award. More his than when he'd begged for her safe return on TV.

He was alone.

Her first stroke of luck in days.

"Daddy!" Winona sobbed immediately, keening in her seat as if she meant it, lying with her muscles and organs, the way he'd taught her.

"Winona?" he hissed. She heard the rustle of sheets as he sat up.

She glanced sidelong at Lucille, who was steering the car with one hand and making a *keep things moving, not much time* spiral with her other.

"Winona, where are you?" he asked. "Tell me where you are, darling."

"Daddy," she choked again. "I don't know—I don't know where they took me. I don't know what they did with Lucille. I—I haven't seen her since they separated us, Daddy, and they won't tell me what they did to her, and I'm *scared*."

Winona checked Lucille for a reaction. She was slack-jawed and silently applauding. Winona turned away to tamp down her smile as her father said in a rush, "Darling, where are you? Look around. Do you recognize your surroundings? Describe them to me."

"I can't," she yelped. "They won't let me talk long. They want money, Daddy. Ten—ten—" She hiccupped and stuttered over the words. "Ten thousand d-dollars."

"Where?" he demanded. "Darling, I'm coming to get you."

No police! Lucille mouthed from the driver's seat.

"They said—they said if you tell anyone, they'll kill me," Winona got out through chattering teeth. "If you bring cops, they'll k-kill me." He was pressing her for more information urgently, but she took the opportunity to evolve into breathless, squeaky sobs for a few seconds.

Hurry! Lucille mouthed again. If TV police procedurals were any indication, some corrupt cop would already be helping them trace the call. Within a few more seconds he would have a lock on their location.

A lock, that's what they always called it. Stormy never again would have a lock on Winona's location, her car keys, her letters from Mom, her pantry.

"They want you to take five thousand to an abandoned gas station and leave it in a brown paper bag at exactly noon tomorrow, then drive to an old shoe factory up the road. They won't meet you until they're sure you've left the first half, and th-that you're alone."

Now Lucille was pantomiming reeling in a fishing line at breakneck speed. Had she been timing the call? Counting in her head? It wouldn't surprise Winona in the least.

"Darling, I need you to—" Stormy began, but Winona cut across him, blurting out the address she'd memorized for the gas station, then the address for the shoe factory.

"Winona," he began again. "I—"

"Please," she wailed away from the phone, clutching it tightly with one hand while her other scrabbled for it, like the halves of her body were controlled by two different brains in complete disagreement. Actually, it was sort of fun, fighting yourself for control. As the war between her hands raged on, she added for good measure, "Please let me just talk to him—No! *Daddy!* Daddy, I love—"

She hung up. Double, triple, quadruple checked the call was ended, then turned, beaming to face Lucille. "And that," she said, "is how that shit's done."

"You absolutely amaze me, Winona Olsen," Lucille said. "You *terrify* me, but you amaze me too."

Winona giggled. "Here." She passed the phone back to her, sliding the ring onto Lucille's finger as she did so. "You're up."

THIRTY-SIX

FOURTEEN HUNDRED AND TWO DOLLARS AND OLLY OLLY OXEN FREE

Lucille texted Marcus. *I'm paying you back. I need the Candy Man's number.*

Good girl, he wrote back, seconds later.

She made the call to the Candy Man on speakerphone.

"I don't know the laws around here," she told Winona as it rang.

"The laws," Winona repeated. "Those are definitely important."

Maybe she was feeling emboldened by Winona's award-winning performance as Abducted White Girl in a Lifetime Movie. (The growl in Stormy's voice was more primal and terrifying than Lucille had imagined. Even if all he wanted was Winona back so he could lock her in her tower again.) Maybe she was thinking, *We're past the point of no return.*

She could probably tell you the exact mile marker when it happened.

"What else do I have to lose," she said to herself as the phone rang one more time and then a gruff voice said, "Lucille."

"Candy Man," she said. "Oh, I'm sorry. *The* Candy Man. Or is it Mr. Candy Man?"

"If you're nasty," Winona added.

"I'm so nasty," Lucille said.

"What the fuck are you talking about?" the Candy Man said.

"I'm talking about paying you back," Lucille told him, pulling onto the highway. "We're sixty miles west of Denver, in Princetown, and we've got your money."

There was a long, long pause. "You have it."

"I have it."

"All of it. All five thousand dollars."

"Isn't that what you wanted?" Lucille said. "Am I speaking fucking Greek?" She could hear the Folgarelli come out of her a little bit then—the thick punchiness of her words, the attitude. (Armie Cinchetto Quinhole would be proud.)

"Then we'll find a place to meet." She heard him cover the mouthpiece, start issuing orders.

"No," Lucille said evenly. "We're arranging a *drop* point. Because I pay you back and I'm gone. I'm a ghost. You don't look for me. You don't talk about me. I don't exist to you."

"Or," the Candy Man said, his voice all static, "I take the money and then I find you and fuck you up the way you deserve, little girl."

Where was that mile marker, the one that told them they'd gone too far? Had it wedged in the parking lot of the Cliffside? Had it been in the Easy Go Motel outside of Iowa City, as Silas paraded in child molesters for them to rob and then knock out? Had it been in the woods outside a scrubby apartment complex in Denver—had it been long, long before that, one rainy night between a church and a police station in Kingsville, Michigan, when two bruised and beaten girls swore that they would bide their time until they got their revenge?

"You'll fuck me up?" Lucille cackled. "Me. You'll fuck *me* up. What are you gonna do, jackass? What are you going to take from me? I don't have anything anymore. Nothing! Go cut off my brother's fingers. He deserves it. Go burn my mother's house to the ground. See what my cousins do to you. Come and try to *kill me*, jackass. Nobody's managed it yet. I swear to God if you get within five feet of me I will take you to the *ground*, I will break *every single one* of your *bones* and I will *floss* with them."

Beside her, Winona let out a low whistle.

"I'll show you *nasty*," Lucille said, and she didn't realize she was speeding until they whipped past the old shoe factory so quickly that it was a blur. "I'll show you *little girl*. I'll make you eat your own *teeth*."

"You're kind of fixated on teeth right now," Winona whispered.

"You pick up the money tomorrow at noon, not a minute sooner," Lucille said, "and then you never see me again."

Static crackled. Lucille waited, counted the seconds. *One, two, three . . .*

"Give me an address," he said finally, and Lucille rattled it off and punched the END button before she turned the car around.

THIRTY-SEVEN

FOURTEEN HUNDRED AND ONE DOLLARS, A TACO BELL CRAVE CASE, AND TWO VERY STIFF NECKS

All Winona had wanted was to crawl into another seedy motel bed, their spread of nacho cheese and fried tortillas spread out between them like a bacchanalian feast, but Lucille was right: checking into a room nearby was too risky at this point.

Winona was fairly sure Stormy wouldn't have tipped off the police, if a little less sure than she was pretending to be for Lucille's benefit, but even if he hadn't, they'd now broadcast their general location to both a pissed-off drug lord and her demagogue of a father, and no amount of five-dollar wigs could guarantee they wouldn't be recognized in a motel registration office.

So instead, they'd driven their box of bean burritos and tortilla chips ("Eat great even late," Lucille said) to the second Walmart parking lot of their trip thus far, put the seats back as far as they would go (not very), and munched in silence before settling down, face-to-face and mostly upright, to catch some sleep.

Winona knew what Lucille's breathing sounded like when she fell into sleep, but that easy rhythm never came. She could be sure of this, because she never drifted off either, though she kept her eyes closed for the better part of the night.

So both of them had been bluffing. Not just to Sir Candy Man, Esquire, and Stormy, but to each other. They *did* still have something to lose. In fact, Winona was sure she'd never had more to lose, except maybe when she still had a mother.

In the morning, they went inside to pee. They splashed their faces like they were in a Clearasil commercial, and then Lucille splashed Winona and Winona laughed and splashed her back like they were in an extremely mild soft porn set in the Princetown Walmart, and when Winona pointed this out, Lucille grinned crookedly at her and said, "I wonder if that exists."

"It totally exists," Winona said, smiling back.

"If not, we should make it," Lucille said. "When all this is over."

"We *should* make movies," Winona said. "We'd be good at it. I bet we will, someday."

"Yeah." Lucille's smile faded. "Someday."

On the way back out to the car, they spotted a green velvet couch. It was small but well made (at least in the perceptible ways; probably it would come apart as soon as you leaned around it and realized it was a two-dimensional cutout for a movie set). "We should come back for that couch," Winona said. "For the apartment."

"Sure," Lucille said, and a cold pit opened in Winona's stomach at the realization that Lucille was lying to her.

Did she hate the couch?

Or did she not believe they'd make it back?

When they got back to the Oldsmobile, Lucille slid into the driver's seat. She turned on the radio as they pulled out of the dead-end town's dead-end center, but she quickly turned it back off. It was hot and sunny. They put the windows down and the day-baked breeze did what the P!nk song playing on the radio could not: it deadened the terrifying quiet between them. It filled all the space their thoughts had been taking up.

They could have been on their way to the lake, to a neighborhood pool, to get ice cream on Winona's birthday, in a world where her father was not the Stormy Olsen she knew.

All signs of life fell away. The cars, the buildings, even the grass. Everything here was either inanimate or dead. Including the masticated possum on the side of the road, which both girls hissed upon seeing and neither seemed able to look away from.

They passed the shoe factory first, smoke-blackened from the fire that had closed it down (they'd read all about it in an extremely short guidebook at the last convenience store they'd stopped to pee in; apparently, it was fairly easy to hire an "amateur ghost tour" of the warehouse, though whether the ghosts or the hosts were the amateurs was difficult to determine), and then, five minutes later, after weaving over equally desolate side streets as directed by Siri, they spied the run-down gas station.

It looked almost like a mirage, standing there in the middle of a scrubby brown field, its white structures, mottled brown by years of dust and dirt, reaching up into the sky like worshipful arms begging a malevolent god for water.

"We're here," Lucille whispered as they neared it. She was decelerating, but didn't seem to notice. Forget about a noon rendezvous. At this rate, Winona would have to get out and walk to make it the final half block before sundown.

Winona swallowed a knot. "No sign of Stormy's car. That's good. He must already be at the shoe factory."

They'd intentionally staggered their arrival a solid half hour past Stormy's drop-off time, so that by the time they got to the money, he'd already be long gone, waiting at the shoe factory for Winona's imaginary kidnapper and finding the Candy Man instead. Now thirty minutes didn't seem like a large enough gap. Not even enough time for the smell of his aftershave to siphon off in the hot sun.

Then again, a lot could happen in half an hour. He could be at the shoe factory. He could be . . . *gone.*

Lucille pulled into the station at a crawl. The asphalt was shredded from neglect, long gray-brown grass sprouting up through cracks like shaggy veins.

"Where was he supposed to leave it?" Lucille's voice was still caught in a whisper, as if she expected Winona's father to jack-in-the-box out of the field beyond the gas pumps at any moment. Winona half expected it too.

"I don't know," she answered, skin crawling. Something felt off. Maybe the heat, the way it made the air wriggle and wave before their eyes, or the sun, its fierce insistence that today was a beautiful near-summer day. Or maybe she was just on edge from a night of C-grade beef and no sleep. "Wait here. Keep the car running."

Lucille nodded, and Winona got out. Her neck was so stiff she couldn't look over her shoulder without turning her body, which only increased the fingernail-on-the-spine tingle she kept getting.

When you couldn't easily look behind you, surely that was when there would be something to see.

Get it together, Winona. The hard part's over.

A couple cars were ambling past in the distance, and she froze until they were well out of sight, then jogged a quick lap around the station, eyes searching the sea of drab green and brown for a brown paper bag full of drab-green money.

Next time they did this sort of thing, maybe they should choose some place where their loot would stand out. A Chuck E. Cheese, or maybe the Met.

She turned bodily to face Lucille, who'd thrust her golden head out of the window to squint Winona's way.

Winona shook her head and gestured to the convenience store. Every bit of glass had been *at least* spiderwebbed with cracks, if not totally shattered. The funniest part was that the doors were still locked, like the last person to rifle through this place for Combos and Bud Lite had broken the glass, unlocked the door, taken a turn about the shop, then locked the door on the way out.

Maybe it had been Stormy.

Winona let herself in, unnerved by the jingle of the bells over the door. The optimism of the sound made the upended shelves, the shattered fridge doors, and the overturned cash register all the more unsettling.

She hurried up and down what was left of the "aisles" with no luck, then went to check the bathrooms. The lights wouldn't flick on: no electricity. She backed out into the hallway, neck prickling.

When she spotted it, she felt immensely stupid. The paper bag sat right there on the counter, awash in a sea of scattered lighters covered in cartoon flames and key chains with "JUSTIN" and "VERONICA" and "DOLORES" printed on them. She reached for the bag, expecting weight and heft and maybe even the smell of freshly minted hundred-dollar bills, but instead her hand shot into the air.

The bag was light as a feather.

No.

Her stomach jolted. She clumsily tore at the paper, as if she needed any more proof, and a business card twirled out, landing among the detritus.

STURGIS "STORMY" OLSEN read the bold green print at the top.

What the fuck was this? Her heart was racing as she reached for it and flipped it over. Words hastily scribbled on the back in the black ink of Stormy's favorite fountain pen:

You'll get all your money when I see my daughter again. Alive.

No, she thought futilely. *No, no, no!* They'd planned this so carefully. This was their way out. The *only* way. She had to think.

At least there was still the shoe factory. At least the problem of the Candy Man was about to be resolved. At least there was still a chance that the issue of Stormy Olsen was being wrapped up at this very minute.

They could find another apartment, she told herself desperately. They could find more money.

Then she heard Lucille's screams.

THIRTY-EIGHT

FOURTEEN HUNDRED DOLLARS AND AN EMPTY PAPER BAG

He dragged her out of the driver-side window by her hair, gun pressed against her temple.

It looked one way in the movies—like your hair could support that much weight, that it wouldn't get pulled out of your scalp by the handful. Like you'd have enough time to make sense of what was happening and fight back.

Like blood wouldn't trickle down your scalp, into your eyes, and through the red-blindness you would have to remind yourself to scream.

"You *bitch*," the Candy Man said, and he must've sat up all night on a red-eye just for the pleasure of dragging Lucille across the loose asphalt of this broke-down gas station. Her feet scrabbled for purchase; one of her slip-ons came off, and her bare foot skidded along the chalky rocks, leaving a red trail amid all that white.

"You thought," he said, huffing, pressing the muzzle of the gun harder against her head, "that I would let you walk away after the way you humiliated me?"

Scream, Lucille thought, *scream*, and she opened her mouth. Nothing happened.

How had she not seen him coming? She'd been leaning out the window, waiting anxiously for Winona, wondering what was behind the smashed-up doors of that convenience store, if it was Stormy with a SWAT team at the ready, if Winona was going to come out in a body bag. If she would come out screaming.

Scream, she told herself again. *Scream! Scream for help!*

She should have heard the car. She should have heard the footsteps. He'd walked right up, within view of her mirrors, in this emptied-out hollow between mountains that somehow swallowed all sound and all hope, and he had taken her by the hair like she was a doll. Like she was what he'd called her: a stupid little girl.

Tears pricked her eyes. She'd lost a toenail to the smash and skidder of the rocks, his fist was twisted in her hair, and he was taking her somewhere to do *something* to her and—

And, as always, Lucille had been so worried about Winona Olsen that she'd forgotten to look out for herself.

There was no changing it. There was no getting around it. There was nothing else to do.

She was screaming now. She couldn't stop—it was a guttural howl, something that came up from her bones, something so hard and loud that it made her choke on it, sputter, made her start screaming again.

"Shut *up*," the Candy Man was saying, yanking her along, the gun shuddering against her head. "Stop it, you little bitch!"

"Hey! Hey, asshole!"

The Candy Man stopped.

Through the blood, Lucille could see Winona stopped short outside the convenience store. In one shaky hand, she lofted a paper bag. "You want this?"

"There's nothing in there. That bag is *empty*," he spat.

(Quietly, Lucille planted one foot, then the other.)

"Try me," Winona said calmly. She was tall and slim and terrifying, with her lopped-off hair sticking up in its longest points and her bald spots catching the light in others, with her eyes like two flat coins.

"It's not like it matters," he said, and pulled the gun from Lucille's head. He pointed it unsteadily at Winona. "I'll find out for sure in a minute. After you're on the ground."

(Lucille, at this point, had positioned her elbow in front of the Candy Man's crotch.)

Winona shrugged. "Go ahead. The cops'll be here any minute anyway. You'll rot away in jail for my murder. That's a big upgrade from being some small-time drug lord. I should *congratulate* you, jackass."

"For what?" he started to ask, but he didn't get the words all the way out.

Because Lucille planted her elbow directly into his balls.

Then she jumped him, and two seconds later, Winona jumped him too.

It was the first time Lucille had gotten a good look at him—the black hair, the waxy complexion, the mouth bloody now too from the fist that Winona was driving into his face, and Winona was yelling, maybe because she felt as cannibalistic as Lucille did right now, like she could destroy him with her mouth alone (or maybe it was because her hand hurt because Winona *definitely* didn't know how to throw a punch), and for a whole minute they had the upper hand.

Lucille with her head in pieces, her fingers scratched and bruised and scrabbling. She had pinned down the arm with the gun and Winona seized on it now, wrestling it from his grip with her nails, her mouth fixed in a triumphant *oh*.

But it wasn't the movies, and Lucille didn't have superpowers, and Winona was almost six feet tall, but she weighed about as much as a large-breed dog. The Candy Man had seventy-five pounds on her, easy, had all those days at the CrossFit box with Ginger Sneakers crushing their girl-named workouts, crushing Ashleys, crushing Madisons, crushing Winonas and Lucilles. When he surged forward, he threw both the girls off him like they were the lightest cotton bedsheets.

Lucille hit the ground face-first, but she could hear Winona rolling and rolling and then the terrifying slap and thud of her smashing against something, and hard.

It took a desperate effort for her to even turn her head, to see Winona's body crumpled against the abandoned gas pump, the gun still in her hand. How had the gun not gone off? How had Winona kept her hold on it?

The Candy Man didn't approach Winona. Didn't go for the weapon.

Instead, he brushed himself off with a deliberate slowness. Then he lifted one heavy black boot and he pressed it down into Lucille's throat.

"Move," he said. "Move a muscle, and I'll crush her."

Lucille couldn't think. Couldn't see. She tried to suck in a breath and coughed and shuddered and tried to breathe again. She lifted her hands in claws, and as her eyesight began to flicker out, she scratched at his pant legs.

She was an animal now. She was on her way to becoming the thing she knew, deep down, she'd always been: nothing.

Nothing at all.

"Where are your white knights now?" she could hear him growl. "Where's your *daddy*?"

That was, as far as Lucille could figure, when Winona lifted the gun and shot him in the head.

THIRTY-NINE

LUCILLE, LUCILLE, ONLY LUCILLE

A handful of birds burst out of the field behind the gas station, black feathers glinting in the light. They took off, up and into the mountains. Winona couldn't hear them over the ringing in her ears. Her legs felt weak and watery. Her nose tickled. It was dripping.

She went to wipe it and found something strange and cool clenched in her hand.

When she registered the gun, her fingers reflexively jerked and it fell from her hand. The sound of the world *whooshed* back in around her. The faint chiming of the car door hanging open. The distant hum of highway traffic on the far side of the retaining wall that wriggled like a mirage in the heat a ways off. Lucille panting raggedly on her back.

Winona panting raggedly on her shaky legs.

Lucille had her hands gingerly braced on either side of her own rib cage, and the blood on her hands and shirt was indistinguishable, as if it had no origin. As if she'd merely rolled through a puddle of it.

The girls locked eyes, catching their breath for a few seconds. Winona stumbled through two steps and stopped in front of the inhuman pile of muscle and fabric and wispy black hair crumpled at her feet.

She nudged the lump with her foot. It rocked back into place. She staggered two more steps and sunk onto her knees a few feet from Lucille. The ground was warm against her skin. Pushing her weight into it somehow soothed the sting of the cuts and scrapes.

Still clutching her abdomen, Lucille peeled herself off the ground and leaned against the gas pump behind her. The wind caught a tuft of her hair and made it dance, the root painted cool blue by the shade of the roof, but the ends splitting into hundreds of shades of gold and yellow beneath the bright burn of the sun.

The paper bag rustled as the breeze carried it right to Winona, and she reached out, exhausted, to pin it flat to the time-bleached blacktop.

After they wiped down the gun, that paper bag would be the only thing connecting them to what had happened here. She pulled the business card back out of the bag and started tearing it into little pieces, stuffing the bits into her mouth as she stared out across the lot, the trail of blood smears sparkling like mica in a creek bed.

"Hungry?" Lucille's voice was weak and raw, and that one word left her wincing and massaging her throat.

"He was right," Winona said. "There wasn't any money. Just a note. He took all the money to the shoe factory to wait for me."

Lucille nodded for a few seconds. She opened her mouth and closed it a few times, building the strength to speak any more. "Does he know? That there's no ransom?"

Winona shook her head. "I don't know."

Lucille studied her for a beat, then held out a hand toward the remains of the business card. Winona tore it into halves and passed one to Lucille, who began to dutifully devour her half. "Deeper in or dead," she whispered.

"Deeper in," Winona said.

But the truth was, there *was* no going deeper in than this. They would either find their way out, or they would realize they'd long since lost track of the way.

Winona carefully maneuvered onto her feet, testing her weight against her left ankle, which had started swelling though she had no recollection of rolling it. She reached out to Lucille and helped her to her feet, and then they stood there, in the warm sun and the soft breeze and the quiet rustle and wave of the grass, the mountains looming in the background, nature overtaking man's world.

They stood there, squinting past the light to see each other, and then they rested their foreheads together, throwing shadows across each other's open, searching eyes, and for a few seconds, they just breathed.

Then Winona went to collect the gun, and the red plastic ring.

FORTY

SOON-TO-BE TEN THOUSAND DOLLARS AND A NEW LIFE

They spotted the oil-slick blur of a luxury car before they even reached the factory's driveway. They'd circled twice to be sure it was alone—that no police cruisers, media choppers, or private investigators in nondescript vans were lying in wait.

The burned-out shell of the building was seemingly void of life, save for one man in a navy Armani suit, leaning against the hood of a car alongside a leather briefcase.

There was no sneaking up on him—he was facing the driveway when Lucille pulled into it, and he pushed off the hood to straighten to his full height—and yet, Winona knew from his posture that he hadn't recognized her yet.

He'd rented the same car he drove at home, a black BMW sedan. Typical Stormy.

The sun had just started sloping eastward, the direction they'd come from, and its light was at their backs, lighting Stormy up for them like he was on fire, while shielding *them* from his narrowed eyes. Like maybe the sun recognized kindred spirits in them, like what had happened back at the weather-beaten gas station had been accepted as a blood sacrifice to the god of dying stars, and now she was on their side.

Blinding Stormy for just a few more seconds.

Another person might have cupped his palms against his brow for a better look, but Stormy was presenting himself, tall and domineering, for a first impression, and he kept his arms coolly at his sides.

The girls hadn't spoken since they got in the car. This was the closest they'd come: Lucille reaching over to squeeze Winona's hand painfully hard, Winona squeezing back until she thought both their bones might snap as Lucille pulled right up to him.

Slow and steady.

The light rebounded off his windshield to splash across theirs. Lucille put the Oldsmobile in park, but didn't cut the engine, and the two of them sat there for a moment, caught in the fiery wash of the light.

Winona reached for her seat belt. She was still wearing it, despite everything, and the blood-crusted handgun was resting on her dusty thigh. Lucille unclicked her belt too, and Winona turned to her, touched her wrist, careful to avoid the new bruises welling there. "Wait here," Winona's voice grated out.

She had to do this alone.

Lucille's eyes went saucer-wide, and her lips pressed into a thin line. She was trying to ask Winona something, but Winona's mind had gone quiet, and for once, she couldn't hear Lucille's voice in her head.

She turned and popped the car door open. This was when Stormy finally had the decency to shield his eyes, to prove he had human curiosity, needed to know who he was facing. Winona squared her shoulders and stepped out from behind the door.

Before she even spotted his wide mouth, his glimmering eyes, those hands that had both cradled and burned her, her chest had pressed tight around her racing heart.

She clocked the exact moment he recognized her. His shoulders hitched. His features seemed to spread across his face.

"Winona!" he gasped, and started toward her.

"*Stop.*" She lifted the gun, and his wingtips scuffled uncertainly in the dirt.

"Winona?" he said, somewhere between confusion and dismay, no more angry or fearful than if he'd just told her to go upstairs and change, and she'd come back five minutes after they were supposed to leave, dressed in a bathrobe. His eyes flicked to the car. "Your hair . . . what have they . . ." He shook his head. "Who's in that car?"

She watched the flaky outer layers of his expression peel away, leaving behind a raw understanding. "What are you doing, Winona?" His meaty hands lifted in front of him, but somehow, the gesture didn't communicate surrender. "Darling, you're not thinking. You have gotten yourself into a very bad situation. I see that now, but I can fix it."

The force of his voice shook her resolve. It sent flashes of memory pinwheeling through her: the scissors sliding up her hair to touch her neck, the sizzle of a cigarette sinking into her skin, that moment of fear that came before the pain washed everything away except the thought *Just let it be over; let me die if I have to, but let it be over.*

The words slipped into the quiet of her mind now. She closed her eyes and shut them out.

"What the *fuck* are you doing?" he hissed, angry now.

There it was, the spike of anger she'd been waiting for, that she'd been fearing since she left. She opened her eyes and tipped her chin toward the briefcase. "Is that the money?"

"Christ, Winona," Stormy said. "Put that down before you get yourself killed."

"Lie down," she answered. " On your stomach."

He balked. She jogged the gun a little.

"Are you going to kill me, Winona?" he asked.

There was a mocking undercurrent to his voice, but it was a good question. *Yes*, Winona wanted to say, but something held her back.

"Open the briefcase," she said instead.

"This is ridiculous," he growled. "We both know you're getting in this car and going home with me."

"Open it," Winona repeated.

Her father sighed and trudged back to the BMW. He unlatched the briefcase to reveal neat rows of bills cuffed in paper slips. It was so like something out of a movie that Winona suddenly doubted it was real. Her mouth went dry. Her finger itched on the trigger, encouraging her to *make it* real.

"Tell me what this is about," Stormy said.

Her weight shifted between her feet. *What this is about?* Could he possibly be that stupid? Or deluded?

"It's your mother, isn't it," he hazarded. "She put you up to this. She needs money, and she's using you to get it."

Winona shook her head.

Stormy scoffed. "Then what? You want to be in contact with that junkie? Fine, Winona. You've made your point. You've had your meltdown, now put down that goddamn gun and get in the car."

"It's not about her," she answered.

Stormy's eyebrows flicked up. His gaze searched her face for answers it would never find. He didn't know her well enough. He only knew the daughter he'd handcrafted, molded from money and high-class genetics.

He couldn't read her, this half-bald woman. She was a stranger.

She watched him realize this. Her stomach fluttered with excitement, a feeling not unlike the one the brush of Silas's hand had given her. A feeling of power.

"Darling," he said hesitantly. "I know you're upset, but I promise you there's a reasonable explanation behind the whole issue of your mother. Just get in the car. I promise—I *promise* I'm not angry."

She wasn't either. What she felt was something deeper than anger, steadier.

"Lie down on your stomach," she told him again.

He took a step toward her, and she jerked the gun toward the ground, firing a shot without any hesitation.

Stormy swore and stumbled back. "Winona," he said, cool, calm. "Darling. My sweet Winona, I can fix this. No one will ever know—I can get you out of whatever situation you've gotten yourself into. I can—"

"That's the thing," she said. "I don't want out."

He stared at her with open shock, utter confusion.

"Now," she said. "Lie. Down."

He only hesitated a couple seconds. Then he slowly knelt, looking at her the whole time. Really looking. Maybe even seeing.

"All the way."

She watched him lower to the ground in his suit, his Rolex, his tie clip and cuff links and belt all designed to match, until he was flat in the dirt. Nothing but an overdressed worm.

She kept the gun on him as she went to collect the briefcase. She sifted through it—not counting, just observing it. Witnessing the proof that this week had happened, and that this chapter of life was almost over.

"NONY!" A voice snapped through the quiet, and she spun, half expecting to see the undead Candy Man standing with his arm wrapped around Lucille's throat again, hauling her out of the driver-side window, an image she would never forget.

The one, she could already guess, that would replace her nightmares about her father.

But Lucille was just standing beside the car, alone, her face a mask of pure terror, and Winona jerked back to face her father in time to understand. From where he lay on his belly, he had finagled his handgun from the back of his belt and was training it on Lucille.

Winona forgot all about the gun in her own hand. Instead she felt like, after nearly eighteen years of life, she'd just finally been plopped down into her own body and understood all that it could do, what it was for.

The itchy tightening of her skin. The flutter of want that came with power. The hunger.

She ran at her father and kicked his wrist with full force, and the gun skidded away, and Lucille was safe, but Winona couldn't stop. She kicked him again, in the ribs. Again, again, until she realized someone was screaming. Until she realized she was screaming.

Wordless anger.

She was dimly aware of Lucille scurrying over to grab the gun. She was dimly aware of Lucille running back to haul her away, of Lucille's voice in a soft rattling hum, trying to whisper her calm.

I am calm, Winona wanted to say, and she was. She was in control. She stopped kicking him to prove it. It wasn't even hard, no harder than it had been to start.

"Get the money," she told Lucille, still calm, still proving she was in control. She stared at her for a beat too long before going to collect the briefcase.

Stormy flipped onto his back and held his hands protectively over himself, gasping for breath. "You're sick," he panted. "You're sick just like your fucking mother. I did everything, *everything* for both of you, you ungrateful little bitch."

"You did nothing for us," she said flatly. "We were your toys."

A gruff, throaty laugh jarred out of him. "Is that so, darling?" he huffed. "I suppose you think I should have let you go with her, when she left. I suppose I should have let you live like the trash you're driving around with. I could have. I could have let you live like I did. That's what your mother would have done.

"Let your clothes get too small while she drank and smoked and snorted every penny she could find in your fucking piggy bank. Let you go to school smelling like shit because she couldn't drag herself off the couch to wash the clothes. She was disgusting, Winona. Is that what you want to be, disgusting?"

He was still breathing hard, wincing as certain words pushed against bruises, but he gestured toward the car. "Ask your little friend how it goes, Winona. Ask her how it feels to have nothing. To be a piece of trash. You think *I'm* the monster? Well, honey, I've got news for you." He nodded with what appeared to be great effort. "You're a spoiled brat. I clawed my way out of the shithole I was born into, and I've done nothing but give you the world, a beautiful life. You're so fucking broken, you fell right back into the trash with Lucille Pryce.

"You leave with her, and you will die, Winona. In a motel, behind a Dumpster, in a fucking ditch. In any number of places where no one will find you, or anyone who does won't care. You won't exist. You will be nothing. Girls like that are *nothing*."

Winona stared at him, hardly able to comprehend what he was saying. Her father never talked about his childhood, his family, his life. For all Winona knew, he'd sprung fully formed from the Universe the day her mother met him on the lawn of Northwestern, grinning, handsome, self-assured as he threw a football to some friends right over her picnic blanket.

Winona didn't know this man any more than he knew her, but that didn't change anything.

She crouched in the dirt beside him, gun lax between her thighs. Then she held it up to his temple and stared into his eyes.

"I gave you everything," he wheezed. Furious? Broken? She couldn't tell. She didn't care. "I gave you everything, and now you're fucking *nothing*."

For the first time in years, she gave her father a real smile.

"Good," she said. "Let me be nothing. Let me fucking finally be nothing."

"You're going to kill me." Tears squeezed out of her father's eyes. Pain? Fear, finally? More lies and manipulation? It didn't matter. The only piece of Winona that Stormy loved were the parts that reflected himself back. She was a whole person, and no amount of waterworks could push her back into the hell of pretending to be one of his appendages.

"No," she said. She understood now what she had been waiting for, why she had held back when she could have ended him. "You don't get that, Stormy Olsen. You get to live in constant fear. You get to be subject to the swings of my mood. You get to feel like your own life—your survival—is within your control, while a secret part of you, every single night, warns that it's not. That there's nothing you can truly do to make yourself safe from me.

"You're not going to look for me," she went on. "You're not going to contact me. You can tell your little audience whatever you want. Let them think it was a misunderstanding—you'd forgotten about a camping trip! I was out with some friends and lost my phone! Or let them think I'm dead *in a ditch*, and you couldn't save me, just like you couldn't save your poor dead wife. I don't care what they think. Because I'm never coming back, unless you give me a reason to kill you. Until then, I am nothing. To them or to you or to anyone else. I am a nothing-girl, so let me be invisible to you and everyone in your world."

She slid the metal barrel off his cheek and stood. She turned toward the Oldsmobile without a backward glance, but halfway there, his voice hit her back:

"What if I told them the truth?" he growled. "What kind of sentence do you think you could get for stealing thousands of dollars from me? From faking your own kidnapping?"

Winona laughed, but still didn't face him until she'd pulled the car door all the way open and stepped behind it. Now he had to squint into the light again. Now the wind made the remains of her hair dance like Medusa's snakes around her.

He would never turn her in. It would be too humiliating for him. The gun was a prop, nothing more. All along, she'd had the power to destroy him.

Winona got into the car, and together, she and Lucille drove off into the sunset.

FORTY-ONE

TEN THOUSAND DOLLARS, EIGHTEEN STITCHES, AND THE ROAD TO KATHERINE OLSEN'S HOUSE

They drove all day, making only the necessary stops.

After Lucille's scalp wounds bled through their bandages for a second time, Winona pulled over into an urgent care clinic in Grand Junction. "That's *it*," she said, despite Lucille's protests that she was fine, and dragged Lucille in to get stitches.

Lucille had considered the different lies she could tell the doctors as to the cause of her injuries—ATV accident (hair got caught in the wheel), fell down the stairs (like forty times), rogue lawn mower (the missing toenail on her foot).

Finally, when the doctor put her hands in her lab coat and said, *Who has been doing this to you*, Lucille told the truth. "My brother," she said. "We got into a fight. But I've left home. I'll be fine. I'm not pressing charges."

The last thing she needed was for the doctor to call the cops. The *very* last thing she needed was to be in an interrogation room. But she had to tell some small truth about what had happened to her, or she felt like she would break. Like she was a spiderwebbed vase, like she was one tap away from spilling out everything onto the floor.

We murdered someone, she thought in a dumb, endless loop, and yes, he was trying to murder her first, and yes, the world was probably better off without him, but—

They had killed someone. And Lucille didn't feel sorry.

Three hours later, swathed in bandages and hopped up on industrial-grade Tylenol, Lucille had done some research while Winona drove them into Utah. It turned out that the Candy Man's real name was Terrance Peterson; she'd learned that from her obsessive Googling of "missing people in the Midwest."

Then, on a whim, she'd specifically looked up "missing people in the Upper Peninsula."

FOUND SAFE was written next to Winona's name.

Lucille told her that, voice cracked from disuse, and Winona nodded with a dignity that Lucille hadn't expected. That she hadn't seen before.

That Winona could *have* that dignity while holding a half-eaten Whopper Jr. in one hand made her an actual work of art.

They got banana smoothies in Salina (they were easy for Lucille to swallow) and in Cedar City, Utah, they pulled over at a Planet Fitness and bought day passes so that they could use the showers.

Winona had protested—"We need to keep going, I want to get you into a bed as soon as possible"—but Lucille wasn't taking no for an answer.

"You," she said, voice flattened to a rasp, "are going to get to wash your face before you see your mom again. Okay? Nonnegotiable."

For a minute, standing there in the sandy parking lot, Lucille was herself again.

The illusion lasted as she took her clothes off in the tiled changing room, as she stepped into the shower and put her hair under the spray. As she watched the dust eddy around her feet. It lasted until she lifted her arms slowly, carefully, to shampoo her scalp—and one of the cuts on her back pulled open.

It was almost audible, the sound of her composure cracking apart.

I want my mom, Lucille thought, gasping into the water. *I want my mom. I want to be put to bed. I want someone to make me pasta and put a hand on my forehead and get me extra blankets and call in my shifts at the diner—*

"Luce?" Winona asked. "You okay in there? Need help?"

"I can still *wash* myself," Lucille said, even though that maybe wasn't true. "Just give me a sec."

You can't have your mom, she reminded herself, *because you never had her in the first place. But that's okay.*

You're going to get Winona hers.

They made it through western Utah in the late morning, the red craggy rocks leading off into the distance. She'd been too sleepy before to notice the easy way that Winona handled the car out here, the road dipping and curving the way it never did back in the straight-and-narrow Midwest.

After every casually handled hairpin turn, Winona would smile a little to herself. The soft line of her jaw, the stubble of her hair, the desert all blown-out bright through the windows—it was more than a little Mad Max, and Lucille told her so.

"Sure," Winona said. "I think everyone in that movie drove a farting Oldsmobile."

Lucille threw a stale fry at her.

They pulled off Highway 15 so that Lucille could see the Vegas strip: the Eiffel Tower at Paris Las Vegas, the dancing Bellagio fountains, the millions of light bulbs blazing even now in the afternoon sun. Like a Disneyland dreamscape. Like a row of collector's piggy banks rattling with money.

All those casinos. All their automatic doors. Every set of them opening and closing and opening again, like mouths, like they were calling her name. *Lucille. Lucille.*

Winona was watching her. "You still want it," she said. "To be the casino queen."

"Yeah." Lucille grinned. It made her face hurt. "I do. I still want it."

They clutched hands across the console.

"Good thing we got it for you, then," Winona said as she pulled onto Summerlin Parkway. "We're almost there—the maps app is saying she lives out here, on the west side."

Lucille rolled the window down and tipped her head against the seat belt, dreaming a little in the heat. That Eiffel Tower on the Strip—there was probably a restaurant in there. They could be hiring waitresses. She could French braid her hair and enunciate her words and make a living off the tips from the tourists paying bank for steak béarnaise. She could take that money and multiply it in the casinos on her nights off.

She could take *that* money and turn it into a degree.

A math degree. She could be an accountant, or something less boring. Investment banker? Wasn't that just high-stakes gambling?

Gingerly, Lucille tested the idea again, like a loose tooth.

It held.

Huh, she thought. *A math degree.*

"This is my mom's road," Winona said, and Lucille blinked her eyes open. Then squeezed them shut, and opened them again.

"Oh shit," Lucille said, ". . . am I dead?"

It was like they had landed on Mars. The B-movie, post-colonization Mars, where everyone thunked their giant ugly spaceships straight down into the sand, then built designer pools behind them.

Each house was bigger than the last. This one had fourteen concrete pillars and a two-story twisty waterslide. The next had a rooftop deck, a giant telescope aimed toward the mountains. All of them had rows and rows and rows of windows, like each house on this road was owned by a different omnipotent god who needed to see in every direction at once.

Those windows gathered up the late-afternoon sun and threw it back at the Oldsmobile as it crept down the road. Lucille had to shade her eyes with both hands.

"A little bungalow," Winona muttered, checking the street numbers.

"What?"

"A bungalow," she repeated. "We thought she'd live in a *bunga-low.*"

"With hibiscus flowers."

Winona was beginning to chortle. "Growing up a trellis. Where would she even put a trellis? Would she hang it off the fourth guest balcony?"

"No. No, that's not the worst part," Lucille howled. "Making her own essential oils!"

"Cutting the fresh sprigs of lavender in her garden. Singing some, like, Carly Simon as she tucks them into her apron."

"*You're so vain—*" In full-on hysterics, Winona clutched at Lucille's arm. "Drying the lavender in bundles over the kitchen sink!"

"Waiting for weeks. Marking the days on her paper calendar. Then, when the time comes, crushing each flower gently, saying a little 'thank you' to each and every one—"

"I can't," Winona said, gasping for air. "I can't. *Essential oils.*"

"I'm sure she sells them at the farmers' market," Lucille said, "for a little extra cash."

Winona coughed and swore and wheeled their car into the driveway of the worst house of them all. "Yeah," she said, peering up at it over the wheel. "I should have fucking known."

It looked like a Jenga game for giants. The house was a riot of metal, pylons sticking out in every direction, like someone had taken a cheese grater to the front of a thirty-first-century fortress.

The front door was lined in purple neon.

Winona and Lucille approached it cautiously. "I feel like he's going to be just inside," Winona said. "Waiting for me."

She didn't have to say who. This house was Stormy Olsen's wet dream. It had to be tens of millions of dollars; nothing this ugly was cheap.

On the front step, before they could chicken out, Lucille rang the bell. "Blasters set to stun," she told Winona.

"This has to be the wrong house," she moaned, but there were quick, cheerful footsteps, the jingle of a dog's collar. "Coming!" a voice called.

The door swung open.

"Mom?" Winona said.

FORTY-TWO

TEN THOUSAND DOLLARS, TWO CORGIS, AND HISTORY REPEATING ITSELF

After the day they'd had, Winona mistook her mother's shriek for a cry of pain. But then the woman was throwing her toned arms around Winona and pulling her into a hug, and the yoga pants, the tan, the twin corgis at her heels might've been new, but her smell—her *mother's* smell—was the same as she remembered, even if she hadn't realized before that moment that she remembered it at all.

"Winona!" she gasped as she pulled back, grinning as sunnily as if she'd just picked her up at the airport for Christmas break. Winona felt herself grinning stupidly too. Her face—that was also the same. She might even have looked a little younger, with her new hairdo and her lithe yoga body, and—had she had *fillers?*

It didn't matter. This was her mother, even if she didn't have the trellis and soft wrinkles Winona had imagined.

"Hi," she said.

An awkward silence followed. When Winona had played this scene out in her mind a hundred thousand times, she'd skipped over this tricky part, assuming that, when the moment arose, the words would just flow, they'd both know just what to say.

Winona did not know what to say. She shifted between her feet, and the woman's brown eyes wandered back to where Lucille stood, a half step behind Winona on the outer-space walkway they'd followed through the . . . well . . . "What is that?" Winona asked, waving vaguely to the steel and cement rectangles they'd passed through.

Not exactly the inspired opening lines she'd hoped for.

"Oh!" the woman said brightly. "The Sculpture Garden? You like?"

Winona shot a helpless look back to Lucille, who stepped up literally and metaphorically to save the day. "Definitely," she said. "We were just marveling at it. I'm Lucille."

"Lucille." The woman nodded, wide-eyed and smiling. The eyes and teeth might've been familiar, but this wasn't an expression Winona had seen her mother wear before. "I'm Kate. Why don't you two come in? I'll have the maid make us lemonade and we can catch up!"

The corgis grunted and shuffled backward as Kate née Katherine led the way through an expansive entryway with black marble floors and some kind of brushed metal wall treatments. All eight corgi-paws clacked pleasantly as the dogs followed Winona's mother, as if she were some barefoot, Pilates-doing Queen of England and they her loyal servants.

Winona and Lucille didn't see much of the house, just followed Kate straight back to a room whose fourth wall opened onto a patio, complete with an Olympic-sized swimming pool and in-ground hot tub. "Lovely, isn't it?" she said, glancing back at Winona, who'd frozen at the sight of the still, blue-green water, the exhilarating pulse of the hot desert wind.

Kate paused by the exterior wall to fidget with the intercom system. She pressed a button and asked someone named Grace to bring them lemonade on the patio. She shot a glance back at Winona. "What about sandwiches? Are you hungry?"

Winona nodded from deep within her daze.

"And sandwiches," Kate told the intercom.

"Grace," Lucille whispered to Winona, her eyebrows flicking up playfully. "The robot maid."

Winona tried to smile, but she was drifting outside her body again. Following her dead mother to an arrangement of patio furniture, watching her gesture to where each of them should sit. The corgis hopped up on the sofa with Kate, panting as they both curled into her lap.

She smiled down at them as she pet their ears. "They struggle with the heat, but I'm too in love to part with them. Last time I impulse-buy a pet, though."

Winona tried again to smile. She felt instead like her mouth slid off her face entirely.

"They're cute," Lucille offered.

Kate smiled that same bright smile. "Thanks!"

"You seem happy," Winona blurted.

Her mother laughed. "I am," she said. "But what about *you?* I want to hear everything—I love the hair, by the way. So bold! Like a young Audrey."

That was entirely inaccurate.

Winona did not look like a young Audrey. She looked like a thumb. Like a not-hot Tom Hiddleston. This was all wrong.

And the question was all wrong too. How was Winona supposed to answer that question: Was she happy?

"Over the last ten years?"

The sunny smile faltered. Kate's hand stilled on the eastern corgi's head. Her eyes dropped. "You must know how sorry I am."

Winona nodded, but what she really meant to say was, *No, tell me. Please tell me. Tell me for hours. Run your fingers through my hair, squeeze my shoulders, and tell me you're sorry.*

Instead Kate sat across the low glass coffee table, flanked in corgis, and gave a troubled sigh. "I'm sure he's told you all about my problem. The drinking, the pills."

"I thought you died," Winona said.

She'd expected to see surprise, but there was none. Just the return of the melancholy expression from all those old pictures that hung in Grandfather Pernet's hallway. "I wondered if he might go with something like that," she said with a nod. "A clean break. Something a little less embarrassing than admitting his addict wife ran out on him in the middle of the night."

"And me," Winona said in a small, pathetic voice. Kate's brown eyes flashed uncomfortably to Lucille. "You ran out on me, too."

Kate's gaze fell and she frowned. "He would've fought me for custody, and there was no way I could win, Winona. He was the gem of my own hometown, and I was the pillhead daughter of a crotchety heir."

Winona wondered if the math of all this was making any more sense to Lucille than it was to her. Kate hesitated as a woman in gray slacks and a white button-up appeared with a tray laden with lemonade and finger sandwiches. Everyone went silent as the maid, Grace, set the tray onto the table, except Lucille, who offered a tiny "Thanks."

Grace ignored her and went back inside, and after a beat, Kate forged on. "I wanted you, baby, you *must* know that. But frankly, I was in no shape to take care of another person. I needed help. I saw my chance and I ran."

"I needed help," Winona said back to her.

"I couldn't have given it to you if I was dead," Kate said a little desperately. "You don't know this, but my relationship with your father was . . . tumultuous. Sometimes he *hurt* me, Winona. Sometimes I was afraid I would die."

Tears swam into Winona's eyes. Lucille shifted closer and took her hand, squeezing it tight, grounding her.

Kate shook her head, and her voice came out hoarse. "When I met your father, he saw a path to the kind of life he wanted in me. And once he realized I was a person, who wanted things he didn't want and did things he didn't like, all bets were off. I went from being an angel of God to the absolute devil in his eyes." She shook her head again. "But he always saw you as an extension of himself. That's how I knew you'd be okay. That's how I comforted myself."

This time the smile was forced, and something in Winona's chest cracked clean in half. It was so unfair, that she had to sit here feeling brokenhearted for herself and simultaneously bear the weight of what the world had done to her mother.

This, she thought, must be what Lucille felt all the time. Like Marcus could wander around in his stupid fake cast and live his one stupid and precious life, while she had to crawl through it under the load of two unsatisfied existences.

Maybe even three. Maybe Lucille looked at Winona and felt this, this simultaneous pity and fury and envy and hate for all the forces that had beaten her into this shape.

Kate stood, and came toward her now, grabbing Winona's hands from Lucille's grip while the corgis watched and tilted their heads from the sofa.

"You *were* safe, weren't you, baby?" she said. "I was right, wasn't I?"

Right? That Stormy saw Winona as an extension of himself. Sure, when she was young. When she was good. As long as she was quiet when he wanted her to be, and charming when he wished her to be, and invisible when he thought she ought to be.

But not in all those between moments when she came alive.

That was the truth.

But her mother was looking at her now with tears in her eyes and—and *love*, everything Winona had wished for, and her hands were soft and feminine, and her sweet smell was wrapping around Winona like a blanket, and she was safe and her mother was safe and Lucille was safe, and wasn't that all that really mattered?

"Nony," Lucille whispered. "Tell her."

Winona blinked back her tears and nodded. "Yes," she whispered. "I was safe."

The sunny smile fluttered into place on Kate's face. She heaved a relieved sigh and released Winona's hands. "I knew it," she said, and settled back onto the sofa. "I just had a feeling everything would work out for you like it did for me."

"Yeah." Winona smiled more fully. "It did."

"It's just so amazing to see you!" Kate said, and clapped her hands together after a beat, all the unpleasantness behind them. "What brings you two through? Post-grad road trip?"

Lucille and Winona exchanged a look, and now the smile came easier to Winona. "Sort of," she said. "We're moving here."

Kate's expression faltered. "Oh? For school?"

"Just to live," Winona explained. "To be close to you. We don't have an apartment yet, but I'm sure we'll find one soon."

"Oh, honey." Kate stood again. The corgis leaped off the couch and circled her like excitable sharks.

Like the sharks locked up back in the Kingsville Aquarium. Who swam and swam and never got anywhere.

"Oh, honey," Kate said again. "I'm so sorry."

A woman crawling over a shattered wineglass, pleading. I'm so sorry.

"I didn't mean to give you the wrong idea."

The wrong idea?

Kate shook her head again. "You can't *stay* here."

Winona laughed uncomfortably. "I didn't mean to assume . . . I wasn't asking you to . . ."

But Kate didn't appear to hear her. "I have a life here, baby. I can't just upend everything."

"Upend everything," Winona repeated, confused.

"I've worked hard, *really* hard to build all this, you know? I'm finally just now in a good spot. I have my privacy, my peace! My freedom. I can't just give that all up."

Winona laughed again, but this time it rang hollowly through her body. "Why would you have to give it all up?"

"She's not asking you to join the circus with us," Lucille piped up beside her, and Kate startled, as if she'd forgotten all about her. "She's not asking you for anything."

"Sweetie," Kate said, like she was talking to a child. Not *her* child, but one who'd rung her doorbell to sell Girl Scout cookies or ask to walk the corgis. "Things are just very complicated right now. Maybe in a few years, they'll settle down, but right now, let's just appreciate that we got to have this chat, right? Maybe we can do a long weekend somewhere soon!"

"Long weekend," Winona repeated through the fog gathering in her brain. Lucille said something else, which included a slew of four-letter words and the phrase, *drove across the country for you.*

Kate's eyes had gone wide. "Honey, you have to know, it has nothing to do with you. You, I love. Believe me, I wish it could be different. I really do. Let's exchange numbers, okay? We'll talk more." Her hand was on Winona's arm. She was trying to physically lift her off the couch.

"Kate?" someone said from within the pseudo-room that opened onto the patio, and her grip fell away from Winona's arm as she faced the hunched old man coming toward them. His suit was as hideously expensive as the house they were in.

"Chaz!" Kate called, so loudly that Winona suspected Chaz might not have the best hearing. Kate hurried toward him and kissed his wrinkly cheek. He didn't smile. He looked like a walrus.

"How's the baby?" he asked her.

Baby. The word hit Winona in the stomach and reverberated up through her suddenly otherwise-empty skull, echoing out again and again, growing louder every time.

Baby. Baby. Baby.

"She's sleeping like a little angel," Kate promised. "How was work?" She quickly regarded Winona and Lucille without making direct eye contact. "My husband is a wonderfully successful businessman. Owns three casinos just in Vegas, and a few international hotels."

Baby.

Wonderfully Successful Chaz looked toward them, and his walrus face remained unchanged.

Baby.

"Who's this?" he asked brusquely, tipping his chin toward them. Lucille stood and pulled Winona up beside her, gripping her hand so tight it hurt. Winona was thankful for it; otherwise she was sure she would've floated away again.

"A couple of girls from Habitat for Humanity—fund-raising to build a children's home. Isn't that nice?"

BABY.

Chaz's lip curled, but he nodded. The intent behind the expression was entirely unclear. Kate jogged his elbow. "I told them we'd *love* to help them. Wouldn't we, baby?"

"Certainly. Not many kids today would be out in this heat, working hard to serve those less fortunate. Have to respect that." His eyes wandered to Winona's hair and he seemed to second-guess his own statement, but he was also reaching into his suit, pulling a checkbook out from the folds of pinstriped fabric. He flipped it open in one hand and with the other, quickly scribbled.

Baby.

Complicated.

Long weekend.

This chat.

Baby. Baby. Baby.

"My husband is a very generous man," Kate fawned as Chaz was starting to tear the check out, and Winona watched him make a quick adjustment to the amount before finishing the tear. Winona was frozen in shock as he held the check out to her.

Lucille cleared her throat and bumped Winona's shoulder. She moved forward. "Thank you," she said, accepting the money. Lucille added something else, probably more convincing, and then they were being led back through the *2001: A Space Odyssey* set to the Torture Garden, and Chaz was shuffling off to see his daughter in some other wing of the modern mansion, leaving them alone.

"Sorry, girls," Kate whispered to them, right there in her own house, in her beautiful new life that she'd worked so hard for. She touched the side of Winona's face and smiled. "Don't be a stranger."

Winona stepped back onto the pathway. "I already am," she said, and then she turned and took Lucille's hand and they walked back under the slowly lowering desert sun and the muddle of soft pastels it splashed across the sky.

They didn't even look at the check until they got into the Oldsmobile, and by then Winona felt like the whole thing had happened to someone else, somewhere far away from here.

Her mother was a stranger to her.

Maybe that wasn't so bad. Maybe that was bound to happen even when you shared a house and life with someone. Winona had been a stranger to herself until a year ago. Everyone in the world was, except Lucille.

Winona looked at the check. "Ten thousand dollars," she read. That was how much her lost childhood was worth. A thousand dollars for each year.

"Holy shit!" Lucille snatched the check and studied it with saucer eyes. He'd left the recipient blank. "Look. He totally added a zero at the last minute. He was *going* to give us one thousand."

"That cheap fuck," Winona said.

"We have twenty thousand dollars total."

"God," Winona said. "That's good. I guess we can use it to hire an attorney?"

Lucille laughed. For a second, they both laughed together, then fell back into silence, sitting there, side by side in front of the heinous sculpture garden, with their seat belts on but the engine off.

She thought about the sharks in the tanks at the Kingsville Aquarium, swimming endlessly, never getting anywhere.

Winona turned the key and the Oldsmobile hummed to life. The sound made her feel just a little bit better. "Ready?"

FORTY-THREE

TWENTY THOUSAND DOLLARS AND WINONA AND LUCILLE

"Where are we going?" Lucille glanced up at Katherine Olsen's house, to the houses on either side. To the shitty apartments she couldn't see but could imagine, two blocks away. Popcorn walls, webbed and cracked. Ants crawling out from underneath the plastic countertops. An aboveground pool, half-full, a single infant-sized inner tube slowly deflating in the warm water.

"I don't know," Winona said. "We could drive around? Scope out some 'for rent' signs? We could start on . . . our future, I guess."

Their future. Their adulthood, really.

Lucille's mom had wanted her to be an adult for so long, and Lucille loved her, and she pitied her, and she had tried to be everything that her mother had needed. And now, finally, Lucille could stop.

Despite the way the world had seen them, despite what it had demanded of them, the lies it had told and the love it had taken away, the insistence that they be both more and less than who they were, despite the rent they had to pay, the utility bills, the days in line waiting for them at the DMV, the interviews for jobs, the meals they would have to make and the floors they would have to clean and the windows they would have to close against the night sky—

Lucille had the confused sense that they were still girls.

At least today.

At least right now.

It was late May in Nevada, and they could both smell the dust and the pollen out the window, could feel the hot sun licking at their hands through the windshield.

"We have twenty thousand dollars, Nony," Lucille said, wiping the sweat from her brow. "Who says we need to start today? Like . . ."

Winona looked at her. "Like what?"

Lucille grinned. "We're five hours from the ocean. Maybe less than that, I don't know, but does it matter? Don't you want to *see* it? We can come back tomorrow, or next week, or never. But right now—don't you want to keep going?"

Following the road all the way to its end. The two of them carrying their shoes across the sand, feeling its kiss burn their soles. The sun would be low, throwing its fierce light across the choppy waves. Neither of them would speak. Maybe they would have one of their telepathic conversations.

Yes, Lucille would say.

Yes, Winona would answer.

Halfway from the scabby parking lot to the water, Lucille just knew Winona would break into a run, and she would follow.

And they would laugh, and Lucille's blond hair would whip around her head, Winona's shabby crew cut blustering around her temples, her mad grin stretched across her face.

When they reached the water's edge, they would find each other's hands and without stopping, without slowing, they would run headfirst into the rushing wave.

Maybe it would crash right over them and they'd open their eyes beneath the surface, look into each other's faces as the wild force of the water pounded against them on all sides, pummeled them.

But they wouldn't lose shape, and they wouldn't be afraid to run out of air.

Together they would keep going, always.

"Yes," Winona said.

"Yes," Lucille said.

Winona took Lucille's hand. She put the car into drive.

ACKNOWLEDGMENTS

We want to thank our incredible editor, Alex Arnold—thank you for your loveliness and insights. We have loved working with you! Thanks, too, to the wonderful Katherine Tegen and everyone at Katherine Tegen Books and HarperCollins, especially Rebecca Aronson and Gina Rizzo. Thank you for letting us do this together. It has been a dream.

Thank you to Lana Popovic, our agent, our angel, and the reason why we are such good friends. Thank you for setting us up!

Thanks to Jeff Zentner for his endless support and wisdom and silliness. You are the third angle of this Friendship Triangle™, and we love you. Thanks to Parker Peevyhouse, Mackenzi Lee (for the secret butchered use of her secret last name), Evelyn Skye, Anna Breslaw, Katie Cotugno, Roshani Chokshi, Candice Montgomery, Tehlor Kay Mejia, Kerry Kletter, David Arnold, Susan Dennard,

Jennifer Niven, Angelo Surmelis, Bethany C. Morrow, Victoria Aveyard, Shannon Parker, Marisa Reichardt, Sarah Schmitt, Alexandra Monir, Rebecca Ross, Stephanie Strohm, Stephanie Garber, Dahlia Adler, and all the other lovely, kind, hilarious authors who make us feel so lucky to be in this community.

Thanks to Mike Aponte, whose thorough, straightforward explanation of counting cards in blackjack helped Lucille to win all that money.

Brittany: I want to thank Mika Perrine, Joe Sacksteder, Laura Osgood Brown, Keith Brown, and all my supportive colleagues at the Interlochen Arts Academy. Thanks to Chloe Benjamin, Becky Hazelton, Jacques Rancourt, Emily Temple, Kit Williamson, and Corey Van Landingham, wonder friends. Thanks to my wonderful family, especially my parents, for their love and enthusiasm. And thanks, of course, to Chase: I love you. You are the best guy I know. Let's go to the bookstore and then snuggle that dog.

Emily: Thank you to Liz Tingue, one of the very first people to take a chance on me, and also to Rhoda Janzen, Steven Iannacone, Daniel Nayeri, and every other instructor who poured time and energy into me. Thank you also to my family, for being nothing like Winona's. A huge thanks to Jordan, my perfect match of a reader and sister, whose excitement I always actively aim for when drafting. Thank you to Megan, Noosha, Alisa, Sophia, Lyric, Merilee, Carly, Morgan, Jill, Stephanie, and all the other amazing women in my life who have found ways to stay tender and good in a world that often isn't. Finally, thank you to Joey, for loving me so well, for being my partner in all things (except crime!!), and for carving out a small corner of the world with me that is always safe, and always home. I love you.

Also, we usually thank each other. So this is us saying thank you, and *yes*.